Praise for LAVINIA

"[A] love song to both the poet and the power of the imagination…as good as anything Le Guin has done." — *Milwaukee Journal Sentinel*

"By telling this story from its heroine's clear, forthright perspective, Le Guin has taken the cipher that is Vergil's Lavinia and given her a new life."
— *Washington Post Book World*

"[E]legant and eloquent." — *Entertainment Weekly*

"[B]rilliant…Read Vergil, read Le Guin and find both writers at the height of their powers." — *Oregonian*

"Le Guin has rewritten the last six books of Vergil's epic poem to create a rich life of the mind for the Latin princess. [T]he novel…is a 'love offering,' and she writes with great affection for both the poet and his hero."
— *Christian Science Monitor*

"*Lavinia* is…ripe with that half-remembered virtue, wisdom."
— Laura Miller, *Salon*

"Brilliant." — *Sacramento Bee*

"[D]elightful…The magic here is that we get to watch Aeneas's story unfold from Lavinia's point of view." — NPR's *All Things Considered*

"[A] narrative rich in physical detail and emotional power. There are passages of astonishing beauty…With *Lavinia*, Le Guin provides the latest installment in a body of work that has established her as one of imaginative literature's most indispensable voices." — *Sci Fi* magazine

"The compulsively readable Le Guin earns kudos for fashioning a winning combination of history and mythology featuring an unlikely heroine imaginatively plucked from literary obscurity." — *Booklist*

"[T]his beautiful and moving novel is a love offering to one of the world's great poets, and former high-school Latin scholars may return to Vergil with a renewed appreciation. Highly recommended." — *Library Journal*, starred review

"Arguably her best novel, and an altogether worthy companion volume to one of the Western world's greatest stories." — *Kirkus Reviews*, starred review

"Le Guin is famous for creating alternative worlds (as in *The Left Hand of Darkness*), and she approaches Lavinia's world, from wh[...]
its course, as unique and strange as any fantasy. I[...]
ranked with Robert Graves's *I, Claudius*." — *Publish*[...]

Other
Houghton Mifflin Harcourt Books by
Ursula K. Le Guin

Tales from Earthsea

The Other Wind

The Telling

Changing Planes

Gifts

Voices

Powers

LAVINIA

Ursula K. Le Guin

MARINER BOOKS
An Imprint of HarperCollins*Publishers*
Boston   New York

First Mariner Books edition 2009
Copyright © 2008 by Ursula K. Le Guin

marinerbooks.com

Library of Congress Cataloging-in-Publication Data
Le Guin, Ursula K., date
Lavinia/Ursula K. Le Guin.—1st ed.
p.   cm.
I. Aeneas (Legendary character)—Marriage—Fiction.
2. Rome (Italy)—History—To 476—Fiction.
3. Legends—Rome—Fiction.   I. Title.
PS3562.E42L38 2008
813'.54—dc22   2007026508
ISBN 978-0-15-101424-8
ISBN 978-0-15-603368-8 (pbk.)

Text set in Centaur MT
Map illustration by Jeffery C. Mathison
Designed by Linda Lockowitz

Printed in the United States of America
23 24 25 26 27 LBC 19 18 17 16 15

sola domum et tantas servabat filia sedes,
iam matura viro, iam plenis nubilis annis.
multi illam magno e Latio totaque petebant
Ausonia . . .

A single daughter, now ripe for a man,
now of full marriageable age, kept the great
household. Many from broad Latium and
all Ausonia came wooing her . . .

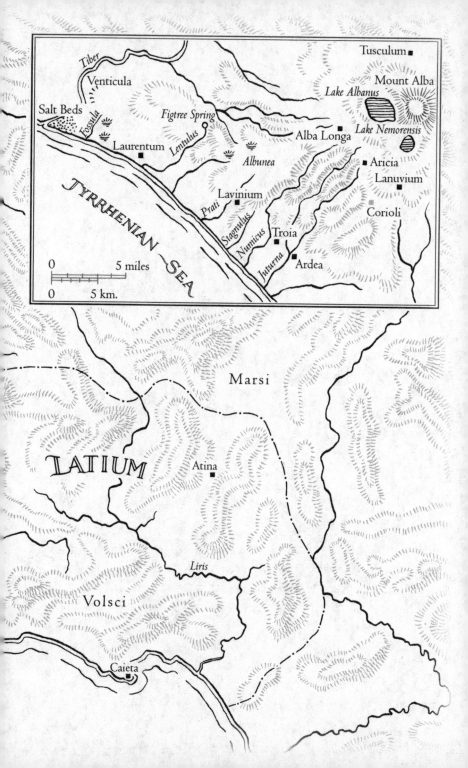

Tusculum

Tiber

Venticula

Mount Alba

Lake Albanus

Salt Beds

Figtree Spring

Lake Nemorensis

Fossula

Lentulus

Alba Longa

Laurentum

Aricia

Albunea

Lanuvium

Lavinium

Corioli

Prati

Stagnulus

Numicus

Troia

Iuturna

Ardea

TYRRHENIAN SEA

0   5 miles

0   5 km.

Marsi

LATIUM

Atina

Liris

Volsci

Caieta

I WENT TO THE SALT BEDS BY THE MOUTH OF THE RIVER, in the May of my nineteenth year, to get salt for the sacred meal. Tita and Maruna came with me, and my father sent an old house slave and a boy with a donkey to carry the salt home. It's only a few miles up the coast, but we made an overnight picnic of it, loading the poor little donkey with food, taking all day to get there, setting up camp on a grassy dune above the beaches of the river and the sea. The five of us had supper round the fire, and told stories and sang songs while the sun set in the sea and the May dusk turned blue and bluer. Then we slept under the seawind.

I woke at the first beginning of light. The others were sound asleep. The birds were just beginning their dawn chorus. I got up and went down to the mouth of the river. I dipped up a little water and let it fall back as offering before I drank, saying the river's name, Tiber, Father Tiber, and his old, secret names as well, Albu, Rumon. Then I drank, liking the half-salt taste of the water. The sky was light enough now that I could see the long, stiff waves at the bar where the current met the incoming tide.

Out beyond that, on the dim sea I saw ships—a line of great, black ships, coming up from the south and wheeling and heading in to the river mouth. On each side of each ship a long rank of oars lifted and beat like the beat of wings in the twilight.

One after another the ships breasted the waves at the bar, rising and plunging, one after another they came straight on. Their long, arched, triple beaks were bronze. I crouched by the waterside in the salty mud. The first ship entered the river and came past me, dark above me, moving steadily to the heavy soft beat of the oars on the water. The faces of the oarsmen were shadowed but a man stood up against the sky on the high stern of the ship, gazing ahead.

His face is stern yet unguarded; he is looking ahead into the darkness, praying. I know who he is.

By the time the last of the ships passed by me with that soft, labored beat and rush of oars and vanished into the forest that grows thick on both banks, the birds were singing aloud everywhere and the sky was bright above the eastern hills. I climbed back up to our camp. No one was awake; the ships had passed them in their sleep. I said nothing to them of what I had seen. We went down to the salt pans and dug up enough of the muddy grey stuff to make salt for the year's use, loaded it in the donkey's baskets, and set off home. I did not let them linger, and they complained and dawdled a little, but we were home well before noon.

I went to the king and said, "A great fleet of warships went up the river at dawn, father." He looked at me; his face was sad. "So soon," was all he said.

I KNOW WHO I WAS, I CAN TELL YOU WHO I MAY HAVE BEEN, but I am, now, only in this line of words I write. I'm not sure of the nature of my existence, and wonder to find myself writing. I speak Latin, of course, but did I ever learn to write it? That seems unlikely. No doubt someone with my name, Lavinia, did exist, but she may have been so different from my own idea of myself, or my poet's idea of me, that it only confuses me to think about her. As far as I know, it was my poet who gave me any reality at all. Before he wrote, I was the mistiest of figures, scarcely more than a name in a genealogy. It was he who brought me to life, to myself, and so made me able to remember my life and myself, which I do, vividly, with all kinds of emotions, emotions I feel strongly as I write, perhaps because the events I remember only come to exist as I write them, or as he wrote them.

But he did not write them. He slighted my life, in his poem. He scanted me, because he only came to know who I was when he was dying. He's not to blame. It was too late for him to make amends, rethink, complete the half lines, perfect the poem he thought imperfect. He grieved for that, I know; he grieved for me. Perhaps where he is now, down there across the dark rivers, somebody will tell him that Lavinia grieves for him.

I won't die. Of that I am all but certain. My life is too

contingent to lead to anything so absolute as death. I have not enough real mortality. No doubt I will eventually fade away and be lost in oblivion, as I would have done long ago if the poet hadn't summoned me into existence. Perhaps I will become a false dream clinging like a bat to the underside of the leaves of the tree at the gate of the underworld, or an owl flitting in the dark oaks of Albunea. But I won't have to tear myself from life and go down into the dark, as he did, poor man, first in his imagination, and then as his own ghost. We each have to endure our own afterlife, he said to me once, or that is one way to understand what he said. But that dim loitering about, down in the underworld, waiting to be forgotten or reborn—that isn't true being, not even half true as my being is as I write and you read it, and nowhere near as true as in his words, the splendid, vivid words I've lived in for centuries.

And yet my part of them, the life he gave me in his poem, is so dull, except for the one moment when my hair catches fire—so colorless, except when my maiden cheeks blush like ivory stained with crimson dye—so conventional, I can't bear it any longer. If I must go on existing century after century, then once at least I must break out and speak. He didn't let me say a word. I have to take the word from him. He gave me a long life but a small one. I need room, I need air. My soul reaches out into the old forests of my Italy, up to the sunlit hills, up to the winds of the swan and the truth-speaking crow. My mother was mad, but I was not. My father was old, but I was young. Like Spartan Helen, I caused a war. She caused hers by letting men who wanted her take her. I caused mine because I wouldn't be given, wouldn't be taken, but chose my man and my fate. The man was famous, the fate obscure; not a bad balance.

All the same, sometimes I believe I must be long dead, and am telling this story in some part of the underworld that we didn't know about—a deceiving place where we think we're alive, where we think we're growing old and remembering what happened when we were young, when the bees swarmed and my hair caught fire, when the Trojans came. After all, how can it be that we can all talk to one another? I remember the foreigners from the other side of the world, sailing up the Tiber into a country they knew nothing of: their envoy came to my father's house, explained that he was a Trojan, and made polite speeches in fluent Latin. Now how could that be? Do we all know all the languages? That can be true only of the dead, whose land lies under all the other lands. How is it that you understand me, who lived twenty-five or thirty centuries ago? Do you know Latin?

But then I think no, it has nothing to do with being dead, it's not death that allows us to understand one another, but poetry.

IF YOU'D MET ME WHEN I WAS A GIRL AT HOME YOU MIGHT well have thought that my poet's faint portrait of me, sketched as if with a brass pin on a wax tablet, was quite sufficient: a girl, a king's daughter, a marriageable virgin, chaste, silent, obedient, ready to a man's will as a field in spring is ready for the plow.

I've never plowed, but I've watched our farmers at it all my life: the white ox trudging forward in the yoke, the man gripping the long wood handles that buck and rear as he tries to force the plowshare through the soil that looks so meek and ready and is so tough, so shut. He strains with all his weight and muscle to make a scratch deep enough to hold the barley seed. He labors till he's gasping and shaking with exhaustion and wants only to lie down in the furrow and sleep on his hard mother's breast among the stones. I never had to plow, but I had a hard mother too. Earth will take the plowman in her arms at last and let him sleep deeper than the barley seed, but my mother had no embrace for me.

I was silent and meek because if I spoke up, if I showed my will, she might remember that I was not my brothers, and I'd suffer for it. I was six when they died, little Latinus and baby Laurens. They'd been my dears, my dolls. I played with them and adored them. My mother Amata watched over us smiling as the spindle dropped and rose in her fingers. She didn't leave us with our nurse Vestina and the other women as a queen might do, but stayed with us all day long, for love. Often she sang to us as we played. Sometimes she stopped spinning and leapt up, took my hands and Latinus' hands and danced with us, and we all laughed together. "My warriors," she called the boys, and I thought she was calling me a warrior too, because she was so happy when she called them warriors, and her happiness was ours.

We fell ill: first the baby, then Latinus with his round face and big ears and clear eyes, then I. I remember the strange dreams of fever. My grandfather the woodpecker flew to me and pecked my head and I cried out with the pain. In a month or so I got better, got well again; but the boys' fever would fall and then return, fall and return. They grew thin, they wasted away. They would seem to be on the mend, Laurens would nurse eagerly at my mother's breast, Latinus would creep out of bed to play with me. Then the fever would come back and seize them. One afternoon Latinus went into convulsions, the fever was a dog that shakes a rat to death, he was shaken to death, the crown prince, the hope of Latium, my playmate, my dear. That night the thin little baby brother slept easily, his fever was down; next morning early he died in my arms with a gasp and a shiver, like a kitten. And my mother went mad with grief.

My father would never understand that she was mad.

He grieved bitterly for his sons. He was a man of warm feeling, and the boys had been, as a man sees it, his posterity. He wept for them, aloud at first, then for a long time in silence, for years. But he had the relief of his duties as king, and he had the rites to perform, the consolation of returning ritual, the reassurance of the ancient family spirits of his house. And I was solace to him, too, for I performed the rites with him, as a king's daughter does; and also he loved me dearly, his first-born, late-born child. For he was much older than my mother.

She was eighteen when they married, he was forty. She was a princess of the Rutuli of Ardea, he was king of all Latium. She was beautiful, passionate and young; he, a man in his prime, handsome and strong, a victorious warrior who loved peace. It was a match that might have turned out very well.

He didn't blame her for the boys' deaths. He didn't blame me for not having died. He took his loss and set what was left of his heart's hope on me. He went on, greyer and grimmer every year, but never unkind, and never weak, except in this: he let my mother do as she would, looked away when she acted wilfully, was silent when she spoke wildly.

Her awful grief met no human answer. She was left with a husband who couldn't hear or speak to her, a six-year-old weeping daughter, and a lot of miserable, frightened women who were afraid, as servants and slaves must be afraid, that they might be punished for the children's death.

For him she had only contempt; for me, rage.

I can remember each separate time I touched my mother's hand or body, or she touched mine, since my brothers died. She never slept again in the bed where she and my father conceived us.

After many days when she never came out of her room, she reappeared, seeming little changed, still splendid, with her shining black hair, her cream-white face, her proud bearing. Her manner in company had always been somewhat distant, rather lofty; she played the queen among commoners, and I used to marvel at how different she was with the men who thronged the king's house than she was with us children, when she sat spinning and singing and laughed and danced with us. With the house people her manner had been imperious, wilful, hot-tempered, but they loved her, for there was no meanness in her. Now she was mostly cold to them, cold to us, calm. But when I spoke, or my father spoke, often I saw the crimp of loathing in her face, the desolate, scornful fury, before she looked away.

She wore the boys' bullas round her neck, the little amulet bags with a tiny clay phallus in them that boys wear for good luck and protection. She kept the bullas in their gold capsules hidden under her clothes. She never took them off.

The anger that she hid in company broke out often in the women's side of the house as fierce irritation with me. The pet name many people called me, "little queen," particularly annoyed her, and they soon stopped saying it. She did not often speak to me, but if I annoyed her she would turn on me suddenly and tell me in a hard, flat voice that I was a fool, ugly, stupidly timid. "You're afraid of me. I hate cowards," she would say. Sometimes my presence drove her into actual frenzy. She would strike me or shake me till my head snapped back and forth. Once the fury drove her to tear at my face with her nails. Vestina pulled me away from her, got her to her room and quieted her, and hurried back to wash the long, bleeding rips down my cheeks. I was too stunned to cry, but Vestina wept over me as she put salve on the wounds. "They won't scar," she said tearfully, "I'm sure they won't scar."

My mother's voice came calmly from where she was lying in her bedroom: "That's good."

Vestina told me to tell people that the cat had scratched me. When my father saw my face and demanded to know what had happened, I said, "Silvia's old cat scratched me. I was holding her too tight and a hound came by and she was frightened. It wasn't her fault." I came to half believe the story, as children will, and decorated it with details and circumstances, such as that I was quite alone when it happened, in the oak grove just outside Tyrrhus' farmstead, and ran all the way home. I repeated that Silvia was not to blame, nor was the cat. I didn't want to get either of them in trouble. Kings are quick to punish, it relieves their anxiety. Silvia was my dearest friend and playmate, and the old farm cat had a litter of suckling kittens that would die without her. So it had to be my fault alone that my face was scratched. And Vestina was right: her comfrey salve was good; the long red furrows scabbed, healed, and left no scar but one faint silvery track down my left cheekbone under the eye. A day comes when Aeneas traces the scar with his finger and asks me what it is. "A cat scratched me," I say. "I was holding her, and a dog frightened her."

I KNOW THAT THERE WILL BE FAR GREATER KINGS OF FAR greater kingdoms than Latinus of Latium, my father. Upriver at Seven Hills there used to be two little fortified places with dirt walls, Janiculum and Saturnia; then some Greek settlers came, rebuilt on the hillside, and called their fort and town Pallanteum. My poet tried to describe to me that place as he knew it when when he was alive, or will know it when he lives, I should say, for although he was dying when he came to me, and has been dead a long time now, he hasn't yet been born. He is among those who wait on the far side of the forgetful river. He hasn't forgotten me yet, but he will, when at last he comes to be born, swimming across that milky water. When he first imagines me he won't know that he is yet to meet me in the forest of Albunea. Anyhow, he told me that in time to come, where that village is now, the Seven Hills and the valleys among the hills and all the riverbanks will be covered for miles with an unimaginable city. There will be temples of marble splendid with gold on the hilltops, wide arched gates, innumerable figures carved of marble and bronze; more people will pass through the Forum of that city in a single day, he said, than I will see in all the towns and farmsteads, on all the roads, in all the festivals and battlefields of Latium, in all my life. The king of that city will be the great ruler of the world, so great that he will despise the name of king and be known only as the one made great with holy power, the august. All the peoples of all the lands will bow to him and bring tribute. I believe this, knowing that my poet always speaks the truth, if not always the whole truth. Not even a poet can speak the whole truth.

But in my girlhood his great city was a rough little town built up against the slope of a rocky hill full of caves and overgrown with thick scrub. I went there once with my father, a day's sail up the river on the west wind. The king there, Evander, an ally of ours, was an exile from Greece, and in some trouble here too—he had killed a guest. He'd had sufficient reason for it, but that sort of thing doesn't get forgotten by our country folk. He was grateful for my father's favor and did his best to entertain us, but he lived far more poorly than our wealthy farmers. Pallanteum was a dark stockade, huddled under trees between the wide yellow river and the forested hills. They gave us a feast, of course, beef and venison, but served it very strangely: we had to lie down on benches at small tables, instead of sitting all together at one long table. That was the Greek fashion. And they didn't keep the sacred salt and meal on the table. That worried me all through the banquet.

Evander's son Pallas, who was about my age, eleven or twelve then, a nice boy, told me a story about a huge beast-man that used to live up there in one of the caves and came out in twilight to steal cattle and tear people to pieces. He was seldom seen, but left great footprints. A Greek hero called Ercles came by and killed the beast-man. What was he called? I asked, and Pallas said Cacus. I knew that that meant the fire lord, the chief man of a tribal settlement, who kept Vesta alight for the people of the neighborhood, with the help of his daughters, as my father did. But I didn't want to contradict the Greeks' story of the beast-man, which was more exciting than mine.

Pallas asked me if I'd like to see a she-wolf's den, and I said yes, and he took me to a cave called the Lupercal, quite near the village. It was sacred to Pan, he said, which seemed to be what the Greeks called our grandfather Faunus. Anyhow, the settlers let the wolf and her cubs alone, wisely, and she let them alone too. She never even hurt their dogs, though wolves hate dogs. There were plenty of deer for her in those hills. Now and then in spring she'd take a lamb. They counted that as sacrifice, and when she didn't take a lamb, they'd sacrifice a dog to her. Her mate had disappeared this past winter.

It was not the wisest thing perhaps for two children to stand at the mouth of her den, for she had cubs, and she was there. The cave smelled very strong. It was black dark inside, and silent. But as I grew used to the dark I saw the two small, unmoving fires of her eyes. She stood there between us and her children.

Pallas and I backed away slowly, our gaze always on her eyes. I did not want to go, though I knew I should. I turned at last and followed Pallas, but slowly, looking back often to see if the she-wolf would come out of her house and stand there dark and stiff-legged, the loving mother, the fierce queen.

On that visit to the Seven Hills I saw that my father was a much greater king than Evander was. Later I came to know that he was more powerful than any of the kings of the West in his day, even though he might be nothing in comparison with the great august one to come. He had established his kingdom firmly by warfare and defense of his borders long before I was born. While I was a child growing up, there were no wars to speak of. It was a long time of peace. Of course there were feuds and battles among the farmers and along the boundaries. We're a rough people, born of oak, as they say, here in the western land; tempers run high, weapons are always at hand. Now and then my father had to intervene, put down a rustic quarrel that got too hot or spread too widely. He had no standing army. Mars lives in the plowlands and the borders of the plowlands. If there was trouble, Latinus called his farmers from their fields, and they came with their fathers' old bronze swords and leather shields, ready to fight to the death for him. When they'd put down the trouble they went back to their fields, and he to his high house.

The high house, the Regia, was the great shrine of the city, a sacred place, for our storeroom gods and ancestors were the Penates and Lares of the city and the people. Latins came there from all over Latium to worship and sacrifice as well as to feast with the king. You saw the high house from a long way off in the countryside, standing among tall trees above the walls and towers and roofs.

The walls of Laurentum were high and strong, because it wasn't built on a hilltop like most cities, but on the rich plains that sloped down towards the lagoons and the sea. Farmed fields and pastures lay all round it outside the ditch and earthwork, and in front of the city gate was a broad open ground where athletes played and men trained their horses. But entering the gate of Laurentum you came out of sun and wind into deep, fragrant shade. The city was a great grove, a forest. Every house stood among oak trees, fig trees, elms, slender poplars and spreading laurels. The streets were shady, leafy, narrow. The broadest of the streets led up to the king's house, great and stately, towering with a hundred columns of cedar wood.

On a shelf on each wall of the entryway was a row of images, carved by an Etruscan exile years ago as an offering to the king. They were spirits, ancestors—two-faced Janus, Saturn, Italus, Sabinus, Grandfather Picus who was turned into the red-capped woodpecker but whose statue in a stiff carved toga sat holding the sacred staff and shield—a double row of grim figures in cracked and blackened cedar. They were not large, but they were the only images in human form in Laurentum, except the little clay Penates, and they filled me with fear. Often I shut my eyes as I ran between those long dark faces with blank staring eyes, under axes and crested helmets and javelins and the bars of city gates and the prows of ships, war trophies, nailed up along the walls.

The corridor of the images opened out into the atrium, a low, large, dark room with a roof open in the center to the sky. To the left were the council and banquet halls, which as a child I seldom entered, and beyond them the royal apartments; straight ahead was the altar of Vesta, with the domed brick storerooms behind it. I turned right and ran past the kitchens out into the great central courtyard, where a fountain played under the laurel tree my father planted when he was young, and sweet daphne and shrubs of thyme and oregano and tarragon grew in big pots, and women worked and chatted and spun and wove and rinsed out jugs and bowls in the fountain pool. I ran across among them, under the colonnade of cedar pillars, into the women's part of the house, the best part, home.

If I was careful not to bring myself to my mother's attention I had nothing to fear. Sometimes, as I grew towards womanhood, she spoke to me kindly enough. And there were a lot of women there who loved me, and women who flattered me, and old Vestina to spoil me, and other girls to be a girl with, and babies to play with. And—women's side or men's side—it was my father's house, and I was my father's daughter.

My best friend, though, was not a girl of the Regia at all but the youngest child of the cattleman Tyrrhus, who was in charge of my family's herds as well as his own. His family farm was a quarter mile from the city gates, a huge place with many outbuildings, the stone-and-timber farmhouse bulking up among them like an old grey gander in a flock of geese. Cattle pens and paddocks and pastures stretched away back from the kitchen gardens among the low, oak-crowned hills. The farm was a place of endless industry, people working everywhere all day; but unless the forge was lit and the anvil clanging, or a drove of cattle was penned in close by for castration or for market, it was deeply quiet. Distant mooing from the valleys and the murmur of mourning doves and wood doves in the oak groves near the house made a continuous softness of sound into which other noises sank away and were lost. I loved that farm.

Silvia came to keep me company sometimes at the Regia, but we both preferred to be at her place. In summer I ran out there almost every day. Tita, a slave a couple of years older than I, came with me as the guardian my status of virgin princess required, but as soon as we got there Tita joined her friends among the farm women, and Silvia and I ran off to climb trees or dam the creek or play with the kittens or catch polliwogs and roam the woods and hills, as free as the sparrows.

My mother would have kept me home. "What kind of company is it she chooses to keep? Cowherds!" But my father, born a king, ignored her snobbery. "Let the child run about and get strong. They're good people," he said. Indeed Tyrrhus was a trusty, competent man, ruling his pastures as firmly as my father ruled his realm. He had an explosive temper but was just with his people; he kept every feast day generously, with observance and sacrifice to the local spirits and sacred places. He had fought beside my father in the old wars long ago, and still had a bit of the warrior about him. But he was soft as warm butter when it came to his daughter. Her mother had died soon after her birth, and she had no sisters. She grew up the darling of her father and brothers and all the house people. She was in many ways more a princess than I. She didn't have to spend hours a day spinning or weaving, and had no ceremonial duties. The old cooks ran the kitchen for her, the old slaves kept the household for her, the girls swept the hearth and fed the fire for her; she had all the time in the world to run free on the hills and play with her pet animals.

Silvia had a wonderful way with creatures. In the evening, the little owls would come to her quavering call, *hu-u-u, hi-i-i,* and alight a moment on her outstretched hand. She tamed a fox cub; when it grew to a vixen she let it go free, but it brought its cubs round yearly for us to see, letting them gambol in the twilight on the grass under the oaks. She reared a fawn her brothers took on a hunt, the hounds having pulled down its mother. Silvia was ten or eleven when they brought the little thing in. She nursed it tenderly, and it grew into a magnificent stag as tame as any dog. He trotted off to the woods every morning, but was always back at supper time; they let him come into the dining room and eat from their trenchers. Silvia adored her Cervulus. She washed him and combed him, and decked his splendid antlers with vines in autumn and flower wreaths in spring. Male deer can be dangerous, but the stag was docile and mild, far too trusting for his own good. Silvia fastened a broad white linen band round his neck as a sign, and all the hunters of the forests of Latium knew Silvia's Cervulus. Even the hounds knew him and seldom started him, having been scolded and beaten for doing so.

It was a wonderful thing to be out on the hills and see a great stag come walking calmly from the forest, balancing his crown of horns. He would kneel and put his nose in Silvia's hand, and folding his tall delicate legs under him, sit there between us while she stroked his neck. He smelled sweet and strong and gamy. His eyes were large, dark, and quiet; so were Silvia's eyes. That is what it was like in the age of Saturn, my poet said, the golden time of the first days when there was no fear in the world. Silvia seemed a daughter of that age. To sit with her on the sunlit slopes or run with her on the forest trails she knew so well was the delight of my life. There was no one in all that country of our girlhood who wished us any harm. Our pagans, the folk of the plowlands, greeted us from their fields or the doorstep of their round huts. The surly bee-keeper saved a comb of honey for us, the dairy women had a sip of cream for us, the cowboys showed off for us, riding bull calves or vaulting an old cow's horns, and the old shepherd Ino showed us how to make piping flutes of oat straw.

Sometimes in summer as the long day drew toward evening and we knew we should be starting home to the farm, we'd both lie facedown on the hillside and push our faces right into the harsh dry grass and the hard clodded dirt, breathing in the infinitely complex smell, hay-sweet and soil-bitter, of the warm summer earth, our earth. Then we were both Saturn's children. We leapt up and ran down the hill, ran home—race you to the cattle ford!

When I was fifteen years old, King Turnus came on a visit of state to my father. He was my cousin, my mother's nephew; his father Daunus, ailing, had given him the crown of Rutulia the year before, and we'd heard of the splendors of the ceremonies of his coronation at Ardea, the nearest city south of Latium. The Rutulians had been close allies of ours since Latinus married Daunus' sister Amata, but young Turnus showed signs of wanting to go his own way. When the Etruscans of Caere drove out their tyrant Mezentius, a savage man who held nothing sacred, Turnus took him in. Now all Etruria was angry with Turnus for receiving and sheltering the tyrant, who had abused his power so cruelly that even the Lares and the Penates of his household had forsaken him. That ill feeling was a matter of concern to us, since Caere was just across the river. The Etruscan cities were powerful and it behooved us to keep on good terms with them if we could.

My father discussed these matters with me as we walked to the sacred forest of Albunea. It lay east of Laurentum, under the hills, a day's walk. We had gone there together several times; I served as his acolyte in the rites there as he praised and propitiated our ancestors and the powers of the woods and springs. In those solitary walks he talked to me as to his heir. Though I couldn't inherit his crown, he saw no reason why I should remain ignorant of matters of policy and government. After all, I'd almost certainly be queen of some kingdom. Perhaps, indeed, of Rutulia.

He didn't talk about that possibility, but the women did. Vestina was certain of it the moment she heard of King Turnus' visit: "He's coming for our Lavinia! He's coming courting!"

My mother looked sharply at Vestina across the big basket of raw wool we were all pulling. Pulling wool, drawing apart the blobs and hunks of a washed fleece to separate the fibers so they can be carded, was always my favorite housework; it's easy and perfectly mindless, and the clean fleece smells sweet, and your hands get soft from the oil in the wool, and the blobs and hunks end up as a huge, pale, airy, hairy, lovely cloud towering out of the basket.

"Now that's enough of that," my mother said. "Only peasants talk about marriage for a girl her age."

"They say he's the most beautiful man in Italy," said Tita.

"And he rides a stallion nobody else can ride," said Picula.

"And his hair is golden," said Vestina.

"He has a sister, Juturna, as beautiful as he is, but she's vowed never to leave the river, they say," said Sabella.

"What a gabble of geese you are!" my mother said.

"You must have known him as a child, queen?" Sicana, my mother's favorite woman, asked.

"Yes, he was a fine little boy," Amata said. "Very fond of his own way." She smiled a little, as she often did when she spoke of her childhood home.

I went up to the watchtower in the southeast corner of the house, above the royal apartments, from which one could see down into the streets and over the city walls and gate. I saw the visitors arrive at the gate and come up the Via Regia, all mounted, with shining breastplates and nodding crests. Then I ran down to the atrium and stood with the house people while my father welcomed Turnus. I got a good look at him, his men, and his high plumed helmet. He was splendidly handsome, well-made and muscular, with curly red-brown hair, dark-blue eyes, and a proud stance. If there was any physical flaw in him, it was that he was rather short for his strong build and deep chest, so that his walk seemed a bit strutting. His voice was deep and clear.

I was summoned to dinner in the great hall that day. My mother and I put on our finest light robes, with the women goose-gabbling all about us and fussing with our hair. Sicana set out for my mother the great necklace of gold and garnets that was Latinus' wedding gift to her, but she put it aside and wore a necklace and earrings of silver and amethyst which her brother Daunus had given her as a parting gift. She looked joyful and radiant. I thought that as usual I could hide behind her, effaced and protected by her imperious beauty.

But during the meal, while Turnus talked affably with both my father and my mother, he looked at me. He didn't stare, but he looked again and again, with a slight smile. I became embarrassed as I never had been. His intense blue eyes began to frighten me. Every time I dared glance up, he was looking at me.

I hadn't given any thought to love and marriage. What was there to think about? When it came time for me to be married, I'd be married, and find out what love was, and childbirth, and the rest of it. Until then, it was nothing to me. Silvia and I could tease each other and joke about a handsome young farmer who made eyes at her, or her eldest brother Almo who sometimes hung around to talk to me, but it was all words, it meant nothing. No man in the house, in the city, in all the country, could look at me as Turnus was looking. My realm was virginity and I was at home in it, unthreatened and at ease. No man had ever made me blush.

Now I felt myself burning red from the roots of my hair clear down to my breasts, to my knees. I cowered with shame. I couldn't eat. The besieging army was at the walls.

Turnus would certainly have recognised the poet's portrait of me as a shrinking silent maiden. My mother, beside whom I sat, was well aware of my discomfort, and it did not displease her; she let me cower, and talked away to Turnus about Ardea. I don't know if she made a signal to my father or he came to his own decision, but as soon as the meat trenchers had been removed, and the boy had thrown the offering into the fire, and the servants were going round with ewers and napkins and refilling wine goblets for the aftercourse, he bade my mother send me away.

"We are losing the flower of the feast," the visiting king protested graciously.

"The child needs her sleep," said my father.

Turnus lifted his cup—the double-handled gold goblet from Cures engraved with a hunting scene, loot from one of my father's wars, our best piece of tableware—and said, "Fairest of all the daughters of Father Tiber, may you have sweet dreams!"

I sat paralysed.

"Get along with you," my mother murmured to me, with something like a laugh.

I slipped out as quick as I could, barefoot, for I didn't want to stop to put my sandals on. I heard Turnus' resonant voice behind me in the hall, but not what he said. My ears were ringing. The night air in the courtyard was like cold water dashed over my hot face and body, making me gasp and shiver.

In the women's side I was of course pounced on by all the girls and women telling me and one another how glorious and gorgeous the young king was, how big and tall, how he'd hung up his helmet and a huge sword and a gilt bronze breastplate like a giant's in the hall, and asking me what had he said at dinner? and did I like him? I couldn't answer. Vestina helped me drive them all away, saying I looked feverish and needed to go to bed. After I'd finally persuaded her too to leave me alone, I could lie in my bed in my small silent room and look at Turnus.

Of course it was foolish to ask if I liked him. A young girl meeting a man, a handsome man, a king, who may be her first suitor, does not like or dislike him. Her heart beats, her blood runs, and she sees him—sees him only: maybe as the rabbit sees the hawk, maybe as the earth sees the sky. I saw Turnus as a city sees a splendid stranger, a captain of armies, at the city gate. That he was there, that he had come, was wonderful and terrible. Nothing would ever be the same again. But there was no need, yet, to unbar the gate.

Turnus stayed several days with us, but I met him again only once. He requested my presence at dinner on his last evening, and I was sent in to the feast, but not to eat with the guests and company,

only for the aftercourse, to hear the singing and see the dancers. I
sat with my mother, and again Turnus looked often at me, making
no effort to disguise it. He smiled at us. His smile was a pleasant,
quick flash. When he was watching the dancers, I looked at him. I
noticed how small his ears were, that his head was well shaped, that
his jaw was square and strong. He might get jowly, later in life. The
back of his neck was pleasant, smooth. I saw that he was attentive
and respectful to my father, who, sitting near him, looked old.

My mother was ten or twelve years older than her nephew, but
tonight she did not look it; her eyes shone and she laughed. She and
Turnus got on well together and were at ease. They talked lightly
across the table, and the other guests joined in, and my father listened to them benevolently.

The day after Turnus left, my father sent for me and my mother.
We walked under the portico outside the banquet hall; he had sent
away all the people that usually were around him. It was a rainy
spring day, and he was wearing his toga, for as he got older he felt
the cold. He paced with us in silence for a while and then said,
"The Rutulian king began to say to me last night that he wishes to
be a suitor for your hand, Lavinia. I did not let him go on. I said
that you are not yet of an age for me to permit talk of courtship or
marriage. He would have argued, of course, but I did not let him
argue. I said my daughter is too young."

He looked at us both. I had no idea what to say. I looked at
my mother.

"You gave him no encouragement at all?" Amata asked, calm
and civil, as she always was with her husband.

"I didn't say that she'll always be too young," my father answered in his mild, dry way.

"King Turnus has a great deal to offer his bride," she said.

"He does indeed. Good land down there. He's a good fighter, too, they say. His father certainly was."

"I am sure he is a brave warrior."

"And wealthy."

We paced on down the portico. Rain pattered in the courtyard, the leaves of the lemon trees nodded. Under the big laurel tree it was still quite dry, and one of the house girls sat there spinning and singing a long spinning song.

"So you might favor the boy if he comes back another year?" my father asked my mother.

"I might," she said coolly. "If indeed he is willing to wait."

"And you, Lavinia?"

"I don't know," I said.

He put his hand on my shoulder. "Don't worry about it, my dear," he said. "There's plenty of time for this sort of thing."

"What would you do about tending Vesta?" I said—I could not bring myself to say, "if I went off to be married."

"Well, we must think about that. Choose a girl to whom you can begin to teach the duties."

"Maruna," I said at once.

"An Etruscan?"

"Her mother is. You took her on a raid across the river. Maruna grew up here. She's pious." By that word I meant responsible, faithful to duty, open to awe. My father had taught me the meaning of the word and the value of it.

"Good. Take her with you when you tend the fire and clean the hearth and make the sacred salt. Let her begin to learn all these matters."

My mother had nothing to say in this; it is the king's daughter who keeps his hearth alight. It was bitter to both my parents, I know, that when we sat to dinner every day the boy who fed the altar fire with our food and spoke the blessing was not their son, as he should have been, but only a servant boy. Now the care of the fire and the storerooms too must go to a substitute, a slave.

My father sighed a little; his large, warm, hard hand was still on my shoulder. My mother paced forward, impassive. As we turned to walk back down under the columns she said, "It might be well not to make that young king wait too long."

"A year, or two, or three," Latinus said.

"Oh," and she winced with disgust and impatience. "Three years! The man is young, Latinus! He has hot blood in his veins."

"All the more reason to give our girl time to grow up."

Amata did not argue, she never argued, but she shrugged.

I read in her shrug her disbelief that I would ever grow to be a match for such a man as Turnus. Indeed I wondered how I could. To mate with such a man I should be deep-breasted and majestic like my mother, fierce like her, and fiercely beautiful. I was short and thin, sunburnt, uncouth. I was a girl, not a woman. I put my hand up on my father's hand on my shoulder and held it there as we walked. I could look at blue-eyed Turnus in the darkness of my room at night, but I did not want to think about leaving my home.

AENEAS' ARMOR HANGS IN THE ENTRYWAY OF OUR HOUSE here in Lavinium, as Turnus' sword and breastplate hung on his visits to Laurentum. I have seen Aeneas wear the armor several times, the helmet, cuirass, greaves, with the long sword and the round shield, all of bronze: he shines as the sea glances and dazzles under the sun. To see his armor hanging there is to realise what a large, powerful man he is. He doesn't look large, or even very muscular, because his body is in perfect proportion, and he moves lightly and gracefully, considerate of who and what is around him, not shoving forward as many big, strong men do. Yet I can hardly lift the armor he wears so easily. It was a gift from his mother, who had it made for him by a great fire lord, he told me. Indeed the man who forged and worked that armor was the lord of smiths. There is in all the western world no work so beautiful as that shield.

The surface of the seven layers of welded bronze is covered all over with a great pattern of figures embossed and delicately carved and picked out with gold and silver inlay. Here and there is a slight dent or scratch from battle. I stand and study that shield often. The picture I like best is high on the left, a wolf who turns her sleek neck back to lick her suckling cubs, but the cubs are human babies, boys, greedy at her teats. Another I like is a goose, all done in silver, who stands with her neck upstretched, hissing in alarm. Behind her some men climb a cliff; their hair is curly gold, their cloaks are striped with silver; around his neck each man has a twisted collar of gold.

Not far from the wolf are figures I recognise from our festivals—some Leaping Priests with two-lobed shields, and a pair of Wolf Boys running naked, brandishing their thorn sticks at laughing women. There are a few women here and there in the pictures, but mostly it is men, men fighting, endless battle scenes, men torn apart, men disemboweled, bridges torn down, walls torn down, slaughter.

Aeneas is not in any of the pictures, and nothing the poet told me about the siege and fall of his city, or his wanderings before he came to Latium, is recognisable on the shield. "Are these scenes of Troy?" I ask him, and he shakes his head.

"I do not know what they are," he says. "They may be scenes of what is yet to come."

"What is yet to come is mostly war, then," I say, looking among them for some that aren't battles, for an unhelmeted face. I see a mass rape, women screaming and fighting as they are dragged off by warriors. I see great, beautiful ships with banks of oars, but the ships are all at war, some are burning. Fire and smoke rise up over the water.

"I think it may be the realm our sons' sons will inherit," he says, very low. Aeneas always speaks out of silence, seldom at length, usually in a low voice. He is never sullen, but he is quiet, he handles words as he handles his sword, only when he has to.

That is my poet's Rome, then, the great city in many of the pictures. I look more closely at the center of the shield, the sea battle. On the stern of a ship stands a man with a handsome, cold face. Fire streams from his head, and a comet hovers over it. I think that is the man made great, the august one.

As I continue looking I see things I never observed before. The city, or some great city, lies all in ruins, utterly destroyed and burned. I see another destroyed city, and another. Enormous fires burst out in a line, one after another, enveloping a whole countryside in flame. Huge machines of war crawl on the ground, or dive under the sea, or hurtle through the air. The earth itself burns in oily black clouds. Now an immense round cloud of destruction rises up over the sea at the end of the world. I know it is the end of the world. I say to Aeneas in horror, "Look, look!"

But he cannot see what I see in the shield. He will not live to see it. He must die after only three years, and widow me. Only I, who met the poet in the woods of Albunea, can keep looking through the bronze of my husband's shield to see all the wars he will not fight.

The poet made him live, live greatly, so he must die. I, whom the poet gave so little life to, I can go on. I can live to see the cloud above the sea at the end of the world.

I burst into tears and clasp Aeneas in my arms, and he holds me tenderly, telling me not to cry, dear heart, don't cry.

THE KING'S HOUSE WHERE I LIVE IS A SQUARE DIVIDED IN four quarters; the great laurel tree is at the crossing, the center. I go out at first dawn from the house and from the city into the fields east of the city.

The pagus where we pagans live is the pattern of the farmers' fields, outlined by the paths between the fields. At the crossing, where four fields meet, is the shrine of the Lares, the spirits of the meeting place. The shrine has four doors, and before each door is the altar of a farmer's field. I stand out on one of the paths between fields, looking at the sky.

The house of the sky is limitless, but with my mind I give it borders and divide it into four. I stand at the center, the crossing, facing south, facing Ardea. I watch the empty sky into which light flows upward slowly. Crows fly from the left, from the eastern hills, circle above me calling, and return into the sunrise that crowns the hills with fire. It is a good omen, but the red sunrise foretells a stormy day.

I WAS TWELVE WHEN I FIRST WENT WITH MY FATHER TO Albunea, the sacred forest under the hill, where sulfur springs running out from a high cave fill the shadowy air with an endless, troubled noise and a mist that smells of rotten eggs. There the spirits of the dead are within hearing if you call. In the old days people came to Albunea from all the western lands to consult with the spirits and powers of the place; now many go to the oracle near Tibur, which bears the same name. This lesser Albunea was sacred to my family. When my father was disturbed in his mind he went there. This time he said to me, "Wear your sacred robe, daughter, and come help me with the sacrifice." I had served as his assistant often at home, as a child's duty is, but I had never yet been to the sacred spring. I put on my red-bordered toga and took a bag of salted meal from the storeroom behind Vesta. We walked for some miles on paths through familiar fields and pastures, then we were in country I had not seen before, wilder, the forested hills drawing closer on both sides. We came to a little stream and followed the north side of its rocky gorge; it was called the Prati, my father said, and he told me of the rivers of Latium: our Lentulus at Laurentum, the Harenosus, the Prati, the Stagnulus, and the sacred Numicus that rises high on the Alban Mountain and is our boundary with Rutulia.

He carried the sacrifice, a two-week lamb. It was April. The thickets were all budding and in bloom, and the oaks on the hillsides bore their long, delicate, reticent flowers of green and bronze. The forests ahead of us rose up and up towards the Alban Mountain, and craggy woods hung like a dark cloud to our left. We entered under the trees. It was dark in the forest, and only a few birds sang, though the fields and thickets had been loud with their chanting. I smelled the stink of the spring nearby, but did not see the vapors, and heard the noise of the water only faintly, a hissing murmur like a kettle coming to the boil.

The sacred place was in a grassy glade deep in the forest, marked out in a rough square with a rock wall no higher than my knee. Within that enclosure the sense of the numen, the presence and power of the sacred, was strong and strange. Tattered, rotting fleeces lay about on the earth inside the wall. There was a small rock altar; my father cut a turf from outside the wall and laid it on the altar. We drew the corner of our togas over our heads. He lighted the fire. I made a garland of young laurel leaves and garlanded the lamb. I sprinkled it with salted meal from my bag, and held it while he prayed. The lamb was docile and fearless, a noble sacrifice; it had its own piety. I held it while my father cut its throat with the long bronze knife, offering this life to the powers we do not know, in fear and gratitude and seeking to be in peace with them. We burned the entrails on the altar fire to augment the power of the spirits. We toasted and ate the ribs ourselves, having not eaten since noon the day before. The rest of the meat I wrapped to carry home. My father scraped the hide and laid it down on the ground, the fleece up, and gathered the remnants of other sheepskins and spread them out. They were damp from the rain a couple of days earlier, and stank of rot and mildew, but that is one's bed at Albunea.

It was quite dark now, the red of the sun was gone from the aisles of the trees, and the sky between the branches was dim. We lay down on the sheepskins, the fleece of our lamb under our heads.

I do not know if the power of Albunea came into my father that night, but it came to me, not as a voice speaking from the trees as it comes to others, but as a dream, or what I took to be a dream. In my sleep I was beside a river, which I knew to be the Numicus. I stood at a ford, alone, watching the clear water run among stones. I saw a thread of color in the water as it ran by, a vein of red. It thickened and blurred into a cloud of red that drifted downstream and was gone. A heavy, heavy weight of grief bore down my heart so that my knees failed and I crouched weeping among the stones. At last I got up and walked upstream and came to a town; its ramparts were of fresh earth. I was still weeping, and held the corner of my garment over my head and face, but I knew that city was my home. Then in my dream I was in the forest of Albunea again, still alone. This time I went past the altar glade and came to the spring. I could not come close to the cave. The hissing, boiling noise was loud there, and all about the mouth of the cave the ground was bog and shallow pools. The stinking, bluish mist hovered over the water and the ground. I heard a woodpecker off among the trees, his tapping on a trunk and his call like a harsh laugh—then he came flying. I drew back, pulling the cloth over my head, afraid, but he did not strike me. I saw his scarlet head flash before me. He drew his wings across my eyes twice, very lightly, like the touch of the softest veil. He laughed as he flew off. I looked up and saw it was not dark under the trees; the forest was full of a still light without shadows, and the water and mist of the spring were luminous.

I woke then, and saw that same still light for a while in the glade, fading as day came.

Before we left, I went on to the spring, and saw it was as I had seen it in my dream, though shadowed.

My father was again silent as we started home. As we came out of the forest I looked south, imagining the course of the Numicus, the ford, and the place where I had seen the town in my dream. I said, "Grandfather Picus came to me while I slept last night, father." And I told him what I had seen.

He listened and said nothing for a time. "That is a powerful grandfather," he said at last.

"He struck my head when I had the fever. I cried for the pain."

"But this time he touched your eyes with his wing."

I nodded. We walked on a while. Latinus said, "Albunea is in his gift. He and the other powers of the woods. He has given you the freedom of it, daughter. He has opened your eyes to see."

"May I come with you again?"

"You may come there when you choose, I think."

IF MY DAUGHTER HAD LIVED SHE NEVER COULD HAVE RUN safe and free through fields outside our domains or along the hillsides among the grazing herds, as I used to run. When my son was a boy the forests were safer for him than the pagus fields. But when I was a girl I walked the open hillsides and the wilderness paths to Albunea with no companion but Maruna. Sometimes she accompanied me all the way, sometimes she stayed the night with a woodcutter's family at the edge of the forest while I went alone to the sacred glade. We could do this because the peace my father had brought to Latium was real and durable. In that peace, little children could watch the cattle, shepherds could let their flocks wander in the summer pastures with no risk of theft, women and girls need not go guarded or in bands but could walk without fear on any path in Latium. Even in the true wild where there were no paths we were afraid of wolf and boar, not man. Because this order had held all my life as a girl, I thought it was the way the world had always been and would be. I had not learned how peace galls men, how they gather impatient rage against it as it continues, how even while they pray the powers for peace, they work against it and make certain it will be broken and give way to battle, slaughter, rape, and waste. Of all the greater powers the one I fear most is the one I cannot worship, the one who walks the boundary, the one who sets the ram on the ewe, and the bull on the heifer, and the sword in the farmer's hand: Mavors, Marmor, Mars.

I kept the storerooms of the king's house: that was my duty as the king's daughter, the camilla, the novice. The food we ate was in my charge. I ground the meal and the sacred salt that blessed the food. Daily and faithfully I cared for Vesta burning on our hearth, the bright center of our lives. But I was not permitted to enter the small room beside the house door where Mars lived—not Mars of the plow, Mars of the bull and stallion, nor Mars of the wolf, but the other one: Mars the sword, the spears, the shields that the Leapers brought out on the day of the new year, shaking him, waking him, rousing him up, dancing and leaping with him in the streets and through the fields. That Mars would be shut away again only when the October Horse had been sacrificed and winter itself, with cold and rain and darkness, ordained the peace.

Mars has no altar in the city. Men worship him. A girl, a virgin, I could have no business with him and wanted none. The house I kept was closed to him, as his was to me.

But I honored the sanction. He did not.

When I was a girl, I did not know him well enough to fear him. I liked to see the Leapers rush to open that locked room on the first day of March and come out in red cloaks and high-pointed hats, dancing, driving out the old year, letting in the new, brandishing the long spears and the shields shaped like an owl's face, cavorting and shouting through the streets of Laurentum, *"Mavors! Mavors! Macte esto!"* We girls ran from them and hid as we were supposed to do, in a dutiful, laughing mockery of fear. Oh how the men like to stick their spears up into the air, we said. Oh how they like to poke their spears and jab their spears. Oh don't they wish their spears were always ten feet long!

Because we were at peace I could laugh at the Leapers, because we were at peace I could sleep alone in Albunea, because we were at peace my father saw no harm in it when more suitors for my hand began coming to the Regia. Let them vie with one another, let Aventinus scowl at Turnus, let Turnus snub young Almo; they dared not quarrel under the king's roof, or break the king's peace across their boundaries. One of them would prove the best man in the end and take me to his house, and the others must make the best of it. My father enjoyed their visits very much, far more than I did. They brought young manhood into the house. He liked to feast them well and give them wine, pouring their bowls full again and again; he liked their gifts of game and sausage and white kids and black piglets; he liked them to see his beautiful fiery queen, so much younger than he, not so much older than some of them. He was a good and generous host, and his geniality disarmed their touchy brashness and their rivalries. They ended up all laughing late into the night at the great table. He made what might have been a cause of quarrels into a way to better friendship among his subject kings and chieftains.

If he had been my only parent I might have taken my suitors lightly, as he did, and with pleasure. Some of them were good fellows. Some were easy to laugh at. Ufens of Nersae, a mountain man, came in wolfskins, with a wolfskin hat, a black curly beard all over his red face, staring around him as if he'd never been in a town before, glowering at everybody except me—he couldn't look at me at all. Tita and the other women teased me endlessly about marrying him, the Wolf Boy, Chinthicket, they called him. And I could laugh with them. But I was polite and cautious and cold to all my suitors, even beyond what befitted my status as virgin prize; for my mother did not take the matter lightly at all, and made my position both difficult and false.

She wanted to marry me to her nephew Turnus of Ardea. That desire had come to possess her. She favored Turnus openly, was all smiles to him and hardly civil to the others who came to stand in his way. Her prejudice made it hard even for rich men like Aventinus to come courting me, and very hard for such a young man as Almo, son of Tyrrhus, the manager of the royal cattle herds, my Silvia's eldest brother. Almo was aiming pretty high in courting me at all, and against such a rival as King Turnus he stood no chance. But he was not merely ambitious, he had fallen in love with me; and having been fond of him all my life as an almost brother, I was sorry for him and kind to him, and so gave him false hope. My mother had no pity on him. She was fiercely jealous of our royal honor. She treated Almo as a cowherd. My father should not have allowed such discourtesy in his hall; but still he let all she did and said go by, and she hid the worst of her behavior from him. It was the game they played, that she could be mad yet not mad because he would not know she was mad.

I did not want to be courted. I did not want to receive the game, the sausages, the kids, the piglets, the stiff compliments. I did not want to sit at the banquet, the silent modest maiden, while my mother Amata spurned and sneered and turned her back on honest men and wooed her sister's son, handsome blue-eyed Turnus.

He did not snub or spurn her, never, of course not, he smiled, he murmured, he lowered his long eyelashes and lifted them again smiling and looked right through her to what he wanted. Could she not see that? Could I, a stupid virgin of seventeen, see it, and she not see it? Could my father sit at the head of the table and not see it?

Drances, an old friend and adviser of my father, was the only person of the household who showed dislike or distrust of Turnus. Drances greatly admired the sound of his own voice and was used to pontificating at our table, but now he had to listen to Turnus' tales of his exploits and triumphs in skirmishes and raids and hunts, and endure the young man's careless, genial, unintended discourtesies. I saw that Drances watched Turnus very keenly, and watched my mother too. Sometimes he would glance at my father, or even at me, as if to say, Do you see? My father was impervious, and I would not return his glance. I wanted nothing to do with Drances; it seemed he knew what I knew, but I did not know what he would do with the knowledge.

I came to the banquets because I must, and left as soon as I could. The only way I could avoid my suitors entirely was not to be in the house at all. These days I could go to Silvia's farm only if I knew poor ardent Almo would not be there. I could achieve absence from the Regia only by going to Albunea.

My mother's anger was chafed by the idea that I had some gift like my father's of conversation with the spirits. It gave me a kind of uncanny importance, which she despised. I agreed with her in my heart: the importance was false. But the gift was real. And it was useful to me as my reason not to be always at home, dressed in white, the meek garlanded sacrifice, while the suitors paraded through and drank their wine, and Turnus flattered my mother and laughed with my father and looked at me as the butcher looks at the cow. Amata tried to forbid me to go to the sacred place, for many good reasons, which she argued eloquently. My father, as always, seemed hardly to hear her. Usually that was how she got her way, but where I was concerned, his deafness was different. He temporised, waved his hand mildly, said, "Oh, it will do the child no harm," or, "Prince Aventinus will still be here, no doubt, when she returns," and let me go. And I put on my red-bordered robe, told Maruna to be ready at dawn, and went.

Turnus came for a visit in late April of the year I was eighteen. He brought a wagonload of splendid gifts to my parents. One was a horrible little creature that he said sailors had brought from Africa; it had hands and feet like ours, and a face like a noseless baby. He brought it in riding his shoulder, dressed in a tiny toga. It clambered all about, chattering, pulling things to pieces, spilling the salt, then stopping to sit and fondle its penis and stare at us with bright black eyes. Everyone at the long table laughed at its tricks. He presented it as a pet for me, and I tried to be kind to the little animal; but I could not like it, and it hated me. It pulled my hair and pissed my dress, and then sprang into my mother's arms. She kissed it and crooned over it. It pulled at the chains round her neck, tugged out the little gold bullas that held my brothers' amulets, and put one in its mouth. Seeing that, a sickness came over me. I had to ask to be excused, and as always my father let me go, though my mother would have made me stay.

I ran out into the courtyard and stopped at the fountain under the great laurel to wash my face and hands and my palla where the animal had pissed it. The night was cool, the stars bright through the leaves of the laurel. How I loved this house! How could I ever leave it, leave the spirits of the tree, of the spring, of my store-rooms, of the hearth, of my people, leave the beloved familiar powers and go serve those of a stranger in a strange place? That would be slavery. I would not do it. Maybe I would marry Almo, and my father would name him his heir, to be king after him, and we would live here, here, nowhere else . . . I knew that could not be. Yet my father had no heir, and someday he must name one, or adopt a son. I thought I did not care who it was so long as it was not Turnus. There was nothing much wrong with Turnus himself, but much wrong in the way my mother looked at him.

I went on to the women's side of the house. I told Maruna we were going to the forest tomorrow morning. Old Vestina said, "The Rutulian prince has just arrived, child! That is scarcely courteous." And Maruna's mother, the Etruscan slave who had taught me to read the birds' flight, a wise and gentle woman, said, "It might be better to put it off a day or two."

"My mother can entertain King Turnus far better than I can," I said, staring them both down, daring them to speak.

Vestina chirped, "But it's you, you he comes to see, how he looks at you, anyone can see you have his heart!" Maruna's mother said nothing. And I left with Maruna at daybreak.

I took my bag of salted meal. The pastures were full of spring lambs, bouncing about, whirling their tails as they sucked at the teat, but I needed no blood sacrifice when I went to Albunea. I scattered salsamola on the altar, slept on the old fleeces of other sacrifices, and sought no vision or guidance. All I wanted when I went there was to sleep there, in that silence, with those spirits around me, in the numen of Albunea. A night there clarified my heart and quieted my mind, so that I could come back home and do my duty.

The walk there was an escape, too, a time of freedom. Maruna was not lighthearted and adventurous like my Silvia, and we did not chatter all day long when we walked as Silvia and I did. Maruna was rather silent, but alert, noticing all things in earth and sky; she was patient, sweet, a good companion. She did not have Silvia's way with animals, but she knew the birds; and she had learned some of her mother's lore, so we talked about what we might read in the calls and flights of the birds in the fields and wild lands about us as we went. And sometimes we talked about what the dead might have to say to us. In Etruria they think much about the dead, and Maruna's mother had been trained in that knowledge when she was a girl in the great city of Caere. I felt ignorant and rustic when she or her daughter spoke of it. To me the dead were best buried, left undisturbed, thought about as little as possible; one did not want to bring their unhappy shadows creeping across the floor, hiding under the table, snapping at dropped food, for they were hungry, the dead were, always hungry. Every spring my father, like every householder in Latium, walked all about his house at midnight with nine black beans in his mouth, and when he spat them out he said, "Shadows, be gone!"—and the ghosts that had infested the house ate the beans and went back underground.

But according to Maruna's mother the matter of the dead was not that simple.

Maybe it was she who had opened my mind so that when I slept at Albunea that night, that night in April when I was eighteen, on that ground that is so thin a roof above the underworld, the poet could come to me, and I could see and speak to him.

Maruna turned off on the path to the woodcutter's hut, and I went on into the forest alone. When I walked there I always remembered the dream I had the first time I went to Albunea, the blood in the river, the city on a hill, the quiet radiance that filled the darkness under the trees.

No one was at the sacred place, but there had been recent sacrifices; fresh fleeces lay on the ground, and a stack of unburned wood by the altar. I scattered salted meal on the altar and all about the enclosure, and wished I could light a little fire, but I had brought none. So I went to the springs while the sun was still up, and sitting on a rocky outcrop above the cave mouth I watched the light grow reddish across the misty pools, and listened to the troubled voice of the water. After a while I moved farther up the hill, where I could hear birds singing near and far in the silence of the trees. The presence of the trees was very strong. For the first time I wondered if I might hear the voice that my father heard speak from among them in the dark. The big oaks stood so many, so massive in their other life, in their deep, rooted silence: the awe of them came on me, the religion. I went back to the sacred enclosure praying, very humbly beseeching these great powers to have pity on my weakness. I was glad I had lit no fire. I made a heap of the fleeces, rolled up in my red-edged toga, for the air was cool, and lay down in the late dusk to sleep.

I became aware that a figure was standing within the enclosure, on the other side of the altar: a tall shadow. For a moment I
thought it was a tree. Then I saw it was a man.

I sat up and said, "Be welcome here."

I was not afraid, but the awe was still in me, the religion
bound me.

He spoke: "What is this place?" His voice was very low.

"The altar place of Albunea."

"Albunea!" he said. I could see that he was looking around,
though it was quite dark, a thin high mist dimming the starlight.
After a minute he said again, wondering, almost with a laugh in his
voice, "So it is!—And you are?"

"Lavinia daughter of Latinus."

Again he repeated the name: "Lavinia . . ." Then he did laugh,
a brief ha! of amazement and amusement. He said at last, "May I
stay a while, Lavinia daughter of King Latinus?"

"The altar place is open to all men." And I added, "There are
fleeces here to sit on, or sleep on. I have more than I need."

"I need nothing, king's daughter," he said. He came a few steps
closer so that the altar was not between us, and sat down on the
ground. "I am a wraith," he said. "I am not here in my body. My
body is lying on the deck of a ship sailing from Greece to Italy,
but I don't think I'll get to Brundisium even if the ship does. I am
sick, I am dying, I am on my way to . . . to Acheron . . . Or else I
am a false dream. But they come from under there, don't they, the
false dreams? They nest like bats in the great tree at the gates of the
kingdom of the shadows . . . So maybe I am a bat that has flown
here from Hades. A dream that has flown into a dream. Into my
poem. To Albunea, the sacred grove, where King Latinus heard his
grandfather Faunus prophesy, telling him not to marry his daughter
to a man of Latium . . ." His voice was low and musical, like the

voice of one talking to the spirits, praying; and that almost laugh came and went in it.

But I said quite sharply, "Did he?" I couldn't help it. Surely my father would have told me if he had received such a warning. Why would he keep it from me?

The man, the shadow, paused; he thought; and he said, "Perhaps not yet."

He knew that he had surprised, disturbed me, and wanted to reassure me. I felt then for the first time his kindness, his searching kindness, sensitive to every suffering.

He went on, hesitant, "I think it has not happened yet. Faunus has not spoken to Latinus. Perhaps it never did—never will happen. You should not be concerned about it. I made it up. I imagined it. A dream within a dream . . . within the dream that has been my life . . ."

"I am not a dream, and I don't think I'm dreaming," I said after a while. I spoke mildly. For he was sad, very sad. He had said he was dying. He was adrift, bereft, poor soul. I wanted to give him comfort, better comfort than can be found in dreams.

He looked at me as if he could see me, as if light filled the glade, light not of sun or moon or star or fire. He studied me. I did not mind it. There was no insolence in him. I could not possibly fear him.

"I believe you," he said. "How old are you, Lavinia?"

"Eighteen last January."

"'Ripe now for a man, of full age now for marriage,'" he said gently, and I knew it was a line of a song, though I did not know the song.

"Oh yes," I said, very drily. I felt no shyness, no falseness, with him.

My response surprised the brief laugh from him again.

"Perhaps I did not do you justice, Lavinia," he said. It seemed he too could say anything to me, whether I understood it or not. That was all right.

"What should I call you?"

He said his name, and I said, "You're Etruscan?"

"I'm a Mantuan. I had Etruscan grandfathers. How did you know?"

"Maru, Maro—it's an Etruscan name."

"So it is. Ah, but how long ago—how long ago you lived, Lavinia! Centuries, centuries! Is there any Mantua, now—yet? Do you know that name?"

"No."

He said, after a pause, and with a kind of wondering, passionate urgency, "Rome. Do you know that name?"

"No. But the Etruscans call—" I stopped. The secret name of the river is not to be spoken to all. Did he know it? But why keep secrets from a wraith, from a dying man? "One of Tiber's sacred names is Rumon."

"She came to Albunea by herself," he said, speaking into the darkness, "and knew the sacred names of the river, and had no wish to be married. And I knew nothing of all that! I never looked at her. I had to tell what the men were doing . . . Perhaps I can—" But he broke off, and presently said, "No. No chance of that." He looked around again, and sighed, and said, "I keep thinking I'll wake up and see the damned deck of the ship, and the gulls overhead, and the sun that goes across the sky so slowly, and the damned Greek doctor . . ."

I have said we understood each other, that we spoke the same language. I did understand him, though he used words I did not know.

We sat in silence for a while. An owl called to the left, an owl answered from the right.

"Tell me," he said, "have they come yet, the Trojans?"

A word I did not know. "Tell me who they are."

"You'll know who they are when they come, Latinus' daughter. I am—" He hesitated—"I am searching for my duty here. How much is it right for me to tell you? Do you want to know your future, Lavinia?"

"No," I said at once. Then I sought in my own mind for my duty, or my will, and finally said, "I want to know what's right to do, but I don't want to know what's to come of it."

"It's enough to know what ought to come of it," he said, gravely agreeing. I felt his smile though I could not see it.

The left-hand owl called again, the right-hand owl replied.

"Oh," he said, "the air is so cool, the night is so dark, and the owls call, and the earth, the dirt—this is Italy, I'm home! . . . I wish I could die here. Here, not on that wooden deck on the sea in the sun. Here, on this dirt. But this isn't my body, this is only my delirium."

"I think you are here," I said, "only your body is not. But I see you. I talk with you. Tell me who the Trojans are."

"No no no. I must not. They are yet to come. Do what's right to do and what follows will be what should follow." He laughed. "Tell me, have you any suitors, Lavinia, 'ripe now for a man, of full age for marriage'?"

"Yes."

"What are their names?"

"Clausus the Sabine, Almo Tyrrhus' son, Ufens of Nersae, Aventinus, Turnus of Rutulia."

"And you favor none of them?"

"I favor none of them."

"Why is that?"

"Why should I? Where can a man take me that is better than my father's house? What do I want with a lesser king? Why should I serve Lares that are not my family's Lares, the Penates of some other woman's storerooms, the fire of a foreign hearth? Why, why is a girl brought up at home to be a woman in exile the rest of her life?"

"Hah," he said, not a laugh this time but a long outbreath. "I don't know, Lavinia. I don't know. But listen. If a man came—if a man came to marry you who was a man among a thousand—a warrior, a hero, a handsome man—"

"Turnus is all that."

"Has he piety?"

The word brought me up short, but I had no doubt of my answer. "No," I said.

"Well. If a man came who was heroic and also responsible, and just, and faithful, a man who had lost much, and suffered much, and made a good many mistakes and paid for them all—a man who saw his city betrayed and burned, and saved his father and his son from the burning, a man who went down alive into the underworld and returned, a man who learned piety the hard way . . . Might you favor such a man?"

"I would certainly pay attention to him," I said.

"It would be wise to do so."

A silence fell between us, companionable.

I said at last, "Have you seen, when the young men have archery contests, sometimes they catch a dove, and put a cord round her foot, and shinny up a high pole and tie her to the top, leaving just enough cord so she thinks she can fly? And then she is the target of their arrows."

"I have seen that."

"If I were an archer I'd break the cord with my arrow."

"That too I have seen. But another man shot the dove as she flew free."

After a while I said, "Perhaps it's just as well that women don't learn to shoot arrows."

"Camilla did. You know of her?"

"A woman archer?"

"A woman warrior, beautiful, invincible. From Volscia."

I shook my head. All I knew of the Volscians was what my father said: savage fighters, faithless allies.

"Well," the wraith said, "I suppose I did invent her. But I liked her."

"Invent her?"

"I am a poet, Lavinia." I liked the sound of the word, but he saw I did not know it. "A vates," he said. I knew that word of course: foreteller, soothsayer. It went with his being part Etruscan, and with the knowledge he seemed to have of what had not happened yet. But I didn't see what it had to do with this woman warrior, who sounded like a mere story to me.

"Would you tell me more about the man who is coming?"

He pondered a little. Even though we were talking with such ease and openness, in perfect trust, as if we were both shadows, harmless and invulnerable, with all eternity before us, still, he was a man who thought before he spoke.

"Yes," he said, "I can do that. What do you want to know?"

"Why is he coming here?"

"That, I think, I should not tell you now. Time will tell. But I think it would not be wrong for me to tell you where he is coming from."

"I am listening." I got more comfortable on the fleeces.

"O Lavinia," he said, "you are worth ten Camillas. And I never saw it. Well, never mind. Did you ever hear of Troy?"

"Yes. It's a little town south of here, near Ardea."

"Ah—not that Troia. This one was a great city. Far east of here, east of the Middle Sea, east of the isles of Greece, on the shore of Asia. There was a pretty prince of Troy named Paris. He and a Greek queen ran off together. Her husband called the other kings of Greece together, and they went to Troy, a great army in a thousand beaked ships, to get the woman back. Helen, her name was."

"What did they want her back for?"

"Her husband's honor demanded it."

"I should think his honor demanded that he divorce her and find himself a decent wife."

"Lavinia, these people were Greeks. Not Ro—not Italians."

"King Evander's a Greek. I wonder if he'd chase after a cheating wife."

"Lavinia daughter of the king, will you let me tell my tale?"

"I'm sorry. I won't talk."

"Then I will tell you the story of the fall of Troy, as Aeneas told it to the queen of Carthage," he said. And he sat up straighter, there on the dark ground, a shadow among shadows, and began to sing.

It wasn't singing like the shepherds' songs, or rowers' choruses, or the hymns at Ambarvalia and Compitalia, or the songs women sing all day at spinning and weaving and pounding and chopping and cleaning and sweeping. There was no tune to it. Its words were all the music of it, its words were its drumbeat, clack of the loom, tread of feet, oarstroke, heartbeat, waves breaking on the beach at Troy away across the world.

I cannot say here all he sang, about the great horse, and the snakes that came out of the sea, and the fall of the city. I will tell only what I have most thought about in the tale.

When the Greeks came out of the horse and let their army into the city, Aeneas the Trojan warrior fought against them in the streets. He fought in a kind of madness, furious, mindless, until he saw the king's high house afire. Then his mind cleared: he thought of his own house and people, and ran there. That house was some way from the center of the city, and it was still quiet there.

As he went through the streets he saw great powers made visible, moving in the darkness, the powers that willed Troy to burn.

When he got home, he tried to get his people to leave the house, escape the city, save themselves; but his father Anchises wouldn't go. Anchises was crippled, could hardly walk. He said he would die in his own house. But the house people wouldn't leave him there, wouldn't go without him. Aeneas was about to give up, rush back into the madness and get himself killed in the street fighting. His wife Creusa stopped him, and told him he had no right to do that. It was his duty and hers to try to save their people. She had their little son Ascanius with her. And as she spoke, someone said, "Look!"—and they saw that the boy's hair had caught fire—a gold flame leaped up over his head. They put it out, but old Anchises, who could read omens, said it was a good omen. Then they saw a shooting star run across the sky and fall into the forest up on the mountain over the city, Mount Ida. Anchises said they should follow that star. So Aeneas told all the house people to scatter out and run, get out of the city any way they could, and told them where to meet: at a mound with an old altar of the Grain Mother, outside the city gate under Mount Ida. Then Anchises carried the household gods in a big clay pot, and Aeneas carried crippled Anchises on his back; he took little Ascanius' hand, and Creusa followed him; and so they set off through the dark streets.

But Anchises saw soldiers down a side street and shouted to Aeneas to run. Aeneas obeyed, turned aside, running blindly in the dark, and lost his way. Finally he recognised a street and made his way, still carrying his father and holding the little boy's hand, to the gate, and came out to the altar where all his people were waiting for him. Only then he realised his wife wasn't with them. She'd been behind him when he turned and ran, and he never looked back to see if she was with him. No one had seen her.

So he went back into the city alone. He ran to their house, thinking she might have gone there. The whole house was burning, full of flame. He ran through the city shouting, "Creusa! Creusa!"—past the ruined buildings, and the fires, and the soldiers killing and looting. And then he saw her. She stood in front of him in the dark street. But she was taller than herself. And she said, "I will not go with you, nor will I be the slave of any Greek. The Earth Mother keeps me here. And you must go a long way for a long time, you must go, my sweet husband, until at last you come to the Western Land. There you will be a king and have a queen. No tears for me, but let your love guard our son!" And he tried to speak to her, and to take her in his arms—three times he tried, but it was like putting his arms around the wind, around a dream. She was gone into the shadow.

So he went back to the altar mound, where a great crowd of people had gathered now, fleeing the city, joining his house people. No Greeks had followed them out of the city, yet. He took his father up on his back again, and led them all up into the hills, where the shooting star had fallen. It was almost morning.

I remember that as the poet's voice died away, a first bird piped up, thin and far off, though there was no light yet in the sky, and no voice answered. Here, too, it was almost morning. I looked where the shadow of the poet had been and there was nothing. I lay down in the fleeces and slept till the sun's light, piercing and flashing through the dark trunks and thickets of the forest, woke me.

I WAS RAVENOUSLY HUNGRY, A WOLF. I WENT STRAIGHT TO THE woodcutter's cottage, where Maruna was waiting for me. It was the old kind of house, one tall round room of stakes with a roof of boughs, all thatched with straw. The woodcutter was already gone to his work in the woods. I asked his wife for food. She had nothing but a scrape of spelt porridge and a cup of sour goat's milk, which she was frightened to offer me because she thought such poor stuff would insult me and I'd be angry with her. I gobbled it up. Having nothing to give her, I kissed her. I thanked her for feeding the she-wolf. She laughed in bewilderment.

"I ate everything you have, what will you eat?" I asked, and she said comfortably, "Oh, he always brings a rabbit or some birds."

"Perhaps I'll wait," I said, but my joke bewildered her again. No doubt she thought we always ate meat at the king's house.

So I set off with Maruna. There was a great joy in me that morning. Maruna saw it and asked, "Was it a good night there?"

"Yes. I saw my kingdom," I said. I did not know myself what I meant. "And I saw a great city fall, all burning. And a man came out of it with a man on his back. And he is coming here."

She listened, believed me, asked nothing.

I could say that, I could talk that way to Maruna, my slave and sister, but not to anyone else.

All the way home I puzzled how I could win my way back to Albunea, soon, as soon as possible, and stay there more than one night. For I was quite certain that the poet would come back, but equally certain that he could not come back for long. His time with me was limited. He was on his way down to the shadow land, and it would not be a long journey for him.

I turned aside from our path and walked to the little river Prati, running shallow and bright on its stones. I was thirsty, and knelt to drink above the ford there, marked with the hooves of cattle. When I looked up from drinking, the ford made me think of the place I had stood in my dream six years before and seen the blood in the water, on the river Numicus. A dread and awe came into me. I stood, and opened my meal bag, and scattered salsamola on the stones.

I looked up at Maruna standing patiently on the riverbank, a tall girl my age, with a long, dark, soft Etruscan face. Tying up the meal bag I said, "Maruna, I need to go back to Albunea, soon. And maybe stay more than one night."

She pondered for half a mile homeward before she said, "Not while King Turnus is here."

"No."

"But when he leaves . . . Will the king ask why you want to go?"

"Probably. And you can't lie about sacred things."

"You can be silent, though," said Maruna.

"I am the king's daughter," I said, thinking how the poet had called me that. "I will do as I will do, and the king will nod his head." I laughed out loud, and then I said, "Look, look, Maruna! There's Silvia's deer! What's he doing so far from home?"

The big stag was walking on an open hillside just above a field where the new crops were coming up green. His white linen neck-piece was torn and dingy, but his antlers were splendid in their new velvet.

Maruna pointed a little way ahead of the stag: a slender doe was drifting along, nibbling a grass stem here and there, ignoring her follower entirely. "That's what he's doing so far from home."

"Mating season or not. Just like Turnus," I said, and laughed again. Nothing could keep my heart down that morning.

So with that courage in me I went to my father as soon as I got home, and greeted him, and said, "Father, when our guest has gone, may I go to Albunea again? Maruna will go with me, and anyone else you wish, if you think I need to be guarded. I wish to sleep there alone, more than one night."

Latinus looked at me, a long look, affectionate, distant, judging. He was about to ask me a question, and then he did not. "I begrudge every night you are not under my roof, daughter. How much longer will I have you? But I trust you. Go to the sacred place when you will, stay as you must, return when you can."

"I will," I said, and thanked him, and he kissed my forehead. Then, because fathers must be stern, he said, "I expect you to be at the banquet tonight. And no sulking, no green swoons."

"Then keep the African creature from me."

"I will," he said, and I saw perfectly well that he was thinking he wished he could keep the man who brought the African creature from me too; but he said nothing.

So I endured the rest of Turnus' visit, meek and maidenly, even saying a word or two at table now and then. Turnus in fact paid very little attention to me. He did not need to. It was my father he must persuade. My mother, of course, was already wooed and won. The tricky bit for Turnus was to encourage her to adore him without offending my father, and to seek my father's conversation and approval without letting her feel neglected. Turnus was a fierce, impetuous man, used to getting his way, not used to watching his tongue. He kept up his cautious courtesies pretty well, but sometimes I knew he was as desperate to get the banquet over as I was. It gave me a fellow feeling with him. As a cousin, I liked Turnus.

The animal from Africa had bitten my mother painfully, and then disappeared. Later on it was found that one of the hounds had got it, eaten its entrails, and left the rest lying by the house wall, where a pregnant weaving woman saw it, thought it was the corpse of a baby, went shrieking into labor, and bore a dead child. That was a creature of ill omen if ever I saw one.

I CAME AGAIN TO THE ALTAR IN ALBUNEA IN THE EVENING OF the Kalends of May. We had started late from home. By the time I had hung up the basket of food I brought with me on a tree branch to keep it from vermin, and blessed the altar place, and laid out the fleeces to sleep on, it was getting dark. Again I wished for a fire, for the cheer of it, but I had left the fire pot with Maruna. I sat and listened and watched the light die. The trees gathered and grew stronger in the dark. One owl called, from the right, far off. None answered.

In the great silence my heart went down, and farther down. What a fool I was to have come here. What did I remember of my last night here? I had had a dream about a man who was dying somewhere else, in some other time. Nothing to do with me. And for that I had come back here, with my silly basket of food.

I lay down. I was tired, and quite soon was asleep.

I woke in the black starless dark and looked past the altar. He was there.

"Poet," I said.

He said, "Lavinia."

A light rain was pattering on the ground and on the leaves of the forest. It ceased and began again and ceased.

He came where he had sat before, not far from me, and sat on the ground again, his arms round his knees.

"Are you cold?" he asked.

"No. Are you?"

"Yes."

I wanted to offer him fleeces to keep off the rain, but I knew it was no good.

"The ship is coming into harbor," he said. His voice was gentle and humorous, charged with passion yet quietly flowing, even when he was not singing his poem. That is what his song was called, he had told me, the first night, an epic poem. "We've passed through the arms of the harbor, where Pompey had his blockade of ships. I can feel how the rise and fall of the waves has diminished. I hated that swelling and sinking when I was out at sea, but I miss it now. We'll be ashore soon, no waves at all. Only a hot, flat bed, and sweat and aching, and more fever and less fever . . . What an escape some kind god has given me! To be here, in the dark, in the rain, to be cold, shivering—are you shivering, Lavinia?"

"No. I'm fine. I wish—" I didn't know what to say. "I wish you were well," I said.

"I'm well enough. I'm very well. I have been granted what few poets are granted. Maybe it's because I haven't finished the poem. So I can still live in it. Even while I die I can live in it. And you, you can live in it, be here—be here to talk to me, even if I can't write. Tell me . . . Tell me, daughter of King Latinus, how goes it in Latium?"

"The spring was early. Calving and lambing went well. The spelt and barley are tall for the season. Everything is well with the

Penates of my house, except the salt is getting low. I'll have to go down to the salt beds at the mouth of the father river soon, and bring dirty salt back, and clean it and leach it and bake it and soak it and dry it and pound it and all the rest you have to do to make it right."

"How did you learn to do all that?"

"From the old women."

"Not from your mother?"

"My mother is from Ardea. They don't have salt beds nearby, down there. They trade for their salt with houses like ours. That's why our women know how to make it. We trade it. But the sacred salt, for the salsamola, I have to make that myself. From beginning to end."

"What would you rather do?"

"Talk with you," I said.

"What do you want to talk about?"

"The Trojans."

"What do you want to know about the Trojans?"

I had trouble getting started, but then it came out: "When Troy was burning . . . His wife Creusa—they were in the streets, trying to escape— He had the child, she was behind him. They got separated. The Greek soldiers killed her. And then she came to him, taller than life, there in the darkness and the burning, and told him he must go on, get out, save his people. And he tried to hold her, three times, but she was only air and shadow."

He nodded.

"But later on—you said he went down to the underworld, and talked to the shadows of the dead there—later on. Did he meet his wife again there?"

The poet was silent, and then said, "No."

"He couldn't find her among so many," I said, trying to imagine the dead.

"He didn't look for her."

"I don't understand."

"Neither do I. And I doubt that I'll know any more when I get there. We each have to endure our own afterlife . . . He had lost her. In the fire, in the slaughter, in the streets. Lost her forever. He couldn't look back. He had his people to look after."

After a time I asked, "Where did they go after they escaped from Troy?"

"They wandered a long time around the Middle Sea, not knowing where to go, getting it wrong. They came to Sicily and stayed a while. His father died there. They set off again to seek the promised land, but a storm scattered the fleet and threw the ships onto a wild coast in Africa."

"And what did they do there?"

"Thanked the gods for safe deliverance, and got themselves some venison, and feasted. And then Aeneas and his friend Achates went off to find out what country they were in, and came to a city that was just being built. Carthage it was called, and the people were Phoenicians, and the queen was Dido. And she welcomed them."

"Tell me about it."

The poet seemed hesitant. I felt at once that his hesitation had something to do with the queen.

"He fell in love with Queen Dido," I said, and felt a curious flatness or disappointment as I said it.

"She fell in love with him," the poet said. His voice was grave. "I think this is not really a story to be told to a young girl, Lavinia."

"But I am not a young girl. I am 'ripe now for a man, of full age now for marriage.' As you said . . . And I am aware that married women sometimes fall in love with other men. Younger men." I doubt he heard the dryness in my voice when I said that. He was thinking about the African queen.

"She was a widow. There was nothing wrong about it. Except that her heart and her will ran away with her. She very much needed a king. She was an excellent ruler, her people loved her; they were founding a beautiful city there, everything going very well; but it's a rare thing for a woman to rule long alone. It makes men uncomfortable. The neighboring kings and chiefs were after her. Courting her, coveting her power, wooing and threatening at the same time. Aeneas came as her savior, her answer to them—a tried warrior, with his own troops—a man born to be a king, but with no country of his own. She needed him before she loved him. She fell in love with his son, first. She took to Ascanius at once, held him and hugged him and promised him good times, and of course the motherless boy liked her, the warmhearted, beautiful, kind, childless woman. And that went to Aeneas' heart. His son was all the family he had left. He promised to help Dido get her city started. And so . . ."

A pause.

"One thing led to another," I said.

"I can never get used to the fact, though I know it, that women are born cynics. Men have to learn cynicism. Infant girls could teach it to them."

I had no idea what a cynic was but I knew what he meant. "I wasn't speaking in contempt. One thing does lead to another. There's no harm in that. How else would husbands and wives ever come to love each other? She needed a man. And he was kind and noble and handsome and shipwrecked. She fell in love with him. Any woman would."

"Let it be an omen," the poet murmured.

"But did he fall in love with her?"

"Yes. He did. She was beautiful, fiery, passionate. Any man would. But . . ."

"He was still mourning for Creusa."

"No. His wife, his city, that was all behind him. Far back. Years and lands and seas between them. He didn't look back. But he didn't know how to look forward. He was caught in the moment, in the present time. His father's death was a hard blow to him. He had depended on Anchises, obeyed him even when the old man led them astray. When he died and took the past with him, Aeneas felt the future was gone too. He didn't know how to go on. The storm that scattered his fleet and took them off course, to lands they didn't know—there was a storm like that in his soul. He'd lost his way."

"What was his way?"

"Here. To Italy. To Latium. He knew that."

"Why couldn't his future have been in Africa? Why shouldn't he stay and help the queen build her city and be happy with her?" I spoke reasonably, though in fact I did not want him to have done that. I counted on the poet's argument.

But he didn't argue. He shook his head. After a while he said, pursuing his thought, "It was a storm that brought them together, too. While they were out hunting. They got separated from the rest of the hunting party. There was rain, hail, they took refuge in a cave. And so . . ."

"Did they marry?" I asked after a while.

"Dido took their love for marriage, called it marriage. He did not. He was right."

"Why?"

"Not even need and love can defeat fate, Lavinia. Aeneas' gift is to know his fate, what he must do, and do it. In spite of need. In spite of love."

"So what did he do?"

"He left her."

"He ran away?"

"He ran away."

"What did she do?"

"She killed herself."

I had not expected that. I thought she would send out ships after Aeneas, pursue him, take fiery revenge. I could not like this African queen but I could not possibly despise her. Yet suicide seemed a coward's answer to betrayal. At last I said so.

"You do not know what despair is," the poet said gently. "May you never know."

I accepted that. I knew what despair was. It was where my mother lived after her sons died. But I had not lived there myself.

"It was a hard death," he said. "Her sword went wide of the heart, and the wound killed her only slowly. She told them to light the pyre she lay on before she was dead. He saw the great fire of it from out at sea."

"And knew what it was?"

"No. Maybe."

"His soul must cringe in him every time he thinks of that. Weren't his people ashamed of him?"

"Even if he'd called himself king there, it would never have been their country. And Dido had stopped building the city, dropped the reins of government. She'd lost her self-respect, she couldn't think of anything but him. Things weren't going right. They were glad to get him away from there." After a time he said, "He did see Dido, down in the underworld. She turned away. She refused to speak to him."

That seemed only right. But there was an awful sadness in the story, an awful shame and sorrow, an unbearable injustice. I felt so sorry for all three of them, Creusa, Dido, Aeneas, that I could not say anything. We sat a long time in silence.

"Tell me of happier things," the poet said in his beautiful, gentle voice. "How do you spend your days?"

"You know how the daughter of a house spends her days."

"Yes, I do. I had an older sister, in Mantua. But this is not Mantua, and our father wasn't a king . . ." He waited; I said nothing. He said, "On feast days the chief men of the city come to dine at the king's table, and visitors from other cities of Latium, and perhaps allies from farther away—and your suitors, of course. Tell me about them."

I sat for a while in the darkness. The rain had passed over and stars were beginning to shine overhead and through the leaves of the forest around us. "I come here to get away from them. I don't want to talk about them, please."

"Not even Turnus? Isn't he very handsome, very brave?"

"Yes."

"Not handsome and brave enough to move a girl's heart?"

"Ask my mother," I said.

At that he was silent. When he spoke again he had changed his tone. "Who are your friends, then, Lavinia?"

"Silvia. Maruna. Some of the other girls. Some of the old women."

"Silvia who has a pet stag?"

"Yes. We saw it down this way, Maruna and I. It was following a doe, just like a dog after a bitch. A dog with antlers. It made us laugh."

"Males in love are ridiculous," he said. "They can't help it."

"How do you know about Silvia's stag?"

"It came to me."

"You know everything, don't you?"

"No. I know very little. And what I thought I knew of you—
what little I thought of at all—was stupid, conventional, unimag-
ined. I thought you were a blonde! . . . But you can't have two love
stories in an epic. Where would the battles fit? In any case, how
could one possibly end a story with a marriage?"

"It does seem more like a beginning than an end," I said.

We both brooded.

"It's all wrong," he said. "I will tell them to burn it."

Whatever he meant, I did not like the sound of it. "And then
look back from out at sea and see the great pyre flaming?" I said.

He gave his short laugh. "You have a cruel streak, Lavinia."

"I don't think so. Maybe I wish I did. Maybe I'll need to be
cruel."

"No. No. Cruelty is for the weak."

"Oh, not only the weak. Isn't a master stronger than the slave
he beats? Wasn't Aeneas cruel in leaving Dido? But she was the
weak one."

He stood up, a tall shadow in the dimness. He paced back
and forth a little. He said: "In the underworld, Aeneas met an old
friend, the Trojan prince Deiphobos. Paris, who ran off with Helen,
was killed in the war. So the Trojans gave Helen to his brother
Deiphobos."

"Why didn't they put her out the gate and tell her to go back
to her husband?"

"The Trojan women asked that question; but the Trojan men
didn't hear it . . . So, then, the Greeks took the city, and Menelaus
came looking for his wife, the woman they fought the war for. And
Helen met him. She took her old husband to the bedroom where
her new husband was sound asleep. He hadn't heard the sounds of

battle. She hadn't wakened him. She'd stolen his sword. So he woke to his death, the Greek stabbing him, hacking him, chopping off his hands, slicing his face in half, crazy for blood, and the woman looking on. And so Deiphobos went down into the dark. Down there, years after, Aeneas saw him, his shadow, still maimed, mutilated, unhealed. They talked a little, but the guide broke in—no time for this, Aeneas must hurry on. And the murdered man said, 'Go on, go, my glory. I am gone. I join the crowd, return to darkness. I hope you find a better fate.' And speaking, he turned away."

I sat in silence. I wanted to cry, but had no tears.

"I will be gone soon," the poet said. "I will join the crowd, return to darkness."

"Not yet—"

"Keep me here. Keep me here, Lavinia. Tell me it is better to be alive, better to be a slave living than Achilles dead. Tell me I can finish my work!"

"If you never finish it, it will never end," I said, speaking only to speak, saying what came into my head, to give him some comfort. "Anyway, how are you going to end it, if not with a marriage? With a murder? Do you have to decide how it ends before you get to the end?"

"No," he said. "I don't, in fact. It's not exactly a matter of deciding. Rather of finding out. Or, as it now stands, of giving up, because I haven't the strength to go on. That's the trouble. I am weak. So the end will be cruel." He paced back and forth once, between me and the altar. I could hear no sound of his steps on the earth. But finally he sighed, a long, rather noisy sigh, and sat down again, his arms round his knees. "Tell me what you and Silvia do, what you talk about. Tell me about her deer. Tell me how you make the salt. Tell me when you spin, when you weave. Did your mother teach you those arts? Tell me how you unlock and clean out the storeroom early in summer, and leave it open for a few days, praying to the Penates that it be refilled with the harvest . . ."

"You know it all."

"No. Only you can tell me."

So I told him what he asked, and comforted him with what he knew.

I SPENT THE NEXT DAY ALONE IN THE FOREST OF ALBUNEA. THE air was heavy under the trees, and the sulfur smell stopped my breath when I went near the springs. Wandering away, I found a path up the steep hill, almost a crag, that rises up over the forest. Clearings at the top gave a wide view west to the bright line that was the sea. I sat up there in the sunlight in the thin grass, my back against a fallen log. I had my spindle and a bag of wool; a woman usually carries some of her Penates with her. I was spinning the very finest thread for a summer toga or palla, so my light bag of wool would last me a good while. I sat and spun and thought and gazed out over the hills and woods of Latium, all green with May. At midday I ate a little cheese and spelt bread and found a spring to drink from. There were shepherds' lettuce and watercress grow-ing at the spring, and I ate that, too, though I had intended to be very sparing, even perhaps to fast; but fasting comes hard to me. Then I explored the hilltop a little more, and when the sun was halfway between high heaven and earth I made my way down into the depths of the woods again. I passed the stinking springs on the windward side and came again to the altar place. There I slept a little, for I had had little sleep the night before. When I woke, in the dusk, big white moths were fluttering in the air within the sacred wall, rising and falling, circling round about one another in an airy maze, wonderful to see. I watched them sleepily, and through their dance I saw my poet standing near the altar.

"The moths look like souls in the underworld," I said, still only half awake.

He said, "It is a terrible place. On the far side of the dark river are marshy plains, where you hear crying—little, weak, wailing cries, from the ground, everywhere, underfoot. They are the souls of babies who died at birth or in the cradle, died before they lived. They lie there on the mud, in the reeds, in the dark, wailing. And no one comes."

I was awake now. I said, "How do you know that?"

"I was there."

"You were in the underworld? With Aeneas?"

"Who else would I be with?" he said. He looked about uncertainly. His voice was low and dull. He went on, hesitant, "It was the Sybil who guided Aeneas . . . What man did I guide? I met him in a wood, like this. A dark wood, in the middle of the road. I came up from down there to meet him, to show him the way . . . But when was that? Oh, this dying is a hard business, Lavinia. I am very tired. I can't think straight any more."

"You're not thinking straight about the babies," I said. "Why would they be punished for not having lived? How could their souls be there before they had time to grow souls? Are the souls of dead kittens there, and of the lambs we sacrifice, and of miscarried fetuses? If not them, then why babies? If you invented that marsh full of miserable dead crying babies, it was a misinvention. It was wrong."

I was extremely angry. I used the second most powerful word I know, wrong, *nefas*, against the order of things, unspeakable, unsacred. There will be many words for it, but that was the one I knew. It is only the shadow, the opposite, the undoing, of the great word *fas*, the right, what one must do.

He sat down, doubling up his tall shadowy figure, and I could see how wearily he moved, how he bowed his head down like a man spent, defeated; but I would not have pity on him.

"If cruelty comes of weakness, as you said, then you are very weak," I said.

He did not answer.

After a long time I said, "I think you are strong." My lips and voice quivered as I spoke, for I did pity him, though I did not want to, and my heart was full of tears.

"If it is wrong, I will take it out of the poem, child," he said. "If I am permitted to."

I wanted so much to be able to help him, to give him a fleece to sit on or my own toga to put round his shoulders, for he sat hunched as if he was shivering cold. But I could do nothing for him, and could touch him only with my voice.

"Who is it that permits or forbids you?"

"The gods. My fate. My friends. Augustus."

I knew what he meant by his fate and his friends. At least I knew what the words meant. The others I was not certain of. And I did not know who his friends were and whether he could trust them. As for his fate, we none of us know that.

"But surely you're a free man," I said at last. "Your work is your own."

"It was till I got sick," he said. "Then I began to lose my hold on it, and now I think I've lost it. They'll publish it unfinished. I can't stop them. And I haven't got the strength to finish it. It ends with a murder, as you said. Turnus' death. Why does it? Who cares about Turnus? The world is full of fine fearless young men eager to kill and be killed. There'll always be enough of them for every war."

"Who kills him?"

The poet did not answer my question. He only said after a long time, "It's not the right ending."

"Tell me the right ending."

Again he was silent for a long time. "I can't," he said.

It was almost dark. Leaves and branches that had stood out sharp black against deep blue had begun to blur away into the dimness of night. Venus shone for a minute low between dark tree trunks in the west, and I prayed to the power of its beauty. There was no wind at all, and no bird or creature made any noise.

"I think I know why I came to you, Lavinia. I have wondered— Of all the people of my poem, why were you the one who called my spirit? Why not my great, my dear Aeneas? Why can't I see him with my living eyes as I saw him so often with the eyes of my art?"

His voice was extremely low, almost breathless. I strained to listen. I did not understand much of what he said, then.

"Because I did see him. And not you. You're almost nothing in my poem, almost nobody. An unkept promise. No mending that now, no filling your name with life, as I filled Dido's. But it's there, that life ungiven, there, in you. So now, at the end, when it's too late, you have it to give to me. My life. My earth of Italy, my hope of Rome, my hope."

There was a desperation in his voice that wrung my heart. His words died away and he sat still, his head bowed. I could barely see him.

I was afraid, knowing that he was drifting away from me into his sadness, his mortal sickness. I was afraid I would lose even his shadow. I wanted to keep him with me. Though I did not and could not understand it as he did, I knew what the bond between us was, and how to use it to bring him back.

I said, "I want to know about Aeneas. After he left Africa, after he looked back over the water and saw her funeral fire burning . . . where did he go then?"

The poet kept his dejected posture for a while. He shook his head a little. He said hoarsely, "Sicily." He looked around, shrugging his shoulders slowly to get the cramp out.

"He'd already been there, hadn't he?"

"He went back to celebrate the Parentalia for his father. While he was in Africa with Dido, a year had passed since Anchises died."

"How did he celebrate?"

"Properly. With ceremony and sacrifice, and then with games and competitions and a feast." His voice had grown stronger. The music was coming back into it. "Aeneas has a very just sense of what's appropriate. And he knew his men needed heartening. Seven years wandering and here they were back where they'd been a year ago. So he gave them games. What he forgot was the women."

"That hardly seems surprising."

"Very well, my cynic. But Aeneas is not a forgetful man. He thinks about all his people. A lot of women had entrusted themselves to him in the escape from Troy. He'd tried to make the long voyaging bearable to them. But when he announced that they were setting off yet again to seek the promised land, it was too much. Juno got into them, she goaded them. They rebelled. They went down to the shore and set fire to the ships."

"What do you mean, Juno got into them?"

"She hated Aeneas. She was always against him." He saw that I was puzzled.

I pondered this. A woman has her Juno, just as a man has his

Genius; they are names for the sacred power, the divine spark we each of us have in us. My Juno can't "get into" me, it is already my deepest self. The poet was speaking of Juno as if it were a person, a woman, with likes and dislikes: a jealous woman.

The world is sacred, of course, it is full of gods, numina, great powers and presences. We give some of them names—Mars of the fields and the war, Vesta the fire, Ceres the grain, Mother Tellus the earth, the Penates of the storehouse. The rivers, the springs. And in the storm cloud and the light is the great power called the father god. But they aren't people. They don't love and hate, they aren't for or against. They accept the worship due them, which augments their power, through which we live.

I was entirely puzzled. I finally asked, "Why does this Juno person hate Aeneas?"

"Because she hates his mother, Venus."

"Aeneas' mother is a star?"

"No; a goddess."

I said cautiously, "Venus is the power that we invoke in spring, in the garden, when things begin growing. And we call the evening star Venus."

He thought it over. Perhaps having grown up in the country, among pagans like me, helped him understand my bewilderment. "So do we," he said. "But Venus also became more . . . With the help of the Greeks. They call her Aphrodite . . . There was a great poet who praised her in Latin. Delight of men and gods, he called her, dear nurturer. Under the sliding star signs she fills the ship-laden sea and the fruitful earth with her being; through her the generations are conceived and rise up to see the sun; from her the storm clouds flee; to her the earth, the skillful maker, offers flowers. The wide levels of the sea smile at her, and all the quiet sky shines and streams with light . . ."

It was the Venus I had prayed to, it was my prayer, though I had no such words. They filled my eyes with tears and my heart with inexpressible joy. I said at last, "Why would anyone hate her?"

"Jealousy," he said.

"A sacred power jealous of another?" I could not understand it. Is a river jealous of another river, is earth jealous of the sky?

"A man in my poem asks, 'Is it the gods who set this fire in our hearts, or do we each make our fierce desire into a god?'"

He looked at me. I said nothing.

"Great Homer of Greece says the god lights the fire. Young Lavinia of Italy says the fire is the god. This is Italian ground, Latin ground. You and Lucretius have it right. Offer praise, ask for blessing, and pay no attention to the foreign myths. They're only literature . . . So, never mind about Juno. The Trojan women were furious at not having been consulted, and determined to stay in Sicily. And so they set fire to the ships."

That I could understand well enough. I listened.

"The whole fleet would have burned if a rain squall hadn't come up and drowned the fires. They lost four ships. The women ran, of course, took to the hills . . . But Aeneas never even thought of punishing them. He realised he'd pushed them too far. He called a council and let them all choose freely: stay in Sicily, or sail with Aeneas. Old people and many women, a lot of mothers with young children, chose to stay. Others chose to keep on looking for the promised land. So, after the nine days of the festival were done, and another day for the tears of parting, they sailed."

"This way? To Latium?"

The poet nodded. "But first he put in at Cumae."

I knew there is an entrance to the underworld there. "To go down? Why?"

"A vision: his father Anchises told him to come find him,

across the dark river. And having always obeyed his father and the fates, Aeneas went to Cumae, and found the guide, and the way down."

"And he saw the marsh where the babies lie crying," I said. "And his friend who was murdered so cruelly that even his ghost was not healed. And Queen Dido, who turned away and wouldn't speak. But he didn't look for his wife Creusa."

"No," the poet said humbly.

"It doesn't matter. I think there is no rejoining, there," I said. "Shadow cannot touch shadow. I think the long night is for sleeping."

"Daughter of Latinus, foremother of Lucretius! You promise me what I most desire."

"Sleep?"

"Sleep."

"But your poem—"

"Well, my poem will look after itself, no doubt, if I let it."

We both sat in silence. It was quite dark. The wind was down. Nothing stirred.

"Has he left Cumae, by now?"

"I think so," the poet said.

We spoke very low, almost in whispers.

"He'll stop at Circeii, to bury his nurse Caieta, who begged to come with him; but she's old and ill, and she dies in the ship. He puts ashore to bury her. That will delay him some days."

A chill of fear had come into me. Too much was coming to me, too soon. I wanted the poet to tell me what was coming, and I didn't want it. I said, "I don't know when I can come back here."

"Nor do I, Lavinia."

He looked across the dark air at me and I could tell that he was smiling.

"Oh my dear," he said, still very softly. "My unfinished, my incomplete, my unfulfilled. Child I never had. Come back once more."

"I will."

I AM NOT THE FEMININE VOICE YOU MAY HAVE EXPECTED. Resentment is not what drives me to write my story. Anger, in part, perhaps. But not an easy anger. I long for justice, but I do not know what justice is. It is hard to be betrayed. It is harder to know you made betrayal inevitable.

Who was my true love, then, the hero or the poet? I don't mean which of them loved me more; neither of them loved me long. Just sufficiently. Enough. My question is which of them did I more truly love? And I cannot answer it. One was my husband, the beautiful man whose flesh my flesh enclosed to make my son in me, the author of my womanhood, my pride, my glory; the other was a shadow, a whisper in shadows, a virgin's dream or vision, yet the author of all my being. How can I choose? I lost them both so soon. I knew them only a little better than they knew me. And I remember, always, that I am contingent.

So, of course, were they. It is only too likely that little Publius Vergilius Maro might have died at six or seven, ashes under a small gravestone in Mantua, before he was ever a poet; and with him would have died the hero's glory, leaving a mere name among a thousand names of warriors, not even a myth on the Italian shore. We are all contingent. Resentment is foolish and ungenerous, and even anger is inadequate. I am a fleck of light on the surface of the sea, a glint of light from the evening star. I live in awe. If I never lived at all, yet I am a silent wing on the wind, a bodiless voice in the forest of Albunea. I speak, but all I can say is: Go, go on.

WHEN I GOT HOME WITH MARUNA THE NEXT DAY, EVERYBODY on the women's side tried to tell me simultaneously that Turnus had sent a messenger to my father, and that Queen Amata wanted to see me right away.

My habit of fear of my mother made me wince inwardly at that. Yet she had not screamed at me or humiliated me in the old way for a long time now. I was ashamed of my cowardice. As soon as I had washed the dirt of travel from my feet and changed my clothes, I went to her rooms. She sent her maids away and greeted me with real eagerness, kissing my forehead and taking my hands to draw me down to sit beside her. Such a show of love might have seemed false, affected, but Amata was not a schemer. She was far too much at the mercy of her feelings to play a part she did not feel. She was truly glad to see me, and her pleasure went to my heart. I had so longed for the approval, the kindness of my beautiful and unhappy mother that the least sign of it was irresistible to me. I sat down by her willingly.

She stroked my hair. Her hand trembled a little; she was very excited. Her great, dark eyes seemed full of light.

"King Turnus has sent a messenger, Lavinia."

"So all the women said."

"It is a formal request for your hand in marriage."

She was watching me so eagerly and so closely, sitting so near, that I could do nothing but look down, speechless. I felt the blush rise to my skin, the wave of heat all over my body, and the sense of being trapped, helpless, exposed.

My shrinking silence did not surprise or displease her. She took my hand and held it while she talked. "It is an unusual proposal. King Turnus is a great-hearted man. He speaks not only for himself, but for other young kings and warriors who have come here court-ing you—Messapus, Aventinus, Ufens, and Clausus the Sabine. Turnus' message is that to avoid dispute and bad blood among these powerful subjects and allies of Latium, the time has come for the king to choose your husband from among them, and so end their rivalry. All are agreed to accept Latinus' choice. He will be sending for you soon to tell you his decision."

I could do nothing but nod.

"It's not an easy decision for your father to make," Amata said, her voice growing less hurried and eager, warmer, now that the message had been given. "He's devoted to you, he doesn't want to let you go. But he's been very worried about the rivalries Turnus speaks of. He's lain awake nights, fearing that the young warriors will come to blows over you or try to force a choice upon him that will upset the kingdom. They're like a box of tinder, those young men. One spark and they'll be in arms. And your father is proud of the peace he has kept, and wishes with all his heart to keep it. He is an old man, past fighting. He needs, in fact, the heart and strength of a young man to defend him—a son-in-law. Which of them would you think best suited to that honor?"

I shook my head. My throat was dry, no words would come from it.

"He will ask you, Lavinia. You must be ready for that. He will not want to marry you to a man you dislike—you know that! But it is time for you to marry, and past time. We can't change that. So you must choose. And it will truly be your choice. He would never go against your heart."

"I know."

She got up and moved about the room a little; she took one of the tiny pots of scent from her table and brought it over to dab the rose oil on my wrists.

"It is rather nice to have young men quarreling over one," she said, with a smile. "I know! It seems such a pity to have to bring all that to an end . . . But it can't last forever. And the impossible choice, when suddenly it must be made, usually makes itself. Among them all, all the young possibilities, there really is only one who is possible. Who is inevitable. Intended."

She smiled again, radiantly. I thought, she is like a girl speaking of her betrothed.

I still said nothing, and she said after waiting a minute, "Well, my dear, you need not tell me your choice; but you will have to tell your father—or let him choose for you."

I nodded.

"Do you wish us to choose for you?"

The eagerness was strong in her voice. I could not speak.

"Are you so frightened?" She spoke tenderly, and sitting down by me again held me close against her, as she had not done since I was six years old. I could not relax, but sat stiff in her encircling arms. "Oh, Lavinia, he will be kind to you, good to you. He is so fine—so handsome! There is nothing to be afraid of. And you can visit back here often with him. And I'll be welcome to come visit you in Ardea—he said so to me more than once. Ardea was my home when I was a child. It is a beautiful city. You'll see. It won't be so different for you from being here. He'll look after you as your father does. You'll be so happy there. You have nothing to fear. I will go with you."

I broke loose from her embrace, stood up; I had to get free. "Mother, I will talk with father when he sends for me," I said, and hurried out of the room. There was a singing in my ears, and the burning flush had turned to a cold that ran in my bones.

As I hurried along the colonnade I saw a great commotion in the central courtyard, a lot of people all gathered around the laurel tree. I tried to get past unseen, but first Vestina and then Tita saw me, and crying, "Look, look, come look!" dragged me out towards the tree. Something was up in it, far in the branches, a fat dark animal—a huge sack of something, writhing—a cloud of smoke, dark heavy smoke, caught in the branches. From it came a humming, droning sound. Everybody was shouting, pointing. Bees, they shouted, bees swarming!

My father came across the court, grave, grey, and erect. He looked up at the great swarm that pulsed and sagged and reformed constantly at the summit of the tree. He glanced up at the clouds beginning to color with sunset.

"Are they our bees?" he asked.

Several voices said no. The swarm had flown in over the roofs of the city, "like a great smoke in the sky," somebody said.

"Tell Castus," Latinus said to the house slave with him. "They're gathering for the night. He'll be able to move them." The boy darted off to fetch Castus, our beekeeper.

"It's a sign, master, it's a sign," Maruna's mother cried. "To the very crown of the tree that crowns Laurentum, they come! What is the omen?"

"What direction did they come from?"

"Southwest."

There was a brief, waiting silence. My father spoke: "Strangers are coming from that quarter—by sea, perhaps. They will come to the king in his house."

As father of the household, the city, and the state, Latinus was accustomed to read omens. He used no mysterious means and preparations, as the Etruscan soothsayers did. He looked at the omen, read its meaning, and spoke it unhesitating, with grave simplicity.

His people were satisfied. A good many of them stayed in the courtyard, chattering about the omen, brushing strayed, sluggish bees out of their hair, waiting to see Castus gather the swarm to take to our hives.

Latinus had seen me, and said, "Daughter, come."

I followed him to his rooms. He stopped in the anteroom and stood by the small table there, facing me. The evening light was bright in the doorway.

"Has your mother spoken to you, Lavinia?"

"Yes."

"So you know that your suitors have agreed to ask me to choose your husband from among them."

"Yes."

"Well," he said with a forced smile, "will you tell me which one you wish me to choose?"

"No."

I did not speak insolently, but the refusal took him aback. He studied me a minute. "But there is one of them you prefer."

"No, father."

"Not Turnus?"

I shook my head.

"Your mother has told me that you love Turnus."

"No."

Again he was surprised, but he was patient with me. He said gently, "Are you quite certain, my dear? Your mother has told me that you've been in love with him since he first came courting you. And she warned me you'd be timid about admitting it. Such timidity is right and proper in a virgin girl. We need say nothing more about it. All you need do is indicate that you will be content if I accept him for you."

"No!"

Now he was puzzled and uneasy. "If not Turnus, then which of the others?"

"None."

"You want me to refuse them all?"

"Can you, father?"

Looking grim, he took a turn round the room; he hunched his broad, muscular shoulders, rubbed his hand over his chin. He had not shaved yet, and the grey bristles stood out on his jaw. He stopped again facing me. "Yes, I can," he said. "I am still king of Latium. Why do you ask that?"

"I know that Turnus' offer contained a threat."

"It can be taken so. You need not concern yourself with that. What do you want, what do you intend, Lavinia? You're eighteen. You cannot go on indefinitely as a maiden at home."

"I would rather be a Vestal than marry any of those men."

We call a woman a Vestal who chooses not to marry or is never chosen, who stays with her father's family and keeps the hearth fire alight.

He sighed, looking down at his big, scarred hand on the table. I think he had to resist the temptation of that idea, that hope to keep me with him. He finally said, "If I were not king—if I had other daughters—if your brothers had lived—you might have that choice. As it is, as my only child, you are bound to marry, Lavinia. You carry my power in you, our family's power, and we can't pretend you don't."

"One more year."

"It will be the same choice in a year."

I had no answer to that.

"Turnus is the best of them, daughter. Messapus will always be under Turnus' thumb. Aventinus is a fine lad, with his lion-skin coat, but he hasn't much sense. You can't live your life up in Ufens' mountains, and I won't send you off among those shifty Sabines. Turnus is the pick of the lot. He's probably the best man in Latium.

He's running his kingdom well; he's feared as a fighter; he's rich. And good-looking. I know all the women think so. And he's a relation. Your mother tells me he's wildly in love with you."

He looked at me hopefully, but I would not return his gaze.

"She tells me all the praises he sings of you. She believes he's so determined to have you that if I give you to one of the others, he'll rebel, despite this agreement they made. She may be right. He's an ambitious, self-confident fellow. But he has reason to be. Your mother has encouraged him. In fact, if you picked one of the others, she might rebel." He tried to make it a joke, but it was not a joke, and I could see misery in his eyes. "She has your welfare and the good of our kingdom very much at heart," he said.

I had no argument, no answer.

"Give me five days, father," I said. My voice came out hoarse and weak.

"And then you will tell me your choice?"

"Yes."

He took me in his big arms then, and kissed my forehead. I felt the warmth of his body and smelled the familiar smell of him, harsh, dear, and comforting as the smell of the earth on the hills of summer. "You are the light of my eyes, daughter," he murmured. That made me cry. I kissed his hand and ran back to the women's side in tears. Everybody was in the courtyard in the twilight, watching Castus talk the swarm together into a great humming dark globe over the fountain, shadowy, swaying, shrinking together always closer and smaller as he talked his spells and made his net ready to capture the bees.

THE FIVE DAYS SEEMED VERY LONG TO ME. I KEPT TO MYSELF as well as I could. Once I got away and ran to Tyrrhus' farm. Silvia was in the dairy; I coaxed her to come away with me. I wanted to talk to her about the choice I had to make, which of course she knew about; it was common knowledge. Very little in a king's house can be a secret. And everyone knew that her brother Almo had not even been included in the list of suitors Turnus offered to my father. When I came to her, she hoped I might ask her to reassure Almo, to tell him that he was my choice and should ask the king directly for my hand. The family had let their hopes run high, thinking my friendship with Silvia raised her brother's status to equality with mine, as indeed it did among us young people: but not among the kings and queens, the mortal powers of our state.

When Silvia understood that I had refused to choose any of the suitors, she began to press Almo's case. When I shook my head and said, "No, Silvia, I can't choose him," she wanted to know why. Had I not always shown him a kindness that had led him to love me? was he not good enough for me? and so on.

I said, "I love him better than any of the others, but I do not want him as my husband. And if I did, if I chose him, it would be the same as killing him. Turnus would be after him like a hawk on a mouse."

It was a stupid comparison, and Silvia took it ill. "Even if your father refused to protect my brother, I think our household has a few good warriors of its own," she said stiffly.

"Oh, Silvia, I'm the mouse—the mouse in the field when they cut the hay and lay the ground all bare—everybody watching me, nowhere to go. I run about and run about in my mind and can't find anywhere to hide. Everywhere I look there's Turnus, with his blue eyes, and his smile, and my—" I stopped myself. "And my mother trusts him," I said.

"You don't?" she asked curiously.

"No. He has no piety. He looks only at himself."

"Why shouldn't he? He's rich, he's handsome, he's a king." Her irony was not entirely ill-natured, but she had no sympathy for me. She was hurt for Almo, and would not let me off easily.

I think she knew I was frightened, but would not ask me what I was afraid of, so I could not speak to her as I longed to.

All the same, we parted friends. She knew well enough that Almo had been in over his head, and that indeed he would have put himself and his family in mortal danger by winning a woman King Turnus wanted. She gave me a long hug and a kiss when we parted, and said, "Oh, I'm sorry all this came up. I wish there weren't any men in the world. I wish we could go down to the river together the way we did last spring!"

"Maybe we will," I said, but my heart was low. I kissed her, and so we parted. I went back through the fields trying not to cry. I was near tears or in tears half the time, and sick of it. There was nobody in the world whom I could talk to, or who could understand me, but the poet. Maruna might have understood, indeed perhaps she did, but I could not talk about my mother to her. To ask slaves to speak or hear dishonor of their master is unjust, it puts them at risk. There are always talebearers, toadies, among household slaves, how could it be otherwise? No room in a king's house is without an ear at the door. I knew I had Maruna's sympathy, and that was much help to me; but, since I could not protect her, I could not confide in her.

Most of the other women and girls simply wondered why I didn't jump at Turnus' offer. Old Vestina sang his praises daily, always to a chorus of sighs and giggles.

And my mother's affectionate pressure and persuasion in favor of Turnus continued, until four days had passed, and I must make my choice the next day. Then her exasperation with me burst out all at once in a fit of fury like those of years ago. She came into my room just after I had lain down to sleep. She was in her sleeping gown, carrying a tiny oil lamp, its flame no larger than a caper bud; she was there suddenly, looming tall and bulky in the loose white gown, her black hair loose round her white face. "I don't know what game you're playing, or how far you think you can lead your father by the nose, Lavinia," she said in a low, harsh voice, "but I tell you now, you will marry Turnus and be queen of Ardea. You don't have to cower and whine about it. If you don't like Turnus, don't worry, he may not like you all that much either, it's a political marriage not a rape. There's one thing a girl is good for, and that's to be married well, and you're no different or better than any other girl. So do your duty, as I did mine. If you ruin this chance I'll never forgive you. I'll never forgive you." It was not what she said so much as how she said it that terrified me: she stood very close to the bed, and every moment I felt that she was about to strike me, to claw me with her nails as she had done long ago. Her voice shook and hissed and her breath came hard.

"Say you will marry Turnus," she said. "Say you will!"

I said nothing. I could not.

A strange noise came from her, a kind of shrieking groan, and she turned and ran out of the room.

After a while I got up, for there was no sleep in that bed, and crept out into the courtyard. No one else was awake. I sat on the wooden bench under the laurel tree and watched the slow sliding of stars over the roofs of the Regia. The chill of the night seemed to come into my mind and make it cool and clear. I saw that I must marry Turnus: it was inevitable. To accept another suitor would be to bring civil war into the kingdom. His agreement with the others meant nothing. Turnus had to compete, to win, to be master; he would never let another man have a woman he had claimed. Marriage was my duty and my destiny. My mother was right, even if she spoke in her own interest not in mine.

In the morning I would tell my father I was ready for him to accept Turnus as my husband.

The great Bears stood high over the father river, over Etruria. The leaves of the laurel whispered in the mild flow of the night wind. I thought of those three strange nights in Albunea, where the faint stink of the sulfur pools always hung in the dark air and I sat talking with a shadow, a dying man who had not yet been born and who knew my past and my future and my soul, who knew who it was that I should marry, the true hero. But here, now, in the courtyard of my house, all that seemed distant, blurred and obscure, a false dream that had nothing to do with waking life. I would not think about it again. I would never go back to Albunea.

For a moment I heard the voice, the voice like no other, in my memory. When the poet first came, when he first stood there in the altar place, he had said that Faunus spoke from the trees of Albunea to King Latinus, telling him not to marry his daughter to a man of Latium. Then, seeing me startled and troubled by that, he said, "I think it has not happened yet. Faunus has not spoken to Latinus. Perhaps it never will happen." And he said that perhaps he had imagined it, that it was a dream within a dream.

And I had imagined it. It had not happened. It would not happen. False dreams, visions, follies.

The roofs were standing hard black against the paling eastern sky when I went in and lay down for a little while.

It was a day of worship, and I was up before the sun. I put on the red-edged toga I wore as a child and still wore for the rites, and went to wake my father, calling with the ritual words at his door: "Do you wake, king? Waken!" And soon he came out, also in his red-edged robe, the loose corner pulled up over his head for worship, and we went to the altar in the atrium.

A number of the house people were with us, among them my mother, who did not usually attend the common rituals. She stood quite close behind me as I scattered the salsamola on the altar. I had the sense that she intended to be close to me, to keep me under her eyes, within reach, all that day, till she got what she wanted. The warmth, the pressure of her body so close behind me was palpable, and I wanted to escape it. I moved closer to my father as he held a little pitch-dipped stick in Vesta's fire and lifted it to light the altar torches, murmuring the sacred words. I do not know if the pitch scattered, or a wind blew in, or a hand moved, but I suddenly saw a strangeness all around me, a flickering movement of brightness. There were voices crying, screaming— "Lavinia, Lavinia! her hair's on fire—she's burning—" I put up my hands to my head and felt a queer soft movement in the air about it. Sparks danced and leapt around me, and I smelled smoke. As I turned I saw through a yellowish, dim cloud my mother standing there not an arm's length from me. She stared with wild eyes at something above my head. I turned and ran from her, ran through the people, through the atrium, out to the courtyard. Flame and yellow smoke followed me, sparks scattered from me, people screamed, I heard my father call my name. I ran to the fountain pool under the laurel and threw myself down, my face in the water, my hair in the water.

My father was there kneeling by me, lifting me up. "Lavinia, little one, daughter, my daughter," he whispered. "Are you hurt, are you hurt, let me see."

I was very bewildered, but I saw amazement dawning through the horror in his face. He passed his hand over my dripping head, down my lank wet hair.

"Can it be you took no harm?"

"What was it, father? There was a fire—"

"A fire above your head. Leaping, blazing. I thought it was your hair—I thought the torch had caught it— Are you not hurt? not burned?"

I put my own hand on my head; I was dizzy, but my scalp and hair felt as usual, only sopping wet. Nothing was burned but the corner of my toga which I had worn pulled up over my head at the altar. All that corner of the white, red-bordered wool was scorched black.

The whole household was gathered around us by now, filling the courtyard, shouting and crying and asking and answering. My mother stood by the trunk of the laurel, her face fixed, blank. My father looked up at her and said, "She took no harm, Amata. She is all right!"

She answered something, I don't know what. Maruna's mother pressed forward; she knelt beside us and touched my head and cheeks gently, a license allowed her as a healer. She looked then at my father and said sternly, imperiously, "An omen, king. Speak the omen!"

And he obeyed the slave. He stood up. He looked down at me, and up into the great tree, and spoke. "War," he said.

All the people fell silent at his voice.

"War," he said again, and then, as if struggling with the words, or as if the words pushed themselves from his throat and mouth without his will: "Bright fame, bright glory will crown Lavinia. But she brings her people war."

GRADUALLY EVERYTHING AND EVERYONE GOT QUIETED DOWN. People scattered out, talking all the way, to their morning work. Vestina took me off to dry my hair and weep and fuss over me, while the red-bordered toga with the blackened, burnt corner passed from hand to hand among the marveling women.

The rite that had been interrupted must be begun again and carried out. That was so much on my mind that at last I broke free from the women to go assist my father; but he sent me back at once to the women's quarters, telling me to send Maruna to help him. I should rest, he said, and come to him later.

I was glad of it, for I found myself shaky and light-headed. "I think I need to eat something," I said when I came back to the women's side, and Vestina cried, "Of course, of course, poor lamb!" and sent girls off to fetch curds and honey and spelt porridge, all of which I ate, and felt better.

My mother had been in the room with us all along, but did not join the chatter. She sat at her great loom. I was a good spinning-woman, I made as strong and even a thread as any, but I was slow and clumsy at the loom. Amata was by far the best of our weavers, working fast, with a steady rhythm and utter concentration; when she was weaving she was aware of nothing else, and her face looked rapt and calm. The very fine woolen thread I had been spinning all this spring was for the piece she was working on now, a full breadth of the finest white fabric, the kind you can gather yards of into your hand and pass through a finger ring. Today, as the women at last began talking about something besides the mysterious flame of fire, and how the yellow smoke had swirled behind me when I ran, and how sparks flew all through the house yet nothing caught fire from them, and so on, and on, my mother turned round from the loom and beckoned to me. I went to her.

"Do you know what it is I'm making, Lavinia?" she asked with the strangest smile, a wide, blind smile that was almost coy.

As soon as she asked me the question I knew the answer. But I said, "A summer palla."

"Your wedding gown. You'll wear it when you marry. See how fine it is!"

"Your weaving's always beautiful, mother."

"You'll wear it when you marry, when you marry him," she said, almost as if it were the refrain of a song, and she turned back to the loom and took up the shuttle. And as she wove she whispered that half song under her breath, "You'll wear it when you marry, when you marry him."

About midday I went alone to my father's rooms. As I crossed the courtyard I paused under the laurel tree and asked the powers of the tree and the spring, the Lar of the household and my dear Penates, to be with me and help me. All I had thought and seen so clearly last night, sitting there on the bench under the stars, all I had so firmly and reasonably resolved, was gone, burnt away in a puff of heatless flame, a coil of yellow smoke. I knew what I must say, but I wanted help in saying it.

My father embraced me and tried to make certain once again that I was quite unhurt, unburnt, unshaken.

"I am well, father," I said. "I was terribly hungry, though. I ate everything they brought from the kitchen." That reassured him, as I knew it would. "Now may I speak to you about my suitors?"

He sat down on the chest against the wall and gave one grave nod.

"I said I would ask you today to give me to one of them."

A nod.

"But because of what happened this morning—the omen—I ask you not to ask me my choice, but instead to go to Albunea, and ask the powers there. Whatever they tell you, I will obey."

As I spoke he looked up at me heavily from under his heavy grey-black eyebrows. He listened. When I had spoken, he thought for some while. At last he nodded once again.

"I will go today," he said.

"May I come with you?"

Again he thought it over. "Yes," he said. Then he looked up at me again with the shadow of a smile and said, "As we used to go together. Do you remember the first time? You were still a child . . ." But his face was melancholy. I saw that he looked very worn.

I kissed his hand, and said, "I'll be ready to go as soon as you like, father."

"Sacrifices," he said. "This is . . . I will need . . . a lamb—two. Is there a white calf? Two lambs and a white calf—at least."

"I'll send to Tyrrhus' Doro, he's with the cows and calves in the long meadow pasture. I can see to the animals, father."

"Good. Do that. There are some things I must see to here before we go— A black calf, better, Lavinia, if there is one. Black, in that place."

That place, Albunea, that lies so close above the underworld that the shadows of the dead can come and go there easily. Black, in that place.

Lambing had been early that spring, and the lambs the shepherd led to me were quite large. The calf old Doro brought was small, a runt in fact, and he was not altogether black, but brownish on the legs and face; not a perfect sacrifice. My father frowned at him.

I said, "He is pious, father. See how he follows along? And he did his best to be black."

Doro nodded solemnly. "He's the blackest we've got, king," he said.

So the king nodded, and we set off.

I wore the toga with the burnt corner, for it was the only sacred toga I had; year after year, my mother had put off making the red dye for a new one. Because we had to lead the animals, and perhaps because my father felt some unease or mistrust in the air, we were quite a troop. It was not as when he and I walked there long ago, he carrying the young lamb, or when I walked with Maruna. She came with me, indeed, but also there was Doro with the calf, and the shepherd's boy with the lambs, and two slaves carrying the other offerings, and three of my father's guards, the men who kept the doors of the Regia and went with him, armed, when he rode out visiting other towns or other kings. They were called his horse-riders, his knights, and they did each keep a horse in the royal stable; but this was a sacred journey, and we went afoot.

One after another we walked through the bright day into the evening. We came to the little Prati and followed it upstream, and I remembered the rocky ford of the river where I had seen blood in the water in my dream.

The knights and Maruna and the slaves stopped at the out-skirts of the forest. The men would camp there. Maruna would go to the woodcutter's house. Doro and the shepherd boy led the animals, and Latinus and I carried the other offerings on into the forest of Albunea.

By the time the sacrifice was completed it was night, the altar fire and torches giving the only light under the dark trees. Doro and the boy took the skinned carcasses back to their camp, where the men would have the first feast on the meat. My father reversed the torches. Their flames died in the earth. He stood before the altar, where the fire still fed on the fat of the sacrifice, his head shrouded, murmuring the words of worship and humble request. I sat on the fleece of one of the lambs, listening. I feared and longed to hear the grandfather's voice speak, answering him, from those dark, silent trees.

But I had scarcely slept the night before, and the day had been long and strange. I was so tired I could not keep my eyes open. I saw the little leaping gold of the altar flame waver and blur. Then I was lying down, looking up into the branch-circled sky dense with stars as the sea beach is dense with sand, a pavement of white fire. And it too wavered and blurred.

I woke. The stars blazed, but other stars. The fire was dead. A small owl called from far on the right, *hii-ii*, and another answered from yet farther, *ii, i.*

He was there, the shadow. He stood between me and the altar. His tall form was vague in the grey starlight. On the far side of the altar, near the wall, I saw a glint of bronze, a motionless bulk on the ground: my father sleeping. The feel of the air was that of the hour before the beginning of dawn.

"The time when the dying die," my poet said, very softly.

I sat up, trying to see him more clearly. I was frightened, distressed, and did not know why, and knew why. I whispered, "Are you dying?"

He nodded.

The nod of a head is such a small thing, it can mean so little, yet it is the gesture of assent that allows, that makes to be. The nod is the gesture of power, the yes. The numen, the presence of the sacred, is called by its name.

"I don't have long," he said.

"Oh, I wish——" But wishes were no use.

"Your father has heard Faunus speak," he said, with a ghost of laughter in his ghost of voice.

"Then——"

"You will not marry Turnus. No fear of that."

I stood up, facing him. Though he spoke so gently I was still frightened.

"What will happen?"

"War. The bees swarmed to the great tree. The king's daughter ran through the house with blazing hair, scattering sparks and smoke. And war and glory followed her."

"Why must there be war?"

"Oh, Lavinia, what a woman's question that is! Because men are men."

"Then Aeneas is coming to attack us?"

"Not at all. He comes in peace, to offer alliance to your father, and marry you, and settle down to bring up his family. He brings the gods of his household here. But he brings his sword too. And there will be war. Battles, sieges, slaughter, slave taking, town burning, rape. And men who rant and boast, and then kill sleeping men. And men who kill young boys. And the growing crops laid waste. All the wrong that men can do is done. Justice, mercy, does Mars care for them?"

His voice had grown stronger, not loud but curiously strident, so that I glanced at my father to see if he had heard; he slept on, unmoving. "I can tell you the war, Lavinia. Shall I?" He did not wait for my answer. "It begins with a boy killing a deer in the woods. There's a good cause for war, as good as any other. First to die is young Almo—you know him. An arrow in his throat chokes off his speech and breath with blood. Next old Galaesus, who's rich and used to being in control, tries to keep them from fighting, comes between them, and has his face smashed in for his pains. And then Turnus sees his chance, and war begins in earnest. No man will spare another man in this battle, though he beg for his life. Ilioneus kills Lucetius, Liger kills Emathion, Asilas kills Corynaeus, Caeneus kills Ortygius. Turnus kills Caeneus, and Itys, and Clonius, and Dioxippus, and Promolus, and Sagaris, and Idas. The blood foams from the pierced lung. The man killed while sleeping vomits blood and wine as he writhes dying. Ascanius shoots his steel-pointed arrow through Remulus' head, and Turnus' javelin pierces Antiphates' throat and lodges in the lung till the steel grows warm, and his sword cleaves Pandarus' skull between the temples so that the man falls to the ground in his brain-spattered armor, his head dangling in two halves from his neck. And when Aeneas joins the battle, his spear crashes through Maeon's shield and breastplate, on through his body, to sever Alcanor's arm from his shoulder. And Pallas drives his sword into Hisbo's swollen chest, and sweeps Thymber's head from his neck, and severs Larides' hand that twitches and clutches with dying fingers at the sword. And Halaesus kills Ladon, and Pheres, and Demodocus, and lops off Strymonius' hand raised against him, and strikes Thoas in the face with a stone, scattering fragments of skull mixed with blood and brains. And Turnus hurls his steel-tipped lance of oak through Pallas' shield and breast, and the boy falls forward eating dirt with his bloody mouth. And Turnus puts his foot on the corpse and tears away Pallas' golden sword belt, boasting of the plunder that will be his death. Then hearing of this, Aeneas rushes out again in blind rage against the enemy, and though Magus begs him for mercy, Aeneas bends the man's head back and cuts his throat, and he kills Anxur, he kills Antaeus, he kills Lucas, he kills Numa, he kills tawny Camers, he kills Niphaeus, he kills Liger and Lucagus, and Turnus is saved from him only by the goddess who loves him and draws him away from the battle. But Mezentius the tyrant of Caere kills Habrus, he kills Latagus, striking him full in the mouth and face with a huge rock, he hamstrings Palmus and leaves him slowly writhing, he kills Evanthes and Mimas. Acron, dying from Mezentius' spear cast, hammers the dark earth with his heels. Caedicus kills Alcathous, and Sacrator kills Hydaspes, and Rapo kills Parthenius and Orses, Messapus kills Clonius as he lies fallen from his horse, and Agis is killed by Valerus, Thronius is killed by Salius, and Salius by Aealces. They kill together and are killed together. Then pious Aeneas obeying the will of fate and the gods pierces Mezentius' groin with his spear, and kills Mezentius' son Lausus as he tries to protect his father, driving his sword through the young man's body to the hilt: the point pierces the shield and the tunic his mother wove for him, blood fills his lungs and his life leaving his body flees sorrowing to the shadows. And Aeneas is sorry for the boy. But when Mezentius challenges him, he goes to meet him with a shout of joy, and though Mezentius rains darts on him, Aeneas kills his horse, then taunts the fallen man, and cuts his throat. And the next day he sends Pallas' body to his father, King Evander, with four prisoners to be sacrificed alive on the grave. How do you like my poem now, Lavinia?"

After a long time I managed to answer him, "That might depend on how it ends."

"With the triumph of the glorious hero over his enemy, of course. He will kill Turnus, lying wounded and helpless, just as he killed Mezentius."

"Who is the hero?"

"You know who the hero is."

"He kills like a butcher. Why is he a hero?"

"Because he does what he has to do."

"Why does he have to kill a helpless man?"

"Because that is how empires are founded. Or so I hope Augustus will understand it. But I do not think he will."

He turned away from me and neither of us spoke. I had begun to cry while he sang his hideous chant of slaughter, and my face was still wet. When the poet spoke again, his voice had softened. "But that's not where it ends for you, Lavinia."

I took a step towards him, for I could no longer see his face. "Tell me, then."

"Not with the end of his reign, after only three summers and three winters. You may think all is over at the bloody ford of the Numicus, but it is not there it ends, nor at Lavinium, nor Alba Longa. Not with your death, or your son's. Not with the Kings, not with the Consuls, the fall of Carthage, the conquest of Gaul. Not even with the murder of Julius, or Augustus' godhead. The great age returns . . . maybe . . . I thought so once. But be of good heart, my daughter, my young grandmother! The gods of Troy are coming to a good house, your house of Latium. And you will marry the son of Spring, the son of the evening star."

I had hated him while he told that tale of slaughter, but I was losing him, now, already, moment by moment, and I loved him, yearning to him. "Wait— Only tell me—your poem, my poem, did you finish it?"

He seemed to nod, but I could hardly see him, a tall shadow in shadows.

"Don't go yet—"

"I must go, my glory. I am gone. I join the crowd, return to darkness."

I cried out his name, went forward, reaching out my arms to hold him, to keep him from death, but it was like holding a breath of the night wind. Nothing was there.

I SAT ON THE FLEECE, MY ARMS AROUND MY KNEES, THE TOGA with the burnt corner wrapped around me for warmth, till the sky was light above the altar place. I went then to my father and said, "Do you wake, king? Waken!" He sat up. We had brought a little drinking water, for there is none near there; I gave him the flask, and he drank a swallow and rubbed a handful of water on his face.

"You heard the grandfather speak," I said.

Looking up at me as if still not fully awake, he said, "The voice among the trees."

I waited.

He looked off into the dark trees and said in the low, level voice of prayer, but clearly: "'Do not let the daughter of Latium marry a man of Latium. Let her marry the stranger that comes, that even now is coming. And the kingdom of her sons will be far greater than the kingdom of Latium.'"

He looked up at me again. I nodded. "I understand. I will obey."

My father got up, stiff and ponderous; he was not used to sleeping out, on hard ground, these days. He rubbed his thighs and stretched his arms painfully. "I am old, daughter," he said. "And now I have to face those young fellows with this refusal." He shook his head, hunched up his shoulders. "If only my sons had lived. I am too old, Lavinia!"

It was not like him to say that. I did not know what to say to him; I was too young to feel anything but surprised, uncomprehending pity, and I did not want to pity my father the king.

He went off into the woods to piss, and when he came back he was holding himself a little straighter. "Don't be afraid," he said. "I'll take no insolence from them. I can still protect my daughter and my house and city." We gathered up the little we had brought, and as we did so, he said, "I could wish your mother hadn't set her mind on your marrying Turnus. But I can see, because he's her nephew, it seems to her like getting one of her sons back. Well. Come along, my dear." He set off, walking heavily, and I followed.

When we came to where the men had camped, they were just waking. The sky was bright behind the eastern hills and all the birds in the world were singing. There was a little brook there, and my father and I both knelt on the bank to wash our hands and faces.

As the knights joined us, I heard my father telling them what the oracle had said. That surprised me again. I had assumed he would announce it formally at home, perhaps summoning the suitors to explain to them that their request had been denied by the powers and the ancestors. To talk about it openly now was to ensure that it would be common knowledge in Laurentum as soon as we got back, and throughout all Latium within a day or two. I could not think why my father had done this, unless he thought he could not face my mother with the news himself, and wanted her to hear it from me, or from hearsay among the women.

But she came to meet us, almost running across the courtyard, flushed and beautiful in her excitement. "I know! I dreamed of you there," she cried. "I am so glad!"

We both stopped, staring like cattle, no doubt. She took my hands and kissed me. "I am so happy about it!"

"About—?"

"Oh! The bridal bed! In Ardea! I saw it all in my dream!"

After a blank pause my father said, loudly and awkwardly, "The oracle forbids Lavinia to marry a man of Latium. She must wait for a foreign suitor."

"No. That's not what it said at all. I saw it. I heard it!"

"Amata, calm yourself," he said. "We will speak of this in private. Lavinia—call the women—take your mother with you—" And he strode off to his rooms.

My mother started to run after him, then stopped, bewildered, and said to me, "What is wrong with him?"

"Nothing, mother. Come with me." I tried to go on to the women's side, but she protested, and only when her women Sicana and Lina came to urge her to come with them did she fall silent, the happy brightness dying out of her face, and follow me.

The news was all over the house and town at once, of course.

The king's daughter is not to marry Turnus, or Messapus, or any of them, she's got to wait for a foreigner to come marry her. That's what the bees meant, that's why her hair caught fire yet didn't burn. War! War! Who'll fight? Who's the foreigner coming? And what will King Turnus have to say to him?

And what will I have to say to him, I wondered, as everybody chattered on.

Amata seemed stunned. She did not tell us what the dream was that she had taken to be a true dream and that the oracle had so cruelly belied. She did not join in the general talk, did not speak to me at all. We kept away from each other. It was easy enough, we had kept apart for twelve years.

By nightfall I was sick of the chatter and commotion and wanted only to be free of the women, away from the house, outdoors, alone, where I could think. My mother was at her loom. I went and asked her permission to go get salt at the river mouth next day.

"Ask the king," she said, not looking away from her work.

So I went to him. He pondered a minute. "I suppose it's safe," he said.

"Why would it not be safe?" I said, amazed. Our possession of the salt beds was one of our great strengths as a nation, and we guarded them accordingly. Nobody had tried to raid them for decades.

"I'll send Gaius with you. And take a couple of your women."

"What do we want Gaius for? I'll have Pico with the donkey, to carry the salt back."

"Gaius will go with you. Go by the west path. Be back before dark."

"I can't, father. We have to dig the salt."

He frowned. "You can do that and be back in a day easily!"

"I hoped to spend the night there, father. By Tiber."

I very seldom pleaded with him. "Well, why not," he said after a long pause. "My mind is vexed, troubled, I hardly know . . . Go on, then. Give worship to our father river. But one night only!" As I thanked him and left, he said, "And look out for Etruscans!"

Everybody always said that when you went to Tiber, as if the northern bank were forever crowded with Etruscans waiting to leap in, swim across, carry you off, and torture you. There were awful stories about Etruscan torture. But we had always been on good terms with Caere, except when Mezentius ruled it. And it would be a mighty swimmer who swam the river there at its mouth. People said, "Look out for Etruscans," when you went to the river the way they said, "Look out for bears," when you went up into the hills—out of habit.

All the same, as I went to find Tita to tell her to find Pico and tell him to be ready with the donkey in the morning, I wondered if the foreigner I was to marry might be an Etruscan.

For when I was not in Albunea, when I was among people, the things my poet had said to me came and went in my mind, sometimes seeming as real as they did when he spoke them, but more often fading away like the shreds of a dream that vanish as you try to remember them. It was a true dream, but you cannot live your life in a dream even if it be true. Hardest of all to remember was what the poet had said last night—was it only last night? He was dying. I did not want to remember that. I did not want to remember what he had sung, the endless hideous deaths. I knew he had told me the name of the man I was to marry, his wife's name and his son's, I knew he came from the far city, Troy, I knew there was to be a war, men would kill men . . . and yet, here in the courtyard of the Regia, passing by the great laurel, where women were gathered talking and singing at their work, the names and all slipped away from me, and I wondered if the foreigner I was to marry might be an Etruscan.

They were foreign enough, the Etruscans. They saw the future in the livers of sheep. I liked Maruna's bird lore, but I could do without the tortures and the sheep livers.

My spirits had risen as soon as I had permission to go, and when we left the city next morning I felt like a sparrow let go from the snare. All the trouble about suitors, the threats, the strange portents, the dark prophecies, dropped away from me. I forbade Tita to say a word about all that. We joked and told stories all the way to Tiber, and even grave Maruna laughed like a child. That was a joyous day, and that night I slept a quiet sleep on the dune under the stars.

And in the twilight of morning of the next day, alone, kneeling in the mud by Tiber, I saw the great ships turn from the sea and come into the river. I saw my husband stand on the high stern of the first ship, though he did not see me. He gazed up the dark river, praying, dreaming. He did not see the deaths that lay before him, all along the river, all the way to Rome.

THERE WAS NOTHING BUT COMMOTION AND DISCUSSION AND agitation in the Regia and the town all that day. Everybody knew what the oracle had told Latinus and they all had to discuss it endlessly—and then word came across the fields of a fleet of ships seen going up the river, and of a crowd of armed strangers making camp on the Latin shore. The talk about that made me think of the great, dark, humming mutter of the swarming bees.

Very early the next morning, I slipped out of the Regia and out of Laurentum without asking permission or telling anyone, and ran through the oak grove to Tyrrhus' farm. Silvia was in the cool stone dairy with some of the dairy women, skimming cream. I said, "Silvia, let's go to the river. Let's take a look at these strangers."

It was usually Silvia, not I, who proposed anything daring or dangerous, and I took her by surprise.

"What do you want to see foreigners for?" she asked—a reasonable question.

"Because I have to marry one."

She'd heard the decree of the oracle, of course. She frowned at first, no doubt thinking of Almo, but after a minute she looked up with a half smile. "You want to see if they have two heads?"

"Yes."

"Maybe these aren't the foreigners you have to marry one of."

"I think they are."

She was standing with the skimmer in hand, her hair tied back, her bare arms shining in the dim cool place and her bare feet on the wet floor; the dairy was kept very clean, sluiced out constantly with water. She couldn't resist the escapade. "Oh, all right!" she said, and gave the skimmer and a few orders to Valenta the dairy keeper, and came out into the sunshine with me. She put on her sandals and we struck off across the pastures. It was six miles or so to the river; we had done it often in our rambles and explorations, and knew the ways through the woods.

We discussed where the foreigners might have landed, for we hadn't heard a clear report yet. Silvia thought they would have tied up at the wooden docks at Sirmo, but I had it in my head that they had not gone so far upstream, but had beached their ships at the place called Venticula, where the river takes a great bend to the north. Though we said nothing about it, we were both aware that if any of our countrymen saw us, whether they recognised us or not, they would rightly tell us to get back home at once, and might make sure we did so. There was a cart road to Sirmo, to Venticula only a path leading through dense woods and past the marshes of the Fossula. We kept off the cart road and the straight pagus lanes, away from farmhouses and shepherds' huts, following the path that wound over old grass-grown dunes and skirted swampy thickets as it neared the river, till we finally scrambled up the low forested hill above Venticula.

As we came over the crest of the hill, we both realised that we weren't alone in the woods: we heard men talking, calling, the blows of an ax, then we saw a couple of helmeted heads across a myrtle thicket, behind which we at once crouched down to hide. Silvia had a fit of wild, silent giggles, which infected me. We crouched shaking with crazy laughter. The soldiers crashed on down the hill, and when it had been silent for a while except for ax blows far off, I wriggled around to the end of the thicket. From there I could look right down the hillside through the trees to the open glades by the shore. I whispered to Silvia, "There they are!" She crawled beside me and we lay watching the Trojans.

I saw my husband almost at once. He stood out among them, not by any ornament or richness of clothing—they were all dressed like soldiers on the march who'd been on duty a long time and crammed into ships on the sea as well, all plain and worn and dirty—he simply stood out, the way the morning star stands out from other stars. He was a man in his forties, with a strong face. He was sitting comfortably on the ground and laughing at something one of the other men said. They were having a picnic there on the grass. Almost all of them were men. They had brought flatbread up from the ships, which were run up stern-first along the beach. They had gathered a great basket of wild greens to pile up on the rounds of flatbread, having no meat or cheese, evidently, as well as no plates or tables. The few women among them were none of them young; one matron, smiling, presented Aeneas with a round of bread heaped with greens, which he rolled up and bit into with gusto. Close to him sat a boy of fifteen or so, who looked enough like him, and looked up to him in such a way, that I was sure it was his son Ascanius. With him were a very pretty boy of his age and a beautiful youth a few years older, wearing a bent-forward red cloth cap. The woman who had served the meal sat down beside him and set his cap straight with an unmistakably maternal fussiness, adoring him.

"They're much better looking than I thought foreigners would be," Silvia whispered to me. "That boy with the red cap is gorgeous." I hushed her with a nudge of my elbow. I was afraid they might hear us, since we could hear them clearly enough, though to be sure the wind was blowing our way.

Red Cap said something about the meal being fit for rabbits not men, and young Ascanius said, "Well, it's not at every meal that you get to eat the table too."

At that Aeneas looked at him as if startled. After gazing motionless for a minute he stood up. They all looked up at him.

"That is the omen," he said, his voice ringing clear and solemn. "'When hunger drives you to eat your tables, there will be your journey's end.' You remember what the Harpy said to us?"

A murmur of assent and awe ran among them all, those travel-weary men and boys and few women sitting there on the grass above the river. They did not take their eyes off Aeneas.

"Euryalus, bring me a myrtle bough," he said, and Red Cap ran to break off a bough. Aeneas bent it into a wreath to cover his head, and stretched out his arms, his hands palm up to the sky. He said, "Dear faithful gods of the house of Troy! This is your promised land at last! We are home, my people, we have come home!" He looked round at them all and his face shone with tears. He prayed again: "Hear us, spirit of this place, and spirits and rivers we do not yet know! Night, and the rising stars! My father in the underworld and my mother in the heavens, hear our prayer!" Then he turned round and drew a deep breath. "Achates!" he shouted in a tremendous voice. "Tell them to bring the wine up from the ship!"

At that moment Silvia nudged me. Seven or eight men with bows and arrows were trotting in single file across the clearing to our left. It was time for us to be out of there.

We crept under the shelter of the cork oaks into thick woods to our right, and through them back over the crest of the hill and so down the way we'd come. We were home before evening. At the farm, Silvia turned to me and gave me a big hug. We were both sweaty from our long run, we stuck to each other when we hugged. We laughed, and Silvia said, "That was a good idea, going there!" So we parted for the last time.

WHEN I GOT BACK TO THE REGIA I HEARD THAT MY FATHER had given orders that no one was to approach the strangers' camp until he had determined who they were and why they had brought longships and armed men into the heart of Latium. I said nothing, of course, about my hare-brained exploit, but slipped into the house, washed and put on a clean tunic, and sat spinning away as if I'd never set foot outside the door in my life.

The word was that the king was going to send Drances with a party of men to talk to the strangers in the morning. But next day before Drances even set out, people ran shouting, "They're coming!"—and a small troop of foreigners came riding up to the city gates.

Their horses looked poorly, as well they might, poor creatures, after a sea voyage, but they were decked out with silver-mounted bridles and trappings, and the men were grand in embroidered cloaks, bronze breastplates, and tall helmets with crests of horsehair or feathers. I could get only a glimpse of the troop from our doorway as they rode up the Via Regia, before the women were sent off to the back of the house; but I saw Aeneas was not with them.

While Drances and other officials brought them in and escorted them to the king's audience hall, I went through the royal apartments and entered the audience hall through the king's door, behind his seat. He had not bidden me to be there; but I had been present with or without my mother at many audiences, as a courtesy to the visitors and to welcome their wives and daughters, and if he did not want me now, he had only to send me away.

I do not think he knew at first that I was there. He was already speaking to the Trojan envoys. He welcomed them with stately courtesy and asked immediately, though politely, where they came from and the cause of their visit to Latium: had they perhaps gone astray or been driven out of their course on the high seas?

A tall, thin Trojan introduced himself as Ilioneus, and in a spate of elegant and respectful language explained that they had come to the kingdom of the great Latinus following the command of fate. Natives of the noble city of Troy, which had withstood a ten-year siege by the Greeks but had fallen at last to treachery, they had escaped from the burning.

As the herald spoke, I heard the poet's voice overlapping his as a sea wave running up the shore overtakes and overlaps the wave before it. I knew then that the high house of the king and all of us in it had being only in those words. And that knowledge changed nothing. The messenger still must speak, the king must listen, the king's daughter must follow her fate.

The messenger spoke on: oracles had bidden them bring the gods of Troy over the seas to the far shore of Italy, where they would find a home. Their lord Aeneas son of Anchises had led them for seven years across land and sea, and though other kings had asked them to stay, he would offer alliance only to Latinus, who reigned over the land promised them by the oracle. And in earnest of his goodwill, Aeneas offered to the king some poor fragments, saved from the fallen city, that had belonged to his father's brother King Priam of Troy.

One of the Trojans came forward and laid at my father's feet a marvelous tall libation cup that looked to be of solid gold carved and jeweled, a silver rod or wand, a thin, old, gold crown, and a delicate weaving of royal crimson embroidered with gold thread.

My father gazed down at these things in silence for some time, neither accepting nor refusing them. At last he asked the envoy to tell him more about the city of Troy and their quarrel with the Greeks, and then something of their seven-year voyage across the Middle Sea, all of which Ilioneus did. My father asked if they had stopped in Sicily, and Ilioneus said that they had left a colony there; he asked if they had been in touch with the Greek settlement south of us, whose king was Diomedes, and Ilioneus said that they had not, Diomedes being a veteran of the siege of Troy and not likely to be well disposed to Trojans. All his answers were both direct and graceful.

My father let silence fall again, looking downward, his eyes moving as they followed his thoughts.

At last he looked up. "Oracles, you say, bade you come to this country," he said. "I will tell you that your coming also was foretold. I think, my friends, that we are to enact what fate will have us do. If your chief Aeneas seeks alliance, if he seeks to settle here with us, I will ask him to come to my city and offer me his hand, even as he has offered me these noble gifts. And I will take it, as I accept them, in sign of friendship and pledge of peace. And say this also to him: my only daughter is bidden by our oracle to marry a stranger, a man who, even as the oracle spoke, was coming to us. I think your lord Aeneas is the man. And if my mind sees truly, this marriage is what I wish. So bid him come." He stood up, and only then, I think, did he see me; but he showed no surprise, he only looked at me with serene, affectionate eyes, a look of perfect certainty, smiling a little.

He did not introduce the envoys to me, but moved among them, admiring their noble gifts, ordering our people to bring out gifts for them. I backed away quietly through the door I had come in.

To hear myself promised as part of a treaty, exchanged like a cup or a piece of clothing, might seem as deep an insult as could be offered to a human soul. But slaves and unmarried girls expect such insult, even those of us who have been allowed liberty enough to pretend we are free. My liberty had been great, and so I had dreaded its end. So long as it could end only with Turnus or the other suitors, I had felt that insult, that bondage awaiting me, the only possible outcome. I had been the dove tied to the pole, flapping its silly wings as if it could fly, while the boys below shouted and pointed and shot at it till at last an arrow struck.

I felt nothing of that entrapment now, that helpless shame. I felt the same certainty I had seen in my father's eyes. Things were going as they should go, and in going with them I was free. The string that tied me to the pole had been cut. For the first time I knew what it would be to fly, to take to my wings across the air, across the years to come, to go, to go on.

"I will marry him," I said in my heart, as I went through the rooms of the Regia. "I will make him my husband, and bring the gods of his house here to join with the gods of mine. I will bring him home."

I turned aside and went across the courtyard, past the great laurel tree, to the domed rooms behind the atrium, the storehouses, my domain, where I and the Penates ruled. Before long it would be the fourth month, June, time to throw open the doors of those storehouses and clean them out, clear them for the new harvest. I sent for a couple of the women who helped me there and we began making ready for the ceremony, recalling and singing to one another the words of the songs of Vesta and Ceres, Fire and Bread, while we carried out empty bins and swept the dusty floors.

There was commotion all through the house and city as the gifts Latinus had ordered were brought out and men chosen to take them. He himself had been out to the stables to select a few good horses, and to send word to Tyrrhus to have a herd of choice bull calves and a flock of lambs driven to Venticula so the Trojans could have sacrifice and meat. He knew what a king's hospitality should be, and enjoyed his own generosity. He looked like a young man as he strode across the courtyard, and I watched him with pride.

But Amata came hurrying to meet him from the women's quarters, her hair loose, her face white, her voice loud.

"Is it true what they say, husband? That you gave our daughter to a stranger—a foreigner—a man you have not seen, know nothing of? Is this wise? Is this kind to the girl?—and me?— Not to say a word to me—"

My father had stopped and stood erect facing her. The geniality had gone out of his face and old age had come back into it. "This is not the place, Amata."

"I will speak—"

"Come with me then. You too, Lavinia." He strode off to the royal apartments and we followed him. Catching up with Amata, I said, "Mother, he did as the oracle commanded, and as I myself asked him to do. Truly I did! This is how it must be. It will be all right!"

She did not even hear me, I think. As soon as we were in

Latinus' office she began to talk, pouring out a torrent of arguments— How could he ruthlessly discard our understanding with Turnus and the other suitors? How could they not see it as pledge breaking? What did it matter if the oracle said the marriage must be with a foreigner?—was Rutulia not a different country from Latium, was Turnus not a foreigner?

"He is a Latin, one of us, one of your house," my father said, frowning. I thought it a mistake for him to answer her arguments at all, and indeed it only inflamed her. She accused him of listening to Drances' counsel, Drances who hated and was jealous of Turnus— faithful Turnus who only sought to uphold and support Latinus' throne in his old age. She berated him cruelly for oath breaking and weakness and indecision, and in the next breath pleaded with him, calling on his strength and wisdom. He stood enduring the flood of words and said nothing, only occasionally shaking his head. At last, as her voice began to get hoarse and shrill, he broke in, also hoarsely: "The matter is settled. Accept it, Amata. Remember you are a queen." And to me he said, "Take your mother back to her rooms and comfort her, Lavinia."

"I will not, I will not go," she shrieked, shaking her arms in the air, and she ran out, whirling across the courtyard like a top that children whip into spinning, screaming that the king had given his daughter to a stranger, an enemy, that the king was mad. And she made for the front doors of the Regia.

The guards did not dare touch her, but my women acted very swiftly, with me, as if we had planned what to do. We surrounded Amata before she had got far into the streets of the city, and talking and soothing and stroking and urging her along, we got her back into the Regia and to her rooms on the women's side. There her hysteria turned to a great fit of sobbing, which left her spent and silent at last.

I thought that collapse into weariness was final. I thought she had given up. That was stupid of me. So was my failure to understand that what she was saying was not only madness or the rage of frustrated desire. She was giving voice to what a great many of our people thought or feared obscurely when they heard what the king had said to the Trojan messenger: that he had welcomed invaders, that, scorning his loyal subjects and allies, he had promised to give his daughter, his inheritance, his country, to a stranger.

I went to bed that night tired and shaken but in peace of heart, and slept well. I woke to a craziness that I can remember only in vivid bits and patches, because nothing in it was sane or clear, none of it made sense. I woke in my mother's world.

It was dark night; women with oil lamps were in my room and one of them was patting my shoulder saying, "Wake up, king's daughter! Wake up!" All about me there was bustle, whispering, laughter. As I struggled awake I saw they were all my mother's women, not mine, and that the slave women were dressed up in fine, ceremonial clothes, in my mother's clothes. I heard Amata's voice, and she came in, wearing the coarse unbleached tunic of a slave. "Up, up, girl," she said with a smile, "this is the Goat Feast, the Fig Feast. We're going to do worship the way my people do, up in the hills. If your father can give you away, I can take you away! Come on, now, we must be there at sunrise!" And I was up, and dressed in an old grey tunic and a ragged shawl, and hurried away among the laughing women—out the back door, through the silent streets of the city, out the postern gate, across the fields, towards the low forested hills that rise east of Laurentum. The tiny oil lamps made a wavering dance down the lane before us and behind us. The eastern skyline was just showing clear against the first beginning of dawn, Mount Alba standing long and dark over the dark world.

We left the last pagus and entered at once into the forest. Night closed around us, it was hard to see the way. The lamps cast wild shadows through the trees and across the uneven path. Women stopped to free their robes from thorns and entangling branches, but Amata urged them on— "Don't worry about that, a tear can be mended, we must be up in the hills, up at the fig-tree spring, when the sun rises! Come on, hurry along!" And she went back down along the line to encourage the women, house slaves, sweepers and washers and cook's helpers and maids of all work, who were struggling along under heavy loads, baskets and jugs of food and drink. She called them by name, cheered them on, and came whirling back up to the head of the line, laughing and talking. "Oh, this is an adventure, at last!" she called to me joyously as she passed me. And indeed there was a wild thrill of strangeness in the hurry and secrecy, the changed costumes, the line of women carrying lights in the forest in the dark—it was all unreal, fantastic, and I was caught up in the excitement of it.

We reached the fig-tree springs as the sky was brightening. Up in the heart of the hills a spring breaks out from a ledge of rock on the side of a deep fold in the hillside, and all around below it, on a level meadow, grow huge old wild fig trees, a kind of natural orchard. I had been there once with Silvia in summer to feast on the black fruit; but we had heard swine grunting and crashing all about, drawn by the fallen fruit, and so did not stay long, a wild boar being about the only thing Silvia was afraid of.

We all straggled up to the grassy level under the trees and set down burdens and drew breath for a while. Amata stood and talked to us, telling us that this was the festival of the Caprotinae as the Rutulians celebrated it in their hills—a festival of women, for women only. "We will set guards," she said. "If a man comes near us, he must be driven away. If he refuses to go, or if he tries to spy on us, it's death for him, worse than death! For if he spies on our mysteries that's the end of his manhood—he'll go back down the mountain a eunuch! Balina brought four sharp swords with her, and four strong women will keep watch day and night on the paths. And the powers of the hills and wilderness wait to curse the man who dares approach us. For Mars must stay below us here, Mars must keep down at the fields' edge and the forests' edge, standing on his boundaries. The heights and the wild forests are ours, ours alone, for our worship and our revels. And look, look, the sun rises! Greet the day, sisters! Sicana, open a wine jug, pass it around!"

So the day began with drinking, and by noon some of the women were too drunk to dance; they laughed and screeched and vomited and fell over and slept where they fell. Amata taught us the dances and songs of her Caprotinae, and a sacred game in which the older women tried to catch the younger ones and whip them with fig branches, shouting out crude joking songs about men's penises and women's vulvas; and we held other ceremonies at altars we raised to Fauna of the wilderness, and the Juno of women, and Ceres who swells the seed in the womb of Earth to be born as the bread of life. Slaves were sent back down to the city to fetch more wine. During the day, groups of women began to straggle in, coming from other households in the city, drawn by curiosity about this new women's rite and by solidarity with their queen. I found myself in an odd position with these townswomen, who were all outraged for me and enraged at my father. They hung about me to commiserate, and pet me, and encourage me in my love and fidelity to Turnus of Ardea. Their indignation and kindness were real and touching, and yet as unreal as all the rest of this escape, this mistake.

I played the part of the meek voiceless maiden all through this masquerade up in the hills. I could not bring myself to tell these sympathetic matrons that I had no love at all for Turnus and wanted only to obey my father and the oracle. To do so would be to betray my mother, and to turn her rage against me. I was a coward. I felt false, frightened, incredulous, scornful, and alone.

My mother had brought none of my women up here to the hills, only her women; and for all her wild gaiety and seeming abandon, she never let me out of her sight. I was very glad when I saw, among the last group of newcomers, Maruna. She had put on my best palla, for that was the rule, the servant to dress as mistress and the mistress as servant. I winked at her to let her know I'd seen her, and seen my best palla, too, but we kept our distance and did not speak. Slight and quiet, Maruna had a gift of going unnoticed, very useful to a slave. She kept with the group she'd come with and did as all the others did, and I think my mother never noticed her.

During the evening Amata began to drink—she had only tasted and pretended, till then—and by nightfall she was not drunk, but mellowed, less hectic, and enjoying the escapade far more than she had pretended to till then. Her laugh came from deep in her belly. I had never heard her laugh like that. It made her seem strange, another woman, a woman she might have been. I felt an aching pang of grief for her.

"Lavinia," she called me, and when I came to her, picking my way among the women sprawled about in the grass amid the little flickering oil lamps and the low boughs of the great fig trees, "Lavinia, I sent for him, last night, before we left. I sent a messenger on horseback. He should be here tomorrow. Your wedding night, my darling!"

I knew who he was, and what she meant; it was all part of the craziness, the unreality, but in her game I had to play the game. "How will he know where to come?"

"The women will tell him. They're looking out for him, they'll catch him before he ever gets into the city. He should be here by this time tomorrow."

"But men are not allowed here among us," I said.

"Oh, this one is," my mother said, in that deep melting laughing voice.

She pulled at my hand to make me sit down beside her. She leaned close to me and whispered in my ear, "There will be such a wedding night here in the hills! And then to Ardea. Home to Ardea! It's all planned. All planned!"

She kept me by her all night. I had to sleep close to her and the group of women she was drinking and gambling with, in the light of their lamps fixed on low branches. I slept only in snatches all night long, waking up always with a start, my mind racing. I kept telling myself not to worry, all I had to do was go along with whatever my mother wanted until her game played itself out, as it must, in confusion and disillusion and retreat. But she had sent for Turnus—what if he came? What if she handed me over to him in a mock wedding, a real rape? What if he took me off to Ardea? There would be nothing, nothing I could do. At the thought my body went stiff, my hands clenched, and I hid my face in my arms. I had to get away from here. I had to find a way to escape. But even if I could creep away, I could not find my way through the forest in the dark: the guards were watching the path we had come by, and it was a long way through wild, broken hills. The best I could hope for was to get far enough away to hide for the rest of the night and then follow a stream down to the lowlands. But my mother's women were all around me, still awake, the tiny lamps still flickering. And beyond them, the guards.

The same series of thoughts—the effort to reassure myself, the shock of thinking Turnus might come, the attempt to imagine a way to escape—repeated itself in my head, round and round, again and again, all night. Sometimes I slept and had snatches of dreams of my poet, not in the altar place of Albunea but here in the wild hills; he seemed to be nearby, near one of the oil lamps, but he was deformed, shrunken into a stump of shadow, mumbling words I could not understand. Then I would wake to the endless repetition of the same thoughts.

I got up at the first hint of light. Seeing Amata asleep at last among her women, I slipped away towards the dell we had been using as a place to piss, and for a moment I thought I could simply walk on—but just past the dell, Gaia was standing on guard, leaning on a naked sword as if it were a cane. She greeted me loudly, with a stupid smile. She was a sweeper, not quite right in her wits; she was devoted to my mother, as were many of these women. If Amata had told her not to let me pass, she would not let me pass. Amata was not a particularly kind mistress, she showed little affection, but she was not stingy, not cruel, and did not play favorites: that was more than enough to win loyalty. And her grief for her lost sons gave her a kind of sanctity among the women of her household. "The poor queen," I had heard them say a thousand times, and it never seemed strange to me that they still pitied her. They were right. She was an unhappy woman.

Many of us slept late and got up staggering. Food and drink had nearly given out, and groups went down to Laurentum to bring stores from their own storehouses and from the Regia. There was a good deal of coming and going, but I could not slip away or join a group going down to the city, as I hoped, for if Amata was not with me, tall Sicana and dour Lina always were, keeping watch.

I and some slave girls were the only young women here; the city matrons had left their virgin daughters safe at home. But women with babies at the breast had of course brought their nurslings, and I passed much of the day relieving tired mothers by rocking fretful babies. It saved me from having to talk with half-drunken adults. And the babies were a relief from the falseness, the insanity of what we were doing. They were solid, real, and needy. They were too young to imagine anything. Looking after them was a comfort to me, for which of course I was overpraised and flattered—look how kind the king's daughter is to the slave's child. Look how kind the slave's child is to the king's daughter, I thought, as a sweet, languid little girl smiled up at me, falling asleep in my arms.

Amata organised dances and whipping games in the afternoon, but they lacked the wild spontaneity of the first day. Everyone knew by now that Amata was expecting Turnus to arrive, and that she meant to marry me to him. Many women were uneasy with the idea of his coming, feeling, I think, like heifers who'd jumped the fence and found themselves in the bull's pasture. And the notion of a marriage so far from the doorway of the house and the Penates and Lares of the family and the city was puzzling and shocking to us all. How could you get married in the wilderness, where none of the domestic powers could help you, and the local powers and spirits had no care for human matters and might well be malevolent? Though Amata continued to talk of a wedding, the others dealt with it by speaking of it as a betrothal. That was something they could look forward to as plausible. So they kept their expectation high all afternoon and evening. When night came and Turnus had not, Amata began to drink again and urge us all to drink. The dances and songs soon broke up into aimless, foolish noisiness. Yet through it all my mother kept me close beside her, with Lina and Sicana; and the guards with swords did not drink, but spelled each other on duty all night long, waiting out of sight, down the path.

Next day a good many women slipped away quietly, and some groups that went down to bring food and drink did not come back. I thought it likely they had lost heart for trudging back and forth, but Amata said their men had locked them up, threatening to beat them if they ran off to the hills again. She ranted about what would happen to those men if they tried to come up here. All our women she sent to the Regia came back, laden with wine and bread: no one had hindered them from raiding the storerooms, and they were told the king had given orders that the women performing religious rites up in the hills were not to be disturbed. But they said also that people were talking about some kind of quarrel with a hunting party of the strangers, in the forest, between Laurentum and the river.

As the day wore on, many of us felt light-headed from little food and much wine and the strangeness of irresponsibility. There was a good deal of weeping, crazy laughter, shouting, quarreling.

As I sat with Tulia's year-old boy, who was teething, trying to soothe him with a lullaby, Maruna appeared beside me for a moment. "Tonight?" she murmured, and I nodded, not looking at her; she whispered, "Owl," and was gone again.

"*Doro, doro, dormiu,*" I sang to the baby, "*papa has a ring for you,*" and wondered what Maruna meant. All I could do was wait and find out.

"You like babies, don't you," my mother said to me, standing above me in her soiled, ragged slave's tunic. Her legs were white and shapely, with fine, soft, black hair on the shins and calves. She looked down at the child in my arms. Her face contorted as if she had toothache.

"He'll breed you," she said. "You can count on that. He's not like the old eunuch. He'll breed sons who live."

She spoke clearly, with detachment. She was drunk the way I'd seen men at feasts be drunk, day-and-night drunk, drunk to the bone. I did not reply, but went on with the lullaby in an undertone, for the baby was beginning to relax at last. I did not want to look up at my mother. I knew her anger was gathering to burst out again.

I knew she knew Turnus was not going to come. I was very much afraid of her.

"*Doro, doro, dormiu*," she sang, mocking. "What a ewe lamb, what a eunuch's daughter you are, Lavinia! All milk and meekness. All obedience to your dear papa who makes up oracles to suit himself. Don't think you're going to have it your way this time. I go where you go. You come with me, my girl. You come with me to Ardea tomorrow."

I bowed my head and said nothing. The child felt the tension in my arms and began to whimper again.

"Shut the brat up," Amata said, turning away. "Sicana! Where's the jug?"

It was an endless evening. After Tulia took her baby off, I dozed, sitting with my back against a great old fig tree. My head ached, my muscles were tight, my mind dull, blank. The sun set in clouds behind the endless trees of the forest, and the night came on very dark. Most women fell asleep early; only Amata's group of gamblers stayed up, still drinking, till even they wore out. My mother came and lay down next to me. "Asleep already, little ewe lamb?" she said. She set down a small oil lamp near her head. "Sleep well. Tomorrow we're off to Ardea. Sleep well. Sleep well." She bunched up the corner of her palla under her head for a pillow, laid her arm over me, not in an embrace, and lay silent. I felt the weight and warmth of her arm, of her body against mine. I lay looking into the darkness, watching the shadows from the small lamp flame move among leaves and branches. After a long time and very slowly I moved out from under the warm, heavy arm that lay across me. My mother sighed, snored once loudly, did not move. I lay watching the shadows die. I was asleep, but awake too, for I heard an owl's thin quavering cry, nearby, to my left: *iii, i, i.*

Without thought or pause I stood up softly and stepped among the sleeping women in that direction. No lamps burned now, but the clouds had thinned and summer starlight was grey on the grass. The owl called softly from farther away, and I followed. I saw Gaia slumped asleep under a tree like a lump of darkness, her sword standing by her, its point stuck in the ground.

I came away from the fig trees, crossed a tiny side stream where I slipped and stumbled, clambered up to a place where trees massed thicker and darker. Maruna was there. I knew her though I could barely see her. She took my hand and we went on together.

Before long she murmured, "I think we've lost the path."

We had; but we got along for half a mile or so downhill before we came into a stream gully so overhung with trees and overgrown with thickets that we could go no farther in the dark. We waited there some hours, curled up together for warmth, dozing, till the wind came up as it will do sometimes an hour before the dawn, clearing off the clouds, and the moon gave us enough light to go on. We struck a downhill path, and took it; it soon opened into a woodcutter's drag, down which we could run. And we ran.

By the time it was light we were out of the high hills, coming into pastures. I knew the country from my rambles with Silvia, knew where we were, and could head straight for the city. We came to the southern gate in the bright early morning. It was shut and there were men guarding it.

I WENT WITH MARUNA TO MY FATHER'S ROOMS, AND AT HIS door I said aloud, "Do you wake, king? Waken!" He came out, heavy-eyed, lumbering, huddling his bedclothes about him, and took me in his arms without a word.

When he released me he said, "Where is your mother?"

"At the fig-tree spring."

"She didn't come with you?"

"I escaped from her," I said.

He looked uncomprehending, confused. His grey hair was tufted and matted with sleep. "Escaped?"

"I didn't want to be there!" I said in anguish, and then, trying to speak calmly, though I could not, "Father, she said she'd sent for Turnus. To betroth me, marry me to him—I don't know. I was afraid he'd come. She kept me guarded. I couldn't get away. I couldn't have got away without Maruna."

"Sent for Turnus?"

It was more than the stupidity of arousal from sleep. He did not understand, he would not understand that his wife had tried to betray him. Feeling that I had already betrayed her, I could not say anything.

"I must get your mother and the other women out of the woods," he said at last. "There's been trouble. Fighting. It could be dangerous for them up there. Is she—will she come back today? What is it she's doing there?"

"Women's rites. Dances her people have." I tried to get my mind to think about what really mattered. "If you send to tell her that there's been fighting, that the women there are in danger, I think she'll come back. But send women messengers, father. Men can't approach. Some of her women are armed."

"But this is madness," my father said.

I was tired, strained, worn out by all the folly and anxiety of the past days and nights. I stared at him. I said, "She's been mad for thirteen years!"

When the poet sang me the fall of Troy, his story told of the king's daughter Cassandra, who foresaw what would happen and tried to prevent the Trojans from letting the great horse into the city, but no one would listen to her: it was a curse laid on her, to see the truth and say it and not be heard. It is a curse laid on women more often than on men. Men want the truth to be theirs, their discovery and property. My father did not hear me.

"Wait," he said, and turned away to his room. I waited.

Maruna slipped away and brought a pitcher of water from the well in the courtyard, and I gratefully drank every drop of it—except a little that I poured out to the Penates first, and a little that I used to wet the corner of my garment and try to clean my face. I was all dirt and dried sweat. The coarse old tunic was tattered and filthy after our night run, and my best palla that Maruna wore was completely ruined. Maruna and I were mourning over the great snags and tears in it when my father came back, dressed. He looked at us with dull puzzlement. "You must go get cleaned up, Lavinia," he said.

"I'd like to, father. But please, what is the trouble, who is fighting?"

"The Trojans were hunting. I told them they could hunt the forests between Venticula and Laurentum. They have to have food." He stopped.

I asked at last, "Did some of our hunters try to stop them?"

"They shot the deer. The stag." His face was stricken as he said it. I could not think what he meant. Why should hunters not shoot a stag?

He said, "Silvia's deer."

"Cervulus," Maruna whispered.

"The creature ran home—to Tyrrhus' farm—bleeding, with the arrow in its flank—crying like a child, they said. And Silvia screamed as if it had been her child shot. They couldn't comfort her. Her brothers and the old man swore they'd punish the hunter. But it was the king's son who shot the deer."

"Ascanius," I said.

It begins with a boy who shoots a deer.

The waves lapped one over another on the shore where the tide was rising.

"If that is his name." I had never seen my father bewildered like this. He groped among words and finally said, "Tyrrhus went into a blind rage, the way he does. He and his boys—they got their farm people together and went out against the hunting party. Armed. With swords, axes, bows. They fought—somewhere over Villia Ridge—they found the Trojans and tried to slaughter them. But the hunters were soldiers. Defending their prince. They killed—"

He looked into my face for a moment and looked away. "Tyrrhus' eldest boy was killed."

First to die is young Almo—you know him. An arrow in his throat chokes off his speech and breath with blood.

I whispered his name as Maruna had whispered the name of the deer.

"And old Galaesus."

Old Galaesus, who's rich and used to being in control, tries to keep them from fighting, comes between them, and has his face smashed in for his pains.

My father said, "I can't believe it. Galaesus tried to interfere, calm them down. He thought young men in a fight would listen to him."

I stood dumb. I stood as I have stood in the shallows of the sea with the tide rising, the waves coming in one over the other, pushing me and drawing away the sand under my feet with the undertow, till all the world was shining and sliding away.

I took Maruna's arm, and she helped me stand. "Please let us go, king," she murmured to my father, and he, finally seeing our filth and tatters and scratched arms, came with us across the courtyard, calling out for women to help us.

"TELL ME SOMETHING I HAVE NEVER UNDERSTOOD," I SAY AS we sit in the small courtyard, the inmost room of our apartment in the Regia. It is a warm morning of June and my husband, who has a great capacity for simple enjoyment, is basking in the early sunlight while we have our breakfast of white figs and new milk sweetened with honey.

"I'll do my best," he says.

"You might rather not."

"Well, let's see."

"Why didn't you come to talk with my father, right away, when he asked you to come affirm the alliance he offered?"

The question interests him. He sits up a little straighter to look back to a year ago. It is of great importance to him that he speak truth as nearly as he can, and since it is always hard to speak truly of things in the past, he thinks about it a while before he speaks. "I was getting together some gifts to bring with me," he says. "Something that would be suitable for you—a betrothal gift. I'd already sent Priam's cup and crown and scepter. The last, best bits of Troy I had. There wasn't anything left, except our gods. But I didn't want to come like a beggar! Euryalus' mother had a shawl woven with silver threads, she'd been keeping it to give to her son's bride when he married, she brought it and offered it to me. Poor soul! . . . Anyhow, while I was worrying about gifts, word came that a band of farmers had attacked our hunting party, because Ascanius had shot a pet stag. Gyas had an arrow nick in his arm, and our men had killed two farmers. That was bad news. A bad beginning.

It looked as if the country people weren't going to accept us, no matter what their king said. Then Drances came to our camp by the ships. Did you know that?"

"No."

"He didn't say he was sent by Latinus, or even that Latinus knew he'd come. He'd taken it on himself to warn us that Turnus was using the quarrel with the farmers to raise the whole country against us—sending off to the Volscians and the Sabines, even to Diomedes down south, for fighting men."

"Drances was always envious of Turnus."

"I wondered why he came to us. But if I'd gone back with him to Laurentum, then, could I have prevented the war?"

"No," I say.

And he does not question my certainty. He accepts that I know some things that I could not, in the ordinary way, know. He does not ask how I know. I have told him that I used to go to the oracle at Albunea with my father. But I have never told him about the poet. I doubt that I ever will.

It has not been difficult for me to believe in my fictionality, because it is, after all, so slight. But for him it would be very difficult. Even if he is at the moment inactive, domesticated, a contented man sitting in the sunlight talking with his wife, the poet's passionate, commanding, anxious, dangerous hero would find it hard to accept contingence, the nullity of his will and conscience. Piety, faithfulness, obedience to what must be rightly done, the *fas*, is the desire of his heart. To know that he has obeyed a poet, rather than his conscience, might be anguish to him—even if he saw, as I see, that the poet obeyed his conscience and followed the *fas*. Why should I trouble him with that, when his concerns are so great and his time so short?

He agrees with my judgment, nodding. "It was time for war. Mars on the march . . . Drances himself said it would be a provocation if I tried to come to the city then. So I hope you see that it was not in neglect of my obligation to you and your father that I failed to come. Did you take it as such?"

Even if he has not worried about it before, his worry about it now is endearing. I want to let him off easily, but perversely I say, "Well, you might have sent a message. I did wonder whether you really wanted the princess as part of the package."

He looks appalled, as he always does when he thinks he's been remiss in duty. "Of course," he said. "Of course I did."

"It was unfair of me to wonder. After all, I had the advantage of you. I'd seen you." He knows that Silvia and I saw his picnic by the river; I told him about it early on, and the idea of two girls hidden in the bushes spying on an army both shocked and entertained him. "And my father could have sent you a message, but he didn't either. So, go on about that time."

I can tell that he is, for once, disposed to talk, to reminisce. He thinks again for a while and says, "I was undecided, that night. Perplexed." I am fond of his understatements when he talks about the decisions he has had to make, on which the lives of his people depended. "We simply weren't a large enough force to stand up to a whole countryside determined to drive us away. The answer might be to get back in the ships and go . . . but where? We'd come where we were to come. That much was clear. So, I went off to think about it, down by the river. My thoughts ran about in every direction at once, trying to see what to do. As if my mind was a bowl full of water reflecting a light, and you shake the bowl this way and that, and the reflections dance over the ceiling, but they don't come together . . . And I watched the reflection of the moon on the river shiver and break apart . . . Then I prayed to the river, Tiber.

And while I prayed, there in the reeds under the poplars, my mind grew quieter. And the river gave me my answer. I thought: upriver, Drances said, is a town with a Greek king, an ally of Latinus but not on good terms with all the Latins. A foreigner like us. Maybe he'd help us. And that came to me as the thing to do. All the broken reflections came together. I got some sleep, and next day I took some men upstream in two of the galleys. I left my son in charge of building up our camp so it could be defended. It was time he took some real responsibility."

"That was a pretty big responsibility for a boy."

"Well, of course he had Mnestheus and Serestus to call on. Good men. Experienced. They had full authority from me. But I didn't realise how quickly the Latins would get their troops and their allies together and attack. And burn our ships, so my people had no way to escape. Ah!" The memory of that makes him clench his fist and scowl in pain. "I thought I had eight or ten days clear to look for some allies of my own. Turnus moved unbelievably fast. A man of immense talent."

Is it self-admiration to admire the man you killed? Is it self-judgment to judge him? I say, "He had courage, but not character. He was greedy."

"It's hard to ask a young fellow to be selfless," Aeneas says, with a rueful smile.

"It seems to be easy enough to expect it of young women."

He ponders. "Perhaps women have more complicated selves. They know how to do more than one thing at one time. That comes late to men. If at all. I don't know if I've learned it yet."

He frowns, brooding; he is probably thinking of what he sees as his worst failing: the fury of bloodlust that overcomes him in battle, making him a mindless, indiscriminate slaughterer, "like a sheepdog gone mad among the sheep," he says. Of course much of his reputation as a warrior rests on this battle madness. Men who faced him were terrified of him. And I cannot see how it differs from the courage he respects in his heroes, men he has told me of with such admiration—the Trojan Hector, the Greek Achilles. But to him it is unquestionably a vice, an abuse of skill, *nefas*. I know he dreads every threat of war from our neighbors, not because he hates or fears fighting; in fact he loves it; but he fears himself. He believes that he murdered Turnus. I have argued with him about this: it was in a fair fight, he couldn't leave an implacable, powerful enemy alive, and so on. He could not deny my arguments; I drove him to silence. But he has not forgiven himself.

Old Vestina appears in the doorway under the colonnade, holding the baby, who twists about in her arms making a noise like a small bellows being squeezed very fast. "He's hungry, queen," she says sternly. The milk is already bursting from my breasts at the sight of him. "Hand him over," I say, and get him settled, although he's so eager he can't find the nipple at first and thrashes his fists in fury, gasping indignantly. "Talk about greed," I say.

My husband's dark eyes rest on me and Silvius with a peaceful, undemanding tenderness. He pours himself another bowl of sweetened milk from the pitcher, dribbles a few drops of it on the ground in worship, and salutes his son with it before he drinks. "Your health," he says.

I BATHED AWAY THE FILTH OF THE THREE NIGHTS SPENT AT THE fig-tree spring, and slept for a few hours in the middle of the day; but it was hard to rest for long, with all the commotion going on in the courtyard and quarters of the house. "Turnus, Turnus"—I heard his name constantly. I got up at last and went to find out what was going on. Turnus had come, but not to my mother waiting for him up in the hills. He was out in front of the city gates, they told me, with an army of herdsmen, farmers, and city folk. I climbed up onto the roof of the watchtower to have a look.

It was a big crowd, and more coming in across the fields all the time. The men all carried weapons, whether they were farm tools or hunter's bows or swords and bronze-tipped lances. As they grouped together they made a dark, endless noise. I looked down from the roof at the top of the laurel in the courtyard where the bees had swarmed. But these men were not the foreigners the bees had foretold. They were Latins, Laurentians, Italians. My people. My enemies.

All that evening the fields were full of armed men; they camped all over the field of exercise and under the slopes of the outer rampart. Next morning I went up to the roof over the front door to look. The crowds outside the city gate and in the city, filling the streets around the Regia, had doubled. Every now and then a shout went up. War, they shouted, war! Drive out the strangers! Send the murderers back where they came from!— I saw a group making their way through the others; some of them were men I knew, herdsmen. They were carrying something long and heavy wrapped in a white cloth stained with blood. "Almo, Almo," they chanted. "Avenge our brother! Avenge our dead!" I glimpsed Almo's and Silvia's father Tyrrhus among them, white-haired, staring wild-eyed, staggering along, half carried by other men. This procession made its way up the street towards the doors of the Regia. There they laid the burden down. The shouting was frenzied now, the air shook and rocked with it. And I saw Turnus. He stood in front of the gates of the king's house, facing the crowd.

"Are we to be ruled by strangers?" he shouted, and the crowd all round shouted like thunder in the streets, "No!"— "Is my promised bride to be given to a foreigner?"— "No!"— "Latinus! King of Latium! I stand at your gates! We demand justice! We demand war!" And the men all shouted, "War!"

After what seemed a long time, the doors of the Regia opened. My father came out, flanked by his guards, with Drances and a few other old counsellors. The shouting died down. Men near and farther called, "The king, the king speaks."

Looking down from almost directly above as I knelt hidden behind the decorative edge tiles of the roof, I could see only the top of my father's head, grey hair gone thin on the skull.

"Men of Latium, my children!" he said in his strong voice, and paused for a long time, so long it seemed he might not speak again. Men shifted from foot to foot. At last he went on, but sounding now more like an old man. "An oracle has spoken. A promise has been given. If you defy the voice that guides us, if you break the treaty I made, you do wrong. You will pay for that wrongdoing in blood. You know that. That is all I can say to you. Turnus, son of my old friend Daunus and sister-son of my wife, if you are determined to lead our people into this guilt, I cannot stop you. I can only say that you rob me of the harbor of peace I hoped for in my last years, the righteous death I longed for."

The silence continued. Without waiting for any answer Latinus turned away and came back into the Regia. His guards closed the high doors behind him, leaving Turnus and the crowds outside, still silent for a little. Then the murmuring and the dark noise began again, and swelled, and grew till it surrounded the house and filled the city.

Now there was a new turmoil in the streets behind the house. I was not the only one up there on the roofs. Maruna and Tita and several girls were up on the watchtower platform over the southeast corner of the house, and one of them was pointing to the east gate. I ran to join them. From the platform we saw another procession straggling up the streets: women—slaves and mistresses, brazen or calm, shamefaced or proud, all with wild hair, with soiled, torn togas and tunics—Amata and her troop from the fig-tree spring.

My mother came into the place in front of the Regia, walking as always with a regal gait. Turnus hurried to meet her there. They met and embraced and talked for a while. Presently a new chant began among the men around them: "Open the War Gate! Open the War Gate!"

The War Gate of Laurentum stands in a little square not far from the actual city gates, a pair of tall bronze-studded oaken doors in a frame of cedar, with an altar of Janus to the east of it and an empty space around it. The doors always stood closed and barred, old and grim and meaningless. There had never been any ceremony there in my lifetime, except at the Kalends of every January when we made libations to Janus. But now everybody was shouting, "The queen, the queen will open the War Gate!" and the crowds were flowing down that way. I could make out my mother for a while among them, and Turnus' high helmet crest. Then the trees cut off my view, and I could only hear the shouting. A great cheer went up of *"Mars! Mavors! Macte esto!"* and people came dancing and calling that the Gate of War was open.

MY FATHER'S BRIEF APPEARANCE BEFORE THE DOORS OF THE Regia seemed to me, to most of us, an abdication. He had made a formal plea, yet not even waited for a reply. "I cannot stop you," he had said to Turnus. It outraged me to think he had said that. How could he say it? How could he hand his power over to Turnus and creep back into the house?

As I look back on it now, I think he was speaking not to Turnus but to the crowd, the men, his Latins. They had, in fact, the power. Turnus could use them so long as they let him, but he could not control them, any more than Latinus could. And so Latinus' plea was made to them, in the hope that they might remember it later. For now, they were afire, mad with excitement. The chance of a fight, the promise of bursting out in violence, vengeance, righteous wrath, that was all they saw at the moment, all they wanted. Every farmer hates a foreigner, and here was a troop of fancy fellows from somewhere who thought they could walk in and take over Latium, shoot the deer, marry the princess, push honest men around—well, they'd find out their mistake. The old king wouldn't stand up against them, but the new one would. What did it matter if he was a Rutulian? We're all Latins. We stand shoulder to shoulder, the peoples of the West, defending our fields, our altars, our women. Once we've driven these strangers into the sea, we can sort out our own affairs.

Latinus had known the enthusiasm of war before and knew better than to try to oppose its first furor, to waste speech on the mindless.

But I was a child of peace, and all I could see was a defeated old man hiding in his palace while fools bellowed in the street. And his queen, in her filthy slave's clothing, striding about, shameless, triumphing in the desecration of daily life, thinking she'd have it all her way.

She wouldn't have me, not while I could get away from her. Even if my father had foresworn his power, he was my hope of resistance. I gathered up my things and told Maruna and a few other women to move with me out of the women's quarter into the royal apartments, the bedrooms my mother had not used for years. Lina and Sicana and all the rest of my mother's devoted attendants, the queen's faction, were already filtering back into the house.

Gaia was brandishing her sword in the hallways. I was not going to let myself come again under the control of those women.

Poor old Vestina was shocked, wept, whined, tried to order me to stay where I belonged, raged feebly when I refused, but I could not reassure her or take her with me; her loyalty was too divided between Amata and myself. I slipped into the royal apartments through the back halls with my little troop and asked my father's guard to tell him that his daughter asked to occupy the queen's rooms.

My father sent for me to come. He was sitting in the audience room with Drances and the others. Rather than ask them to leave, he rose and came to talk to me in the space behind the throne. He looked tired and grim, the wrinkles heavy on his cheeks and around his eyes. "Why did you not consult me about this change of rooms, daughter?"

"I was afraid if she heard of it, the queen would forbid me."

"Do you not owe her obedience?"

"Not when obedience to her is disobedience to you."

He frowned, turned half away, controlling anger. "Say what you mean."

"If she can—if I'm in her power—she'll marry me to Turnus."

He made an impatient, dismissive noise.

"That was why she took me up into the hills. To meet him there. To defy the oracle and betray the alliance you offered the Trojans."

"She would not," he began, but he could not say, "She would not dare," knowing she had opened the War Gate. He stood scowling and indecisive.

"Let me stay with you, father. Let me have one of your guards at my door. I'm trying to obey you and the oracle. I will not marry Turnus."

After a while he said, "Do you dislike him so?"

His voice was weak, the question was weak. I tried to suppress my impatience. "You promised me to the Trojan leader. He is my husband. I will have no other."

"It looks as if the people will go to war to prevent it, daughter," he said, with a show of making light of it.

"Father, I know what I have to do. And I will. My mother won't stop me, and all the men in the kingdom shouting for war won't stop me." Only you can, I thought, but I did not say it. The thought, however, weakened my resolve, and my voice shook somewhat when I said, "I beg you to let me do as I must, and protect me so that I can."

I do not know what was going through his mind, what he might have said, when Drances came forward. He had of course heard us, and being always very sure of his mind and free with his tongue, and encouraged in his freedom, he did not even ask leave to break in on us. "King," he said, "your daughter is right, and wise, and brave. If Turnus were to take advantage of the queen's favor, in this time of confusion, and defy the oracle, defy you—the crime could not be undone. Ruin would be upon us! Have patience. Our people will come to their senses. But as you said yourself, they must see what color blood is first. Keep the maiden safe with you, away from danger, away from the Rutulian. Let your guards defend her. She is our pledge of honor. In her, the sacred powers are with us."

Drances always said too much, went too far, but maybe he had to rant, now, to make my father hear him.

"Very well," Latinus said slowly, ponderously. "You may stay in your mother's apartments, Lavinia. I will set a guard at the door. But

I will have no more disrespectful, rebellious talk about the queen. You understand?"

I bowed my head, murmured thanks, and slipped away.

It was a great deal easier to talk with the king's guards than with the king. I had known them since I was a baby—Verus, Aulus, Albinus, Gaius and the others; some of them still called me by my childish title Camilla, altar girl. The pick of Latinus' fighting men in his fighting years, they were all middle-aged, grizzled, a bit thick in the waist under their bronze corselets, fond of their food and drink but not slow in their wits. They were keenly aware that the Regia was now a house divided. To my relief I found that they shared my antipathy to Turnus, even if they did not want to think ill of their queen. "The Rutulian's got the queen tied round his finger," said Verus, "being her sister's son, see, she's made a son of him, he can't do wrong. It's how mothers are." I didn't mind how they explained it so long as they saw that I might be in danger from Amata. And they did see that, for without my asking, one of them was near me wherever I went in the Regia to carry out my ritual and housekeeping duties.

Those were strange days, when half my own house was foreign to me. I never entered the women's quarters, my home for so long. I was entirely estranged from my mother, and on terms of embarrassment with women I'd known all my life. Most of them could not believe I was insisting on my betrothal to the foreign chief, the enemy, or could not understand why I did. Amata let them say that I was mindlessly, slavishly obedient to my father, and whisper that he was quite senile. And indeed, hiding away in his quarters, eating in privacy, seeing almost no one, Latinus seemed to give proof of his weakness. I saw him only when I assisted him at a rite performed in the house or the city; he never went out the city gates.

Neither did I, though I spent a good deal of time up on the roofs and the watchtower looking out over the city walls. Up there, I could get away from the curiosity of some and the ill will of others. Verus or one of the other guards was always on duty at the foot of the stairs that led up to the platform in the southeast corner, the highest place in the city, from which you could see the exercise field, the plains and pastures and groves as far as Tyrrhus' farm, the blue hills eastward, and westward the Lentulus winding down among its marshes to the dunes. I took my distaff and went up with Maruna or one of the other girls; we put up an awning, for the summer sun was getting hot. Sometimes women asked if they could join me and came to sit with me a while, with their work or their baby, as if things were as they used to be. It was brave of them, for it was a defiance of my mother, in whose power they were. Some of them told me about her behavior, which clearly worried them. Every day she ordered that the banquet hall be made ready and animals butchered, so that Turnus and his ally chiefs could have a feast. But the chiefs were all busy riding about the countryside raising troops; and arrogant as he was, Turnus would hesitate to eat at the king's table without the king's invitation. He sent excuses. Amata always said, "He'll come tomorrow. We must be ready for him." So the house sweepers and the stable boys were living on choice cuts of beef and mutton, the women said, shaking their heads over the waste and folly of it.

I felt safe up there on the tower. I watched the men drilling on the exercise field, practicing at swordplay, grouping and charging as the officers shouted orders. It all seemed like the games boys play. Sometimes Verus or Aulus stood at the parapet with me and told me what the maneuvers were for. "They're not using the trumpets," Verus remarked. Latinus had told me once how he had realised, years ago, in Etruria, that the Veiians were telling each other across the battlefield where they needed reinforcements, when to attack or retreat, by the sweet piercing signals like bird calls. He captured two Etruscan trumpeters and had them teach their tricks to some of his boys; and he had won the advantage in more than one fight, he said, from those trumpet tunes. But Turnus was evidently not one for innovations or foreign ways. His men bellowed their orders. The endless, raucous shouting, like dogs barking, wore on all our nerves.

The numbers of men encamped to the north and east of Laurentum grew daily. Ufens arrived with his rough Aequians. An even rougher troop came from Praeneste, men in wolfskin caps, who went into battle with one foot shod in leather and the other bare. From my platform I could see the captains conferring, among them my old suitors, Ufens and handsome Aventinus, flaunting his lion-skin cape. Mezentius the Etruscan, who had been tyrant of Caere, came up from Ardea with his son Lausus. I looked at Mezentius to see what a traitorous, murderous tyrant looked like. I expected something more sinister than this tough old soldier, clearly very fond of the slender, dark-eyed son whom he kept close by him.

Turnus was waiting for Messapus to come with his horse troops from Soracte. He arrived at last on the same day as a troop of Volscians, also mounted, black horsehair crests on their helmets. I looked for the woman warrior my poet had said would ride with the Volscians, but I did not see her. But then, he said he had invented her. But had he not invented all of us? I tried to take comfort in that, to pretend that it was all a pretense, all the shouted orders and clashed weapons and sharpened swords, the nervous horses and swaggering men. The horrible list of carnage my poet had told me on the last night, that was what they were making ready for. But why, what was it for? For a pet deer? For a girl? What good would that be?

Without war there are no heroes.

What harm would that be?

Oh, Lavinia, what a woman's question that is.

They all gathered the next morning, our Latins nearest the city walls, then the Oscans, Sabines, Volscians in their bands, the Rutulians out in front, and Turnus on his splendid stallion leading them. Women and children and old men on the city walls cheered and threw down flowers as they rode off north, towards the river.

My poet could tell how heads were split and brains spattered armor, how men with a sword in their lungs crawled gasping out their blood and life, how so-and-so killed so-and-so, and so on. He could tell what he had not seen with his mortal eyes, because that was his gift; but I do not have that gift. I can tell only what I was told and what I saw.

What follows I was told, then and since, by men returned from the battle.

Aeneas had gone upriver to the Greek settlement hoping to bring reinforcements. He had been gone now for eight days. The Trojans had had no word from him. They completed a steep ditch and earthwork round their camp, which was built into the bend of the river so that it was protected on two sides by the Tiber; their ships were drawn up stern first on the beach within the earth-work.

The forces of Latium attacked the camp. The older men among the Trojans, veterans of the ten-year siege of Troy, managed a fierce and skillful defense. Young Ascanius was wild to make a sally and chase the Latins off, but Aeneas had left orders that if attacked they were not to attack. The captains he left in charge followed those orders, though it was hard to restrain the young Trojans when the Latins began to taunt them as cowards hiding behind their ramparts. "Is that all the Italian land you want?" they shouted. "That little bit of riverbank? Why don't you come out? We'll give you dirt to eat!" They repeatedly tried to force the gate or swarm up over the rampart, but the Trojans drove them back, hand to hand and with showers of darts and javelins. A rain of iron, Rufus Anso called it.

We women of the Regia took in as many wounded as we could, and looked after them as best we could. Rufus Anso was a farmer from the royal lands just west of the city, who was brought back to the city wounded. He was about my age. A javelin had gone right through his belly below the navel, they had pulled it on out from the back. Our healing women told me he would die. He was not in much pain yet, only frightened; he wanted to talk, not to be left alone, and I sat with him that night. I had sent for his mother, but she could not come till the next day. He said, "The air went dark all at once, like rain. It was like a rain of iron."

A dart had hit his arm near the elbow, and he complained more of the pain of that small wound than the other. He seemed incredulous that he had been hurt at all. He thought it unfair, bad luck. I wondered why a man would go into battle expecting not to be hurt, what he thought a battle was. He was impressed by the Trojan defense and said they were good fighters. But he had expected to kill, not to be killed, and lay puzzling about the injustice of it. His mother came next day, and he was carried off home, where he died in agony a few days later.

What weapons did to men was all I saw then of warfare. I did not have to watch them fighting, yet.

A report came back to us just after dark. While his men made a showy attack on the gate of the Trojan camp, Turnus, alone, got round the ramparts on the river side, lighted a torch, and ran from one beached ship to the next, firing them. The dry wood was caulked with resin, and the ships lay close side by side: the fire caught, the downriver wind spread it from ship to ship: in no time they were all aflame. Turnus escaped before the Trojans saw the fire towering up over the river at their back. All they could do was cut the lines, push the mass of flaming ships out into the water, and watch them drift out on the current and lurch and burn down to the waterline and sink.

Rufus Anso listened to the man who reported this to us and said, "Well, seems they won't be going back where they came from, those Trojins!" He thought it a good joke. And there was much cheering and high spirits among the wounded men and the women of the Regia.

I was confused and troubled. Should I not be happy at this feat of daring, this victory for my people? Here among my own people, caring for men of my own people hurt by the invaders, how could I be on the invaders' side?

But if our purpose was to drive the foreigners out of Italy, why burn their ships? Evidently Turnus meant to exterminate them, not drive them away—if he had acted with any intention except to do immediate harm and carry off an act of bravery.

I thought again and again of the treaty Latinus had made with them, which we had violated. Tyrrhus and the herdsmen had attacked in anger, the Trojans had responded in self-defense. The matter could and should have stopped there. If there is any sacred thing, it is a treaty. How could the powers of our earth, our land, be with us if we not only defied the oracle they gave us, but did one of the great acts of evil—the deliberate breaking of a promise?

My mind went round and round on these thoughts and my heart was torn and miserable, wanting to rejoice with the people around me but unable to. I felt myself a traitor, as if I had done the great wrong, had caused it simply by being who and what I was. My mother had taught me that self-pitying guilt, and I had known it most of my life. Though I fought against it, knowing it childish and mistaken, under this stress and pressure it was all too easy to be childish, to be mistaken, to drop back into it.

The few men who came back to Laurentum later in the evening said our army had set sentinels around the enemy camp and settled down to feasting and drinking, content with their day's work and ready to break into the camp next morning and finish off the Trojans. So then, if Turnus had a plan, it was extermination.

I know what happened that night from tales told next day by men coming back to the city, and then much later, by Serestus the Trojan, when he became my friend. He took part in a grim conference in the Trojan camp that evening about their chances of holding out until Aeneas returned with the hoped-for allies. Not knowing he had gone from Pallanteum to Etruria, they were desperately anxious about his long absence.

Two soldiers, young Euryalus and his older friend Nisus, came to the conference and volunteered to creep out through the Latin encampment and carry word to Aeneas. Distressed over the loss of the ships, craving his father's presence and support, Ascanius sent the pair out heaped with praise and promises. When Aeneas came back and won the war, he said, Euryalus would receive all the lands belonging to King Latinus as a reward, and twelve Latin matrons to use as he pleased. I remember the wave of pure rage that came over me when Serestus told me that.

So the two sneaked over the ramparts in the deep dark of night, and threaded among the burnt-out watch fires, finding their enemies sprawled asleep, full of food and wine. Instead of hurrying through the Latin camp and on upriver, they fell to slaughtering sleeping men and stealing their drinking cups and armor. They cut the throats of ten or twenty helpless, drunken men before their bloodlust and greed were sated and they finally hurried off, burdened with stolen stuff. A patrol saw the gleam of stolen armor, heard the clinking of it, fell on them, and killed them. Their heads were cut off, stuck on poles, and paraded in front of the Trojan ramparts at dawn.

When Silvia and I hid and spied on the Trojans, we saw Euryalus on the grass, joking with Ascanius. Gorgeous, Silvia had called him. We had seen his mother straighten the red cap on his head. She was the woman who offered Aeneas a weaving she brought from Troy for her son's bride gift. She saw the heads on the poles.

Later in the morning the Italian troops made an all-out assault. Against heavy odds, the Trojans held on: their archers shot Rutulians and Aequians dead as they worked their way through the ditch, and their swordsmen met attackers clambering up over the earthworks, sword to sword, and repelled them. The Trojans fought so well that by noon half our army had fallen back, unwilling to charge that ditch and wall again. They fought so well that some young Trojans, sick of being on the defensive, began to shout victory, and opened the gates of their camp to charge out and drive the enemy back. Turnus, utterly fearless, hacked and hewed his way in that opened gate, not even looking to see if his men were following him. Alone, he cut his way through the enemy camp, so mad with the fury of killing that the Trojans ran from him, till he got down to the river. He leapt in, in full armor as he was, swam downstream, and came ashore among his friends.

That feat of reckless courage was the last of the day. Both armies were worn out, there were no more assaults. Both camps were silent that evening.

We got news all day and in the evening, little by little, as

wounded men were brought or made their way back to Laurentum. They were still limping in after dark. Some of them were not
wounded, only tired or frightened; they had left the siege, left the
battle, they wanted no more fighting just now. These were Latins whose homes were in or near the city, whose relatives would
take them in. No Rutulians, no Aequians or Volscians were among
them.

One of our royal herdsmen, Urso, came with a sword wound
in his thigh. I asked him about Tyrrhus and his sons, Silvia's two
remaining brothers. He said they had all been in the fighting, both
days, and that "the old man was like a wild boar, mad with rage. But
he wore out," he said. Urso was not a man I had known well, and
he did not even recognise me until one of the other women called
me by name. Then he stared at me, and his face flushed and broke
out in sweat. He raised himself up on his elbow. "It's all about you,
woman," he said. "Why wouldn't you marry our Almo? or that King
Turnus? All this killing for a girl's whim!"

The women hurried over and hushed him and hissed at him,
scandalised, but I said, "Let him alone. He had to fight for me." My
voice shook, and the fierce red blush of shame and anger ran over
my face and body as I spoke. "I'm doing what I have to do, Urso,"
I told him. "We all are." He lay staring at me but said no more.

We had turned the courtyard into an infirmary. It was full of
wounded men by now, and women looking after them, in a murmur of low voices and moaning and the glimmer of oil lamps in
the warm night under the restless leaves of the great laurel. The
women's quarter remained closed, and my mother stayed there. She
gave orders for supplies when asked, but she had not come out of
her rooms all day.

Early the next morning, long before sunrise, I saw her striding
under the colonnade to the royal apartment, alone. Verus, on duty

at that door, bowed his head to her. She went in. I got up from my half-sleeping vigil beside a dying man and followed her. I do not know why. Maybe I thought I should defend my father from her.

As I came down the corridor I heard her voice in his room, coaxing at first, then becoming hard and fierce. "It's not too late, Latinus," she was saying. "The foreigners will be destroyed today. They can't hold out any longer. Their great chieftain has run away up the river. He won't be back! Send to Turnus. Tell him he is your son, your daughter's husband. Put the reins of power in his hand. Why not? You've given up your power. So, why are you delaying? Why are you hiding in the Regia? You could have gone out and watched the battle, at least! You could have taken a little of the credit for saving the country! Have you been hiding here thinking the foreigners would come and rescue you and Lavinia? Did you really think they were going to defeat Turnus?" She said the name "Turnus" with passionate energy.

I stood in the dark corridor, just past the door. Inside the bedroom it must have been even darker.

"What is it you want, Amata?" My father's voice was thick with sleep, low and slow. "What do you think you want?"

"I want you to save a little of our pride. It is shameful that Turnus should have to be ashamed of his father-in-law! Get up and go out there. Act like a king."

"What am I to do?"

I did feel shame, hearing that.

"Act like a man, for once, if you can't act like a king. If you want to know how a king acts, look at Turnus."

There was a silence, then a sound of movement, a shift or scuffle, in the dark room, a sharp "Ah!" from my mother.

"Enough," my father said, even lower, but with a different tone. "Enough of Turnus. He is not my son, or yours. He is not Lavinia's husband. Or yours. Go back to your rooms now. Keep silent. Do not send any more messengers to Turnus. My men have intercepted them. Even if the Trojans are defeated, that will not make Turnus king of Latium. I will never make him king of Latium. Nor will you! Now go."

He must have been holding her, and now pushed her out of his room—she came out staggering wildly and nearly fell. She turned back to the doorway at once, but he menaced her in some way, for she stopped and stood clenching her fists and shaking them in front of her shoulders, crying out broken words I could not understand. She whirled round with a strange moan, like a hurt dog, and ran back down the corridor. She had not seen me standing just past the door. I was trembling so that I could hardly move, but I managed to creep on past the dark doorway of the room and follow my mother back to the courtyard full of hurt and dying men, where the paling sky dimmed the light of the small lamps.

"THE WORST MOMENT?" AENEAS PONDERS FOR A WHILE. "THE worst moment was coming up the river in the Etruscan ships— my few men, and the Greeks Evander had sent with me, and the Etruscans from Caere. I was counting on getting up to our camp at sunrise. I had no idea what had been going on, of course, but I was worried. Young Pallas had been hanging around me all night, talking, asking questions—King Evander's son."

"I knew him when we were children," I said. "He took me to the wolf's den near Pallanteum."

"He was a nice boy. Very excited, the night before his first battle. Poor boy, poor Evander . . . Well, Pallas kept chattering, but the feeling that something was wrong kept growing on me. We came over the bar, into the river, as the air began to get grey. I saw stuff floating downstream all around us. Driftwood, I thought, from a storm higher up the river. But it was all black. A big chunk bumped up against our prow. It was the stern of a ship, charred, eaten away by fire. The river was full of pieces of burned ships floating along with the current.

"Tarchon and Astur from Caere came up beside me, and Astur asked after a while, 'Are they yours?' I said yes. I had seen the figure-head of the *Ida* go by. Achates was with me there, and after a while he said, 'It must be the whole fleet.' I thought so too.

"I said, 'No bodies.' For there was nothing but the fragments of the ships. But that was no cheer. It looked as if they'd taken our camp, burned the ships, slaughtered the people.

"I said to Tarchon, 'I fear I've brought you to a lost battle,' but he shook his head. 'Wait and see,' he said. The Etruscans are strange people, they seem to live half in the other world. So we put on ar-mor, in case of arrows from shore when we landed, and we rowed on up the river thick with broken burnt wood. You could smell the stink of burning.

"We rounded the long curve just as the sun rose. I saw our fort, our camp. The ships were gone but the earthworks were stand-ing, and there were men on them, guards—in Trojan helmets. My heart gave a leap, and I held up my shield as high as I could and shouted out to my people in the camp. The first sunlight struck the bronze in a great flare of light. And the men on shore shouted back, first the guards, then a roar from them all. They weren't dead, they weren't asleep. They were ready. After that, I never really worried much about the outcome of it all."

I remember Aeneas' words as I remember the poet's words. I remember every word because they are the fabric of my life, the warp I am woven on. All my life since Aeneas' death might seem a weaving torn out of the loom unfinished, a shapeless tangle of threads making nothing, but it is not so; for my mind returns as the shuttle returns always to the starting place, finding the pattern, going on with it. I was a spinner, not a weaver, but I have learned to weave.

MY JUDGMENT OF TURNUS IS THAT HE COULD NOT LOOK farther than the moment. His response to emergency was instant, active, complete; where he failed and wavered was in following through, holding to a purpose. That of course is where Aeneas excelled. In emergency, at the moment of choice, Aeneas might hesitate, confused, looking to the outcome, torn between conflicting claims and possibilities: in a torment of indecision he groped for his purpose, his fate, till he found it. Then his choice was made and he acted on it. And while he acted, his purpose was unwavering. Afterwards he might agonise over it all again, question his conscience endlessly, never fully satisfied that he had done the right thing.

But Turnus never looked back, as he never looked forward.

I think he was truly fearless: but a man without fear is one who lacks a quality of humanity. Men followed him for his brilliant daring, but he did not take charge of them. He met the event as it came, and so events buffeted him and blew him about, and he lost sight of what had to be done, and seemed to act on whim. So he broke a treaty, twice, without a thought. So more than once he left the battlefield, abandoned his men without guidance. And at last, when he had to face the implacable, he seemed to act in a kind of panic. But it was not fear, even then. It was recklessness meeting the reckoning.

Aeneas, who does not forgive himself, will not grant me even this tempered judgment; he will say of Turnus only, "He was young."

At any rate, Turnus certainly could rise to the unforeseen. He pulled his Rutulians and their allies together at the first sight of the Etruscan ships sweeping up the river in the sunrise, and was ready with a fighting force to meet Aeneas and his allies as they landed.

Some of the ships could land within the Trojan earthwork, but the current brought others to shore outside it, and the men disembarking were at a great disadvantage as Turnus' men attacked them. Archers and lancemen on the ships covered them with the iron rain, and the Trojans sallied out of their camp to defend them. Many Italians, Trojans, Greeks, Etruscans never saw the noon of that morning. And the killing went on and on. Up the riverbank they fought, and over the green lawns and through the thickets of the shore. The Trojans were tremendously heartened by their leader's return, and Aeneas had to keep them from wild charges that would scatter them out, since even with the new reinforcements they were far outnumbered. He kept them, Serestus told me, in good defensive order around their camp and the Etruscan ships, so they had a fallback if they needed it. And the battle went on in the heat of the June day, hour after hour, man against man.

Turnus was enraged with Evander for allying with the Trojans against him. When he saw Evander's son Pallas dueling with young Lausus, he saw a chance of vengeance. He shouted out that this was his fight, and made Lausus stand back. Pallas made a brave attempt to fight, but Turnus killed him with one awful blow of his bronze-pointed oak spear through his shield and through his body. Then he stood over him. "Send him back to his traitor father the way he deserves to get him," he said, and putting his foot on the dying boy, he yanked with main force at the heavy, gold-plated weapon belt across his shoulder till he tore it off. And he strode off with the trophy, waving it in the air and laughing.

When Aeneas heard of this, the fury came into him. He told Serestus to keep the Trojans together, and went looking for Turnus. He killed men along the way, left and right, ruthless, relentless. He was the mad dog among the sheep now. The Latins fell back from him as the Trojans had fallen back from Turnus in the camp.

But Turnus himself was nowhere. After killing Pallas, he disappeared. No man I ever talked to knew what became of him during the long hour that Aeneas stalked him through the battlefield, challenging him, calling out to him to come fight. No doubt he was resting, catching his breath somewhere up the hill in the shade, but he chose a strange time to do it.

It was Mezentius, the old Etruscan tyrant, who met Aeneas face to face. Men who saw it said the two fought as equals. When Aeneas wounded the older man in the thigh with a spear, Mezentius' men gathered round him and got him mounted on a horse, while his son Lausus covered their retreat. Young as he was, Lausus came bravely at Aeneas. After shouting in vain at him not to try to attack, Aeneas killed him with a single sword stroke. Then he followed Mezentius to the riverbank. When they told him his son was dead, the old tyrant turned and called out to Aeneas: "Come on, then! What does my death matter now?" and charged. Aeneas had to kill the horse with a blow between the eyes. Wounded, pinned under the fallen horse, the old man fought like a bear until Aeneas cut his throat.

Many Italians who saw that fight asked why it was Mezentius, not Turnus, fighting the Trojan captain.

The fury went out of Aeneas then. He went back to where Pallas lay and gave orders, in tears, that the boy's body be wrapped to carry back to his father, Evander, with a guard of honor, though not with slaves to be sacrificed, as the poet said; I do not know how my poet could think his own Italian people would commit such barbarity. Perhaps the Greeks might. Though all my poet sang was true and is true, yet there are small mistakes in the truth of it, and I have tried to mend those tiny rents in the great fabric as I tell my part in it. So, then, Aeneas withdrew his men from the field. The Italians were already withdrawing, not to their siege position round the Trojan camp but miles farther back towards the city.

Laurentum itself was full of wounded men and refugees now, and more kept straggling in. Everywhere was a sense of exhaustion, confusion, lack of purpose. But when Turnus came, he appeared unaware of any such mood; he rode in the city gate on his fine stallion, tossed the reins to a stableman in the street before the Regia, and strode in, handsome and smiling, broad and erect in his high-crested helmet, Pallas' ornate gold sword belt glittering over his shoulder. I watched him arrive with Messapus and Tolumnius, the Rutulian soothsayer, from my watchtower. Soon I saw my mother hurry across the courtyard to the reception rooms, picking her way round the makeshift beds of wounded men. I went downstairs then. My father was not in his apartments, so he had come out of hiding and gone to meet Turnus and the other captains. I was glad of that. There was a lot to be done for the people in the Regia, and I was busy with that all the evening, till Drances found me at the granary room.

Now, I had never much liked Drances. He was not like the old farmer warriors who made up most of my father's circle of friends and counsellors. He was soft, flexible, enthusiastic. He did not lay down his opinion like a large rock on the table, as they did, and challenge anybody to move them from it; his opinions seemed to weigh very little, to be light and airy, a mere waft of words; but he got his way, more often than not. He was a city man, a politician. To him, my mother and I were unimportant persons in tactically important positions. We had to be managed. He saw women as he saw dogs or cattle, members of another species, to be taken into account only as they were useful or dangerous. He considered my mother dangerous, me negligible, except insofar as I might be made use of.

Yet he had an acute perception of relationships, more like that of a woman than of many men. He knew I was afraid of Amata, that I had run away from her and taken refuge in the royal apartments, that she was in love with Turnus, that I was not, that my father and she had quarreled. All this was grist to his mill. He had always opposed betrothing me to Turnus, I suppose because he saw Turnus as a threat to Latinus' power encouraged by Amata's favoritism, and was envious of Turnus' splendid, contemptuous manhood, and wanted to thwart it. As I came out of the granary he stopped me and said, out of hearing of anyone else, "Daughter of Latinus, have no fear that your father will let you be given to the Rutulian. Our king could not prevent the breaking of the treaty, but no sacrilegious marriage will follow, be assured. Trust me."

I thanked him and stood with lowered eyes. I knew what he thought of me, the girl who understood nothing, the nobody that everybody was fighting a war about.

All the same I was grateful to him for saying what he did. Though the war had not gone as they expected, and many of them were troubled about the broken treaty and the flouted oracle, still most of our people backed their queen and her local hero against the foreigners. And they assumed that whatever my parents chose was my choice. My father's weakness had left me alone, isolated; there was nobody I could tell the truth to, nobody to hear me speak my heart. Maruna was loyal beyond question, but I could not lay my burden on the shoulders of the powerless. She knew my heart, but we could not talk freely.

The next morning, Latinus sent messengers to the Trojan camp requesting a truce for the performance of rites and the burial of the dead. Corpses were lying all over the riverbank and the ground for a mile inland.

Drances was one of the messengers, and when he came back to Laurentum he made a point of seeing me and telling me about the parley. He said, "We told the Trojan leader that since he surely had no quarrel with the dead, would he not allow decent burial to men who might have been the hosts, the fathers-in-law of his men. He answered at once, very directly: 'You ask peace for the dead: I would grant it to the living, if I could! Why are we at war? If Turnus will not honor his king's treaty, if he wants to drive us out of Latium, then let him alone meet me alone with sword in hand. We two could have spared all these deaths!' Ah, you should have seen him as he said that—what a man he is—the man you're promised to!"

"I have seen him."

That brought Drances up short. He stared.

"I spied on the Trojan camp from the hill, the day after they landed," I said. "Aeneas is a tall man, with a deep chest, and big hands. He speaks rather softly. His eyes are full of fire, smoke and fire, because he saw his city burn."

Drances continued to stare. The dog had talked.

"You speak the truth, king's daughter," he said at last.

I looked down at my spindle and let it drop, twisting the wool into thread as it fell. "Please go on telling me about the parley."

Drances pulled himself together and went on. He had thanked Aeneas, he said, and promised to revive the treaty with Latinus. "I told him, 'Let Turnus seek his own alliances. We would rather help you rebuild your Troy here, with us!' And so we made a twelve-day truce. And now the Trojan knows that Turnus is still not the ruler of Latium. It was a good day's work. I doubt our people will go back to war, whatever Turnus and Messapus decide to do."

"That is for the king to decide," I murmured.

"Indeed, indeed. But take heart, Lavinia! Your father will never defy the oracle!"

He presumed too much, I thought. I bowed slightly and walked away from him. He might pat the dog, but it declined to wag its tail.

FROM THE FARMS AND FROM THE CITY PEOPLE WENT OUT that afternoon and found their sons and fathers and brothers dead on the field. Some carried home the bodies of their dead to wash them and mourn them and bury them. Others made pyres there where they fell, so that evening all the fields north of Laurentum were clustered with fires, and smoke dimmed the stars. All the woodsmen in Latium brought wood in from the forests, and next day a huge common pyre was built outside the city walls for men who lived too far to be carried home for burial. It burned all day. Grief hung as dark and heavy in the city as the smoke.

We were told that the Trojans were burning their dead on the shore of the river. Those who saw the ceremony said that young men ran round the pyre three times on foot, then horsemen galloped round it three times, while people wailed aloud and blew conch shells. Warriors threw the weapons they had taken from their enemies onto the fire that consumed their friends. The rite was not like ours and yet it was like enough, there was nothing alien in it.

The next days passed in a curious suspense and inactivity. We looked after wounded men in the Regia and in houses all over Laurentum; some healed, some died. No word came from the Trojans.

Evidently they were waiting to hear what we would say to Aeneas' offer of single combat with Turnus and a restoration of the treaty. But my father sent no messengers to them. Like his people, he was uncertain what to do.

Drances had made sure that Aeneas' words to him were heard everywhere, and many people in the anger of their grief cried that this war was accursed. It was Turnus' fault; he had broken the truce Latinus made. If Turnus claimed the king's daughter, let him win her fighting the Trojan hand to hand, let one life pay for all. But there were as many who, fearing foreigners, said that the war was our salvation, that the Trojans and their allies had come to overrun the land, and Latinus could save Latium only by sending Turnus with our forces to destroy or drive out the invaders.

When Latinus at last called his counsellors, they came in that same division of mind. And they were met right away with bad news from Diomedes, the Greek who had founded a city in the south, whom we had sent to for troops. He refused. He politely told our envoys that we were fools to take on the Trojans. "We fought them for ten years," he said, "and though we beat them, how many of us ever came home? Our victory brought us shipwreck, death, exile. Aeneas is no ordinary man. He brings his gods with him. Keep the peace, keep your treaty with him, sheathe your swords!"

Amata and I were at that meeting, sitting far back in the shadows behind Latinus' throne, and veiled. With us was the princess Juturna, Turnus' sister, who had come up from Ardea to be with him. She was very beautiful, with blue eyes like his, but hers were strange eyes that seemed to gaze through water at the world. She had vowed chastity, people said; some said it was because the river Juturna, for which she was named, gave her certain powers so long as she remained virgin; others said she had been raped as a girl and since then would speak to no man but her brother. I do not know the truth of these stories. She spoke to us only in the barest civility, very softly, calling Amata aunt and me cousin, and sat listening to the council, a translucent grey veil over her head and shoulders.

When the Greek's messenger was done, the counsellors broke into muttering, and then discussion, and they would have been shouting soon, but the king stood up and lifted his arms slowly, with open palms upturned, in the gesture of invocation. They fell still. Latinus bowed his head, and the silence deepened. He sat down on his high seat again and spoke. "I wish we had settled this great matter sooner! Better not to convene the council when the enemy is at the gate. My people, we are fighting an unrighteous war against an enemy who will not be conquered, because they follow the will of earth and heaven, while we do not. We have broken our obligations, they have held to theirs. We cannot defeat them. I know my mind has wavered on this, but I am certain now. Hear what I propose. Let us give them the land I own out beyond Sicania, all the rough foothill farmland there and the pine forests of the mountains: let us ask them to build their city there and share our realm. Or, if they wish to leave, we will rebuild the ships we burned. Let us send them envoys, with gifts to seal the treaty, now. Consider well what I say, and take this chance to spare our shaken people from defeat!"

Silence followed, but not a cold silence. They knew their king was a brave man, a warrior, who would not surrender lightly, and a man of piety, who had received the clear word of an oracle and held that it must be obeyed. They were thinking it over.

Unfortunately, Drances got up and began to talk. He talked vividly and fluently as always, but with burning malevolence, addressing Turnus directly. He told Turnus the war was his doing, the defeat was his doing, and it was up to him to end it—unless he was so smitten with glory and so lustful for the dowry of a king's daughter that he would lead our armies out again, "leaving our worthless lives scattered over the fields, unburied, unwept, unknown. But if you had any real courage at all, you'd stand up to the man who challenged you!"

At this Turnus of course burst out and called Drances a coward who had never yet been on the battlefield, whose tongue talked of courage while his feet were running away. The Latin alliance was not defeated, far from it! Had not the Tiber run red with Trojan blood? Maybe the Greek Diomedes was afraid of Aeneas, but Messapus was not, and Tolumnius was not, and the Volscians did not know what fear was. "And does this hero challenge me to fight him alone? I hope he does. Better that I appease the angry powers by my death or win deathless fame by my courage. Better I than Drances!"

There was a growl of applause for that from the old counsellors, but Latinus intervened to stop the exchange of boast and insult and was about to speak again, when a messenger ran in under Verus' escort, shouting, "The Trojan army is advancing on the city!" He was followed by other messengers, and through the opened doors of the room by a great noise of people in alarm, like a flock of geese or swans startled up crying and cackling on the marshes.

Turnus seized the moment unhesitating. "To arms!" he shouted. "Shall we sit here praising peace while the enemy attacks us?" And he ran out, calling to his captains, ordering who should defend the city and who should ride out with him. Latinus could not have stopped him if he had tried. He did not try. He sat motionless on his throne while the council broke up and the counsellors hurried out to see what was happening. Drances tried to talk to him but Latinus paid no attention, ordering him with a gesture to stand away. At last he got up and walked past us women, going to his apartment. He did not look at us or speak.

Amata took my hand.

Without thought, as if her touch were ice or fire, I pulled my hand away from her and stood facing her, ready to fight or run if she tried to touch me again.

She stood staring at me.

"I won't hurt you," she said at last, almost childishly.

"You have hurt me enough," I said. "What do you want?"

She spoke hesitantly, still staring at me as if she scarcely knew me. "I thought—I think we should show ourselves to the people— at the altar of the Lar Popularis."

She was right. With the king in hiding and the enemy attacking, the people needed immediate reassurance that all was well with their royal family and the powers that guarded the city. I nodded. I set off, then turned and said to Juturna, "You come too." I had no business giving orders to a king's sister, but she came without a word, pulling her grey veil about her.

We went out and walked through the streets to the square where the shrine to the protective spirit of the city stands. As we walked women joined us, coming out of every house, running down the streets. When we came to the place there was a great crowd around us. Amata had walked ahead, and she lighted the incense, but it was I who had stood with the king before this altar a hundred times, and it was I who knew and spoke the words he used to speak, offering the people's duty and honor to the Lar, the spirit and indwelling power of border and boundary, walled city, place of our people.

The women around us bowed their heads or knelt down, and the people crowded into the streets and up on the walls and roofs fell silent listening.

I felt flow into me from them a loving trustfulness, a flood of feeling that humbled my mind and yet gave me a sense of great and reliable support. I was their daughter, their pledge to the future, a powerless girl yet one who could speak for them to the great powers, a mere token for political barter yet also a sign of what was of true value to us all. I stood among my people in silence when the ritual was done, all of us quiet as the birds that stand in hundreds at evening on the sea beach, seeming to worship together.

And so we could hear the noise outside the walls—rumble and clash and crash, neighing and yelling and thunder of hooves and feet, the noise of an army making ready for war.

THE MEMORY OF THE SWEETNESS OF THAT WORSHIP AT THE shrine of the Lar of the People was a solace and shield to me in the dark time that followed. Something had changed in the weighting of the balance. I no longer had to hide away, isolated from the current of public feeling; I was buoyed up by it, borne on it. My courage was restored.

Yet there seemed no reason why I should feel such confidence. Any hope of obeying the oracle, or following my fate as the poet told it, seemed lost. When my father proposed placating the Trojans by giving them land or building ships for them, he had not even spoken of my part in the original bargain. It seemed I was not worth mentioning. My mother had what she wanted—war against the foreigners, with Turnus in control of it, lord of the kingdom and the king's daughter. Yet she went back to the Regia with that same bewildered look on her face and shut herself up in her rooms, while I was released from my seclusion. I found a kindness in the eyes of the men in the streets, the women of my household. They spoke my name tenderly. I felt welcomed, protected. My home was my own again, even if it was under siege.

I went to the king's apartment and talked with him very briefly.

Haggard and aged, his eyes red and swollen, he told me to come to him with any news of great importance, otherwise to let him be; he was not well. I asked him to rest and sleep. Verus and I would meet the messengers, I said, and come to him if need arose. So I spent some of that day in the atrium and at the doors of the Regia with Gaius and other men of the king's guard, receiving couriers from the battlefield.

There was a constant flow of men and news between the city and the fields in front of it, where the Volscians and the Latins were taking up position for battle under Messapus and the Volscian captains. Scouts reported that Aeneas had sent his horsemen and the Etruscans forward, while he led the rest of his troops up into the hills northeast of the city—Verus said it looked as if his goal was to come at our army from two directions. So Turnus had taken his Rutulians up into the hills, intending to set an ambush for the Trojans at both ends of a pass. I knew the place, Golo Pass the shepherds called it, a narrow dark gorge. An army might well enter it and be trapped.

Such news came to us quite steadily for a while. In the early or midafternoon there was a pause. Leaving Verus in charge at our front doors, I ran up to my watchtower, just for a look, I thought.

I stood at the parapet to look out over the roofs and walls to the exercise grounds and fields north of the city. In several long irregular lines beyond the earthworks stood the ranks of Volscians with their black helmet crests, and behind them our Latins, very motley in their helmets and hand-me-down armor. Horses fidgeted, and their riders let them dance and curvet. Archers and men with long, light lances stood around in front of the Volscians, some fidgeting like the horses, others looking bored, leaning on their lances, chatting together.

The watchtower had the widest view in the city, and we on it may have been the first to see the glint of light on the metal tips of lances far off over the fields in the north.

A boy on a pony came scouring across the pastures, the pony white with lather, the boy yelling—I could not hear his words but he was surely yelling, "They're coming!"—and they came.

It was very beautiful, the bristling glitter of lance heads far off there, moving quickly nearer and nearer. The air was shaken with the thrilling drum of the feet of horses at the gallop. All along the lines of men drawn up in front of the city, spears and lances reared up into the sunlight, and horses began to whinny and shift and fight the reins. Then the Etruscan horns and trumpets sounded their battle signals, some deep and hoarse, some silvery sweet. The attackers came on: the defenders stood firm: for a moment everything seemed to stop, hold still. With a blare of the horns and a great shout of men's voices, arrows and javelins and lances went up from both sides, a swift darkness passing and crossing in the air between the two armies. Under the iron rain they met face to face, men afoot and horsemen, body to body.

I tell you what I saw as I saw it, not understanding it. I saw men running towards the city, converging on the gate. I thought they were the attackers. I could not understand why they suddenly began turning around, running back towards other men who, when they met, fought them, swords rising and falling. Then men were running away from the city, holding their shields behind them as they ran, and mounted men and riderless horses ran with them, and other men followed them, until suddenly those being chased turned around and the swords went up and down again, and there was the horrible noise of men screaming. And it all happened over again. It was like sea waves approaching the city and washing back from it. But the spray was dust, thick, dark, summer dust. After that there was no running and turning, only knots and pairs of men chopping at one another in the dust with swords, and throwing and pushing heavy lances at one another, and blood running where the sword bit and the spear point hit. *Mars, Mavors, macte esto.* I do not know how long it went on. I stood clutching the parapet of the platform, Maruna and other women with me, and women and children stood on all the roofs and on the walls, watching men kill men.

The snarling trumpets rang out again. A group of horsemen far out in the fields moved forward in a solid mass like a shadow across the ripening crops and the pagus paths through the hot slanting light full of dust. Before that mass the lines and knots of fighting men gave way. Very quickly the movement involved them all: they were turning and coming back to the city, the Volscians with their black horsehair crests, they were all running back towards the walls. Both armies, all the men down there in the fields were running towards the walls in a cloud of dust that half hid them, fine dust of the plowlands billowing up brownish gold, sunlight making strange hollows and aisles in it through which loomed the shapes and shadows of horses and men.

The city gates were open. They had been open all through the fighting. I thought: I must go down and give orders that they be shut! Maruna held my arm. I did not understand why I could not hear what she said to me. She put her mouth almost on my ear, crying, "The guards will defend the gate! Stay here! Stay up here!" As she drew away, something passed us perfectly silently and lay still on the platform. A bird, I thought, they shot a bird, but I saw it was an arrow. It lay there with its long, bright bronze point and stiff clipped feathers, harmless. I could not hear anything because the noise down at the gate and the noise on all the roofs and walls of the city was so huge: a screaming, a howling that filled all the world and the mind. From the watchtower we could not see what was happening at the gate. But we could see those who could see, standing on the walls above and near the gate. Some of them were watching their son or husband die, cut down by a bronze sword in front of the locked gate of his city.

We saw the Etruscans pull away, and the black-crested Volscians follow, though fewer, and slowly. The Volscians stopped just outside the ditch. The Etruscans went on a hundred paces or more before they stopped, wheeled their horses, and stood motionless in the dimming, settling dust. There was a long pause, the sound of shouting fading slowly away, rising in pitch as it grew less, till it was only the crying and moaning of the wounded and bereft.

"Look, look," somebody said, and where she pointed we saw a column of men coming at a quick pace, though in the distance it seemed slow, down out of the western hills. "It's Turnus, Turnus is coming!" people shouted from roof to roof. An old man's voice shouted, "Where's he been all day?" but he was drowned out by cheers and acclamations for Turnus and the Rutulians. The cheering rang thin and did not last long. Somewhere down near the gate a woman was keening, a gasping ululation, intolerably shrill and full of pain.

I went down, back to the doors of the Regia, then; so I did not see, as others did, Aeneas lead the Trojans down out of the hills on the same road Turnus had taken, not far behind him.

The Etruscans drew back farther to join with the Trojans. What was left of our men and the Volscians camped, with Turnus' Rutulians, between the earthen rampart and the city walls. They spent the evening digging the ditch deeper, setting up defenses for the gate.

I did not see that. At first I was with the women looking after the new lot of wounded men in our courtyard, and then I saw my mother pass under the colonnade, going to the council rooms. At once—though I stopped at the fountain under the laurel tree to wash blood hastily off my hands and arms, and bathe my face in the blessed cool of the water—I followed her.

I joined her and Juturna at the back of the council room. My father sat on his throne with its curved crossed legs; he did not look like the shaky old man I had last seen, but sat erect and stately in his red-edged toga, listening to Turnus. Drances was there, and Verus and several of the other guards and knights, but only a few of the king's council. Most people were caring for their wounded or mourning their dead, or were out helping fortify the walls for siege.

Turnus was still in battle gear, though in fact he had not fought that day. He was dusty, and his face was strained and pale. He was not strutting now. He looked young, anxious, handsomer than ever. Amata and Juturna both stood watching him with yearning eyes. He was giving a report of the conditions of the allied army to Latinus, not trying to disguise that his ambush had failed, or deny that the Volscians had broken and run, nearly bringing the Etruscans after them into the city. But he praised Messapus and Tolumnius and the Latin troops, and the citizens too, for rallying at the city gate and holding firm.

"Tomorrow," my father said, "you and your men will be with them. And Aeneas and his men will be with the Etruscans."

"Yes," Turnus said. There was a pause. He shifted his position, stood with his legs a little farther apart, his head back. "I do not hang back. There is no delay in me," he said rather strangely, his voice growing louder. "If people say the treaty was broken, if the Trojans think so, I give them the lie. Repeat the rites, King Latinus, renew the terms of the agreement, tomorrow morning, before all the people! I swear to you here and now, I will by myself clear our people of the taint of cowardice. This Trojan, this man who ran away from his conquered city, let him meet me, let him meet me

alone, in fair fight. Let all Latium be on the city walls to see it.
Either my sword will take all shame from us, and take Lavinia from
him, or he will rule a defeated people and have her as his wife."

He glanced at us three women standing behind the throne as he
finished speaking, but his eyes did not meet mine.

Latinus answered him with a slow, thoughtful firmness. On the
eve of defeat, confidence had returned into him, as it had into me.
"Turnus, no one questions your courage. It is so great, in fact, that
it obliges me to move slowly, to hold back. Consider: your father
gave you a noble kingdom, you're rich and have the goodwill of
your neighbors. You know that I am your friend, your kinsman by
marriage. And there are many girls of good family, unmarried, in
Latium. Weigh all that in the balance! For whatever happens, I cannot give you my daughter. It is forbidden. It cannot be done. My
wish to make the bond strong between us, my wife's pleading, my
own weakness led me to do wrong. I broke the pledge. I let it be
thought that the promised wife could be taken from the man she
was pledged to. Wrongly, I let this war begin. Let it end, now, before
a final defeat. Why have I changed back and forth like this, hiding
from the inevitable? If I was and am willing to take the Trojans as
allies while you're alive, why should I wait for your death to do so?
Consenting to this duel, I betray you to your death. Let it not be so.
Let my old friend, your father Daunus, see you come home alive!"

"My sword can draw blood too," Turnus said; he had been pale,
but was now red-faced, his blue eyes glittering. "You needn't try to
protect me, Father Latinus. The story is that some power hides this
Aeneas from his enemies in battle. But here, on our ground, the
powers are with me. I will defeat him!"

At this Amata started forward, ran to Turnus and took his arms,
half clinging to him, half kneeling as a suppliant. Her black hair

was loose and she was in tears, her voice high and shaking. "Turnus, if you ever loved me—you are our only hope—the only savior, the honor of this disgraced house. All our power is in your hands. Don't throw it away! Don't throw away your life! What happens to you happens to me! I will not be a slave to foreigners! I have no one but you! If you die, I die!"

Hearing her begging, I blushed with shame till tears filled my own eyes. I felt the red blood color my face, my neck and breast and body. I could not move or speak.

But Turnus looked over my mother's head straight at me, the bright unseeing stare that had frightened me the first time I ever saw him. He spoke to her, though he kept looking at me. "No tears now, mother, no ill omens, please. I'm not free to put off death. I've already sent a herald to the Trojan. Tomorrow morning there will be no battle. The treaty will be resworn. He and I alone will meet. Our blood will settle the war. And on that field Lavinia will find her husband."

He smiled at me, a wide, fierce smile. He put Amata away from him, pushing her hands away. She cowered down sobbing.

"The messenger has gone?" Latinus asked. His voice was dry.

"He may be there by now," Turnus said proudly.

Latinus moved his head once, the nod of acceptance. "Then go make yourself ready for your fight, my son," he said, with kindness, and stood up, dismissing the others. He turned around as they left, and I think he was about to tell me to look after my mother, but he asked, "Daughter, are you hurt?"

I saw where he was looking: there was a great smear of half-dried blood all down my palla, which I had not seen in the twilit courtyard. "No. I've been with the wounded men, father."

"Take some rest tonight, my dear. Tomorrow will be a long day, for some. Go, sleep well. Juturna, go with your brother. If you can persuade him out of this duel, do so. There is no need for it. We will restore the treaty and the peace."

She hurried after Turnus. When the others had all left the room, Latinus went back to Amata, who was hunched down on the floor, her hands plucking and tugging at her hair. He knelt by her and spoke softly. I could not hear what he said. I could not bear to watch them. I went back out across the courtyard, and to my room.

AS I MEET THEM IN THE COURTYARD OF OUR HOUSE, ASCANIUS is saying something jokingly to his father, "You said it yourself— come to you for work, but not for luck!" Then he goes off to do whatever it is that Aeneas has asked him to do. And I ask Aeneas, "What did he mean?"

"Oh, it's something I said to him when we couldn't get that arrowhead out of my leg. I said, 'You can learn a man's work from me, son, but if you want good luck, go to somebody else!' I was in a foul mood."

"What arrowhead?"

"The last morning of the war."

I puzzled it over. "But Turnus didn't have a bow. He was using his sword."

"Turnus?"

"The wound in your leg—"

"Turnus never wounded me," he says grimly. Then his face changes. "Oh. I see. I lied to you. To some extent. I lied to everybody, actually."

"Explain, please."

We sit down side by side on the bench under the laurel sapling.

"Well, it was just after that augur, that Tolumnius, threw his lance to break the truce. I saw him do it. He killed a young Greek on the spot. Then of course they all went mad. I was trying to get our men together, out of it, keep them from fighting— Fighting there. At the altar! Where you were standing!"— His face goes dark again at the thought of it. "And in all the confusion, somebody got me in the leg with an arrow."

"You don't know who?"

"Nobody ever claimed the honor," he says with a bit of mockery. "Serestus and Ascanius helped me get out of the mess, back to our camp. Seeing the captain down is frightening to the men. I had to hop along leaning on my spear, bleeding like a sacrifice. So, old Iapyx did his best, pulled out the shaft, but he couldn't get the arrowhead out. It was barbed, you see. And everything was going to pieces, back there. So I said, tie it up, man, I can't stand around here all day, I have to find Turnus and finish this thing. I made Iapyx do it. Once he'd stuffed the hole with dittany and had it tied up tight, it didn't hurt. You don't notice that sort of thing much, in the thick of it. So I went back, looking for Turnus. And couldn't find him. I'll never understand it. What was he doing? I'd see him not too far off now and then, and then he'd disappear, like a swallow in an atrium—flit past, gone again. I'd go where he'd been and he wasn't there. I was running out of patience. And just then Messapus knocked off my helmet crest with a spear, and I lost my temper. So I called for an attack on the city." He looks down, frowning, at his hands clasped between his knees. "I am sorry about that. It was wrong."

"So Turnus didn't wound you? You were already wounded when you fought him?"

He nods, rueful at having deceived me, or at having been caught at it. "As soon as I got back to camp, afterwards, Iapyx got the

162 | Ursula K. Le Guin

point out—it practically jumped out, then." He looks at his tough brown thigh and pokes the dent, a hand's breadth above the right knee, deep and red among other, older dents and scars. "Healed up amazingly fast," he says, as if this excused everything.

"Why did you let me think it was Turnus that wounded you?"

"I don't know. I suppose a lie extends itself, somehow. I had to pretend it didn't amount to anything, you know, while the fighting was going on. As I said, it worries the men. We were so outnumbered, it was always chancy. And I had to find Turnus and fight him to end the whole thing—it was the only way. So, then, afterwards, when I could admit that I'd been hit—in fact as you remember I was pretty lame for a while—it didn't seem important how it had happened. I didn't know you thought it was Turnus who did it. It doesn't really matter, does it?"

He asks this not boyishly, seeking excuse, but gravely, to find out if it does matter very much to me. I have to think about it a while.

"No," I say. And I lean down and kiss the scarred dent in his thigh. He puts his arms around me and lifts me up against him. His hands under my loose gown are large, warm, rough-skinned, and strong. He smells of salt and incense.

I DID SLEEP, THAT LAST NIGHT OF THE WAR, SLEPT SOUNDLY, DEEPLY, so that my waking was slow. At first it seemed to me that there was something I must do for my mother, but I could not think what it was. Then I came a little farther out of sleep and thought that there was to be a ritual and I should help my father with it. Then I woke, and saw my small window just showing the first beginning of light in the sky, and a hundred images of bloody wounds and dying men I had seen yesterday went through my mind in a rush, and with them the poet's voice chanting, and then came the knowledge that today we would either renew the treaty of peace, or the fighting would be in the city itself and my people defeated, destroyed.

I got up and put on my old red-edged toga with the scorched corner and ran to my father's apartment to wake him; but he was up and about already. He did not question my presence or my intention to go with him. Together with Drances and a couple of older men we got the ritual implements together, and I brought out the bowl of salted meal to the stable yard, where the animals were to be selected from herds brought in from farms overrun by the fighting. By the time we had picked them, it was time to lead them out to the sacrifice.

Soldiers on guard opened the city gates for us, hailing the king with a clash of weapons on shields. They made to shut the gates behind us, but Latinus said, "Let the gates of our city stand open!" He strode ahead of us, holding up his oak scepter like a lance, the wide purple-red edge of his toga showing bright in the dawn. Our army was drawn up all in order, facing outward from the walls and the earthwork that had been built up outside the ditch. Across a narrow space of farmland, trampled to dust now, the Trojans and Greeks and Etruscans were just forming up their ranks. A space between the armies had been lustrated, marked out as sacred, and an earthen altar set up in the center. Old men from the city were busy piling up firewood in the hearth they had made beside it.

Latinus strode directly to the altar. He held out his hands, palm up. Young Caesus, our salt boy, was ready with a fresh-cut piece of turf and put it square on the king's hands. Latinus set it on the altar. Just as he did so, the sun shot its first ray over the eastern hills, and Aeneas came forward between the armies and stood across the altar from the king of Latium. Everything happened as if it had been planned and rehearsed a hundred times, everything happened as it should and must.

With Aeneas came his son, Ascanius, standing behind him, and Turnus came to stand behind Latinus at the altar. Aeneas wore the magnificent armor and carried the shield I came to know later. The crest of his helmet was a red plume that looked like the flaming cloud of a volcano. Turnus was as splendid in gold-washed bronze, with a plume that towered up white and streamed in the wind of morning. His sister stood near him in her grey veils. My father had pulled up the corner of his toga over his head, as I had done.

The walls and roofs of Laurentum, when I looked back and up at my city, were dark with people—women, men, children. They were all silent, and the men of the two armies were silent.

I stepped forward with the bowl of salted meal. My father took up some in his hands and sprinkled the sacrifices with it, a young white boar and a two-year-old sheep with very fine white wool. Aeneas came forward and took up meal in his cupped hands from the bowl I held out to him. It was the first time I was ever close to him. He was a big man, all bone and muscle, tanned dark, his face seamed and weathered, worn and fine. He was the man I knew and had known since the poet spoke his name in the glade of Albunea. I looked up at his face, and he looked down at mine. I saw him recognise me.

He turned away to sprinkle the meal over the animals. I gave my father the little ritual knife I carry, and he carefully cut some hair from the forehead of the pig and the sheep. He gave me back the knife. I held it out to Aeneas. He took it and cut a bristle or two and a curl of wool and gave the knife back to me. Then they both stepped to the hearth and dropped the offerings into the fire. Caesus brought the wine jug and the old silver cups on a tray. He poured the cups full and gave one to each king. First Latinus, then Aeneas poured out the libation over the green grass on the altar. My father spoke the ritual words in a low chanting voice, invoking the powers of the earth, the hour, and the place. Aeneas stood gravely listening.

In all this time there was hardly a sound from all the people gathered there. A baby's wail up on a rooftop in the city; a clink of bronze as a soldier shifted his stance; birds singing far off in the trees of the city streets; and the broad, sweet silence of the brightening sky over all.

My father's prayer was done. He stepped back a little. Aeneas drew his sword. The hiss of bronze on hardened leather was loud.

He held the sword up over the altar and said, "Let the sun be witness to what I say, and this land also, to which I have come through much suffering. Let Mars who rules the war, let the springs and rivers of this earth and the sky above it and the sea that washes it, bear witness. If Turnus is the victor, my people will withdraw to Evander's city in defeat, and my son will leave this land, and never return to it in war. But if I am, as I may be, given the victory, I will not make the Italians my subjects, nor claim rule over your land. Let both our peoples, unconquered, pledge eternal treaty. With me come my gods. Latinus, my father-in-law, will keep his sword and his rule. My people will raise up a city. And Lavinia will give it her name."

He looked directly at me as he said that, not smiling, but with a brightness in his face and eyes. I looked back at him and nodded once, very slightly.

He lowered and sheathed his sword. My father stepped forward to face him and held up his heavy oaken staff over the altar. "By the same powers I swear, Aeneas, by earth, sea, stars, the lord of lightning, and two-faced Janus, and the shadows under earth. I touch the altar. I swear by this fire and the powers that stand between us: Never shall this peace and truth be broken, whatever may come. Never shall my will be changed, not until this staff, the ancient scepter of the lords of Latium, bear branch and leaf!"

He nodded to the men who held the animals. They brought them forward, with the long sacrificial knives, and Latinus cut the sheep's throat while Aeneas cut the boar's, each with one quick experienced stroke. And at that the people, soldiers standing by and citizens up on the walls, broke the silence with a long, soft, quavering *aaahhh* of release, relief, fulfillment.

Now an Etruscan haruspex came forward to look at the entrails of the sacrifice, a matter the Etruscans consider very important; and the animals had to be cut up and the meat spitted and cooked over the fire. This all took a good deal of time. Aeneas and Ascanius stood back from the altar, keeping silent, as did my father; but Turnus began to talk with his sister and with a Rutulian chief, Camers, who stood beside her. Despite his gilded armor and gorgeous plume, Turnus looked pale again, and tired, as if he had not slept; he kept gazing around at his men with a grieving, pleading face. And the Rutulians began to gather around him. Camers talked to them not loudly but earnestly, and they listened, looking grim. The augur Tolumnius moved about among them, also talking. The haruspex took forever poking about in the livers and hearts and kidneys, the attendants put too much meat on the fire at once and nearly put it out so that it had to be rebuilt to burn high, the murmur and mutter of talking grew louder through the ranks of the Italians. The sacred moment was lost, past. The sun was getting higher, the day was beginning to be hot.

People looked up and pointed to a faint clamor in the sky. A great flight of swans was coming from the river, heading south past us and the city, flying lazily, left to right. The Greek and Trojan troops followed the birds' flight as we Italians and Etruscans did. And so all saw the sudden eagle, arrow-fast from the east, seize the lead swan in its talons in a shower of feathers and shoot on in a wide curve over us, heavily carrying its prey. Then, most strangely, the whole flight of swans turned as one, flying low and fast, the shadows of their wings passing over us, chasing and driving and harrying the eagle, crowding it till it dropped the dead swan and flew up and off over the western hills. A hesitant cheer went up from some of the watchers, but most were silent, wondering at the meaning of the sign.

Into that silence Tolumnius shouted out, "An omen! An omen! Rutulians, Latins, obey the omen! Attack the attacker! Close ranks, defend your rightful king!" And as the men around him shouted and shook their fists in the gesture of Mars, Tolumnius heaved back his six-foot spear and threw it straight into the ranks facing him across the sacred ground.

A man bent forward over the shaft making a strange noise like a cough or laugh, clear to hear in the last moment of the silence.

Then the world was filled with the enormous bewildering roar of men shouting, drawing weapons and clashing shields. Men rushed past me, this direction and that, shouldering me unseeing. I could see nothing I knew any more except the altar. I pressed up close to it. My father was there with the boy Caesus, trying to take up the sacred dishes, his hands shaking. "Help me, Lavinia," he said, and I took and carried what I could. Keeping close together we struggled away from the altar through the confusion of running men and plunging horses towards the city gate. Caesus was not with me, and I stopped and looked back for him. I saw an Etruscan in splendid armor trip and fall backward, sprawling head and shoulders right across the altar. Another man leapt at him and struck down at his exposed throat with a massive blade-headed spear, and the Etruscan's blood spouted up over men crowding in to tear the armor and weapons off him. Some Rutulians had pulled long burning sticks out of the sacrificial fire and were using them as weapons, shoving them in men's faces, so there was a stink of burning hair. Beyond them, for an instant, I saw Aeneas, taller than the others, his hand up, calling out in a great dark voice. Then somebody shoved me so that I nearly fell, and the boy Caesus, his face distorted with tears and terror, was tugging at my robe. I hurried on after my father. The gates of the city stood open above us. My father's guards had gathered around us, and they brought us in.

The confusion in the streets was almost as bad as outside the walls. People were shouting that the Trojans had broken the peace and treacherously attacked the king at the altar. Many old men and boys, even slaves, rushed out to join the battle; the king's guards kept the great gate open for them and for the wounded to take refuge. Women stood up on the walls screaming insults and throwing down clay bricks and whatever they had to throw at men fighting at the ditch and rampart. Other people rallied to the streets between the great gate and the Regia to protect their king if the enemy broke into the city. Others were feverishly burying their treasures in their garden or trying to wall up their doors and windows so they could hide inside their house.

I followed the king directly to his council room, where Drances and others who had escaped the fighting gathered. Drances was gibbering with terror and talked only about where we should hide. My father was shaken, out of breath, and grey in the face, but he sat on his throne and began to consult with Verus and the others and give orders for the defense of the city and the house. Seeing myself unneeded there, I ran to the women's side, where there was nothing but dismay and rumor and wailing. My mother was in her apartment, but she came out to meet me. She spoke to me with savage contempt: "So! that's how your great Trojan keeps a treaty!"

"He swore peace," I said.

"He attacked your father across the altar!"

"He did not. He pledged peace with him. He asked to fight Turnus hand to hand. He swore if he lost they'd leave, and if he won, Latinus would still be king of Latium. And father swore to that oath. But Juturna and the Rutulians didn't want that, and Tolumnius called an omen and threw the spear that broke the truce. I was there. That is what happened."

"It is not true," she said, but she knew it was. After what I had seen I had no fear to spare for her. I heard my voice ring out stronger than hers, I felt taller than her as I stood facing her.

"If Turnus had come forward to fight Aeneas, there'd be no war now, the city would be safe," I said, for my heart was hot with anger. "He betrayed us."

"Turnus would never," she began, and then, her voice shaking, she said, "It was for, it was for you."

"Turnus doesn't care a stick for me or you either," I said. I heard myself speak with the sneering stridency I had so often heard in my mother's voice. I thought of the clarity of the sky above the altar between the armies as the two kings swore the treaty. A great swell of shame and passion ran all through my body. I knelt down before my mother and took the hem of her white palla. I said, "Mother, forgive me. Let us have peace between us!"

"Never, he would never," she said. She looked around as if bewildered. "Is it my fault?" she cried. She turned away, pulling her gown out of my hand, and hurried back into her own apartment and closed the door behind her.

I crouched there weeping for a while. Tears that had been pent up in me through these terrible days poured out. Then they were done, and I put back the hair from my forehead and wiped my face with the edge of my palla and stood up, looking at the women who were watching me in awe and concern and confusion.

"It was Turnus' people who broke the truce, but it will be the Trojans and Etruscans besieging the city," I said to them, groping for the truth I needed and the reassurance we all needed. My voice quavered. "So we have no true friends but our own Latin men fighting out there, and ourselves. What can we do to make the house safe, and wait out the siege?"

They all gazed in silence, some of them sniveling, until Maruna said, "The storerooms are full."

I said, "Praise be to our Penates, the storerooms are full, and the fountain runs. Is there plenty of firewood for the cooking stoves?"

That was indeed a problem, and something within our scope. A discussion arose about it, and Tita said, "We could cut down the laurel tree." At that Sicana, the tall grim woman who had always served and sided with my mother, said, "Are you mad, Tita? Go wash your mouth out and beg all that's sacred to give you the wits of a rabbit! Cut down the king's tree? Idiot! There's the old poplars back of the stables, to start with." I put Sicana at once in charge of finding men with axes to fell and cut up the trees; then there were a hundred other things to be done, and women willing to do them.

The battle outside the walls went on all this time, all that morning. I saw none of it. I heard the noise of it only when there was some pause in the business of the house. I can tell only what I was told. The Rutulians at first, in the surprise of their assault, drove the Trojans and their allies back, but after that the battle moved steadily nearer the rampart and ditch outside the city walls and gate. Messapus was in charge of the Rutulians; Turnus was here and there, "but never staying in one place," said the man who brought us the clearest report. This man, Mellus, had been among our recovering wounded in the Regia, and went out to fight again; his wound, a bad sword cut, reopened as he fought. He managed to get back inside the city while the gates were still open. He reported to the king that the Trojans were not trying to get closer to the gate, but were holding their position on the rampart while Aeneas hunted for Turnus, claiming his right to settle the war by single combat, and Turnus rode here and there through the fighting, mounted on his horse, dealing out death, but never letting Aeneas meet him. After Mellus had made this report clearly and quietly, he fainted from loss of blood; and though we did what we could for him in our courtyard hospital, he died that evening. He was a Latin farmer, with a small farm and orchard in the foothills south of the city.

I was trying to direct the sweepers to use mops and soaked rags to keep the courtyard pavement clean of blood from the wounded men who were continually carried in, when the roar of noise swelled up immediately outside the city gate. All of us in the house looked up from what we were doing, and some ran up onto the walls and the watchtower to see what was happening. They reported to us that the Trojans had crossed the space between the ditch and the walls and were attacking the city gate, led by their tall captain with the red crest on his helmet, although the crest had been sliced off short. One of the girls who had gone to the wall above the gate said the captain was shouting that the Italians had broken the treaty twice and their king was faithless.

"And he killed Verus," she said. She was white as whey and talked in a high, monotonous voice, repeating things over and over. "He just sliced off his, his head, just sliced off his head, off his body."

"Verus," I said, not comprehending yet; there was too much to do. I was aware, even inside the Regia, that there was a great movement of people in the streets. Some were pressing to get down to the gates and throw them open in surrender, others were trying to get down there with pikes and poles and axes and kitchen knives to keep the attackers out of the city. The noise within the city was a dull mindless roar. Somebody shouted, "Fire!" and at that I did run up onto the platform to see if the Regia was threatened. Flaming missiles were flying up over the walls in a couple of places, but people in the streets below rushed to put them out. Still the cry of fire was repeated again and again, and the dark buzzing wailing noise of the people all over the city was so loud one could not think.

Through that noise there came from down in the house a shrieking of women, so keen and sharp I turned and ran down the stairs again and to the women's side.

There the screaming and high wailing rang and echoed so I could not hear what Sicana, coming at me with her mouth open in a square and her eyes unseeing, cried to me. I followed her to my mother's rooms. I saw Amata hanging from the noose she had made of twisted cloth and tied over a beam. Her feet were bare. Her long black hair hung down all round her face and body.

Sicana and I pushed back the table under her and Sicana held her while I cut the cloth noose with my small knife. We laid her down on the long table there in her anteroom. She still wore the little gold bullas my brothers had worn. "Wash her," I commanded Sicana and the others, for she had soiled herself in her agony, and I could not bear for her body to be shamed.

What I had to do was tell my father.

He had heard the frenzy in the women's side and was coming across the courtyard, Drances and some others following him. I stopped him under the laurel tree. I am not sure what I said. He stood a while. His face looked very tired and sad; he embraced me, and I held to him. I said, "Come to her." At that he let me go, and slowly got down on his knees, and picked up dirt from around the roots of the laurel tree, and rubbed it into his grey hair.

I knelt by him, trying to give him comfort.

I realised that though the wailing went on in the women's rooms, the noise of the city and the war had sunk down almost to quietness.

I looked up and saw people standing motionless on the walls of the house and the platform.

They were still. It grew still.

Then there was a great sound like a deep breath, like the earth breathing, all around the walls. I thought it was earthquake, the sound earthquake makes as it comes. But it was the sound of the end. The war was over. Turnus was dead. The poem was finished.

NO, BUT IT WAS LEFT UNFINISHED.

Didn't you tell me that, my poet? here in the sacred place, where the stinking sulfur water comes up from under the earth to make pools on the earth, and the stars shine between the leaves? Once you said it was not complete, and should be burned.

But then again, at the end, you said it was finished. And I know they did not burn it. I would have burned with it.

But what am I to do now? I have lost my guide, my Vergil. I must go on by myself through all that is left after the end, all the rest of the immense, pathless, unreadable world.

What is left after a death? Everything else. The sun a man saw rise goes down though he does not see it set. A woman sits down to the weaving another woman left in the loom.

I have found my way so far, even though the poet did not tell me the way. I guessed it right, without mistake, from things he said, the clues he gave me. I came to the center of the maze following him. Now I must find my way back out alone. It will be longer and slower in the living, but not so long, I think, to tell.

THERE WERE MANY WHO SAW TURNUS DIE, FOR IT WAS BEFORE the gates of Laurentum that he finally stopped hiding from Aeneas and turned to fight him. Both men threw their spears, and missed. So they met sword to sword, but Turnus' sword broke, and he turned and ran again.

Aeneas tried to chase him, but was too lame to run. He stopped and tried to pull out his spear from the wild olive trunk it had hit. That was a sacred tree. I had done worship to Faunus there many times. The Trojans had cut it down in a rage of destruction when they occupied the ramparts, and nothing but the stump was left. The spear was big and heavy and had gone deep, and the tree would not let it go. While Aeneas was struggling with it, Juturna ran up to Turnus and gave him a sword. Aeneas pulled his spear free at last and came for Turnus, shouting, "This is a fight, Turnus, not a footrace!"

Serestus was close to them then. He told me he saw an uncanny thing: an owl, a little owl, flew round Turnus, there in the broad daylight. He said that Turnus tried to keep it from his face. He seemed dazed, bewildered, like a man already mortally wounded. He ran off a short way again till he came to a terminus stone, a boundary marker. He stopped at it, turned, picked the huge stone up, grappling it in his arms, and threw it at Aeneas. It fell short by far. Then he stood there with the same bewildered look, holding his sword but doing nothing, till Aeneas brought him down, sending his heavy spear through Turnus' thigh.

Aeneas came limping up and stood over him breathing hard. Turnus couldn't get up. He struggled to his knees. When he'd got his breath he spoke clearly and quietly, as if his confusion had passed. He said, "You've won. I ask no mercy. Do as you will. If you kill me, send my body home to my father. Lavinia is your wife. Don't take your hatred further." Aeneas listened to him and drew back, as if to spare him. Then he saw Turnus had on the gold sword belt he had torn off dying Pallas. He shouted out, "Did you let the boy live? It's he, it's Pallas who makes this sacrifice!"—and he drove his sword into Turnus' heart.

JUTURNA HAD STAYED ON THE BATTLEFIELD ALL THROUGH THE fighting. They say she had more than once hidden her brother from Aeneas who came stalking him, lame and dire. She came forward now through the broken Rutulian ranks and knelt by Turnus' body, her grey veils falling over him, and keened.

Aeneas stood there leaning on his sword until Achates and Serestus came to him; then he sheathed the sword, and with an arm round his friends' necks, they helping him to walk, he began to hobble slowly back to the Trojan camp. He turned round as they crossed the rampart, and called out, "King Latinus! Our treaty holds!"

Latinus was not there to answer him; he was in an inner room with his dead wife, dust in his hair. But the Latin troops replied, many-voiced, "The treaty holds," and people on the walls repeated it.

The few that were left of the Rutulian captains—for in his final fury Aeneas had killed every man who dared meet him—gathered their troops together and formed a group to take up and carry the bodies of Turnus and Camers and Tolumnius. In silence they began their long walk back to Ardea. The leaderless troops scattered out to find rest or find their dead comrades. Next day they too would straggle back to Rutulia, or Volscia, or the hill country.

Juturna went alone, northward; people saw her go, but she was never seen again, and it is thought she drowned herself that night in the father river.

The Latin army dispersed as the allies did. Some came into the city for rest or healing, but many went to find their dead brothers or neighbors on the battlefield and carry them home, back to the farm down the valley or over the ridge. Already from the nearby homesteads slaves with carts drawn by an ox or a donkey were coming out, sent by the farmwife or the old farmer to help carry the wounded and the dead.

That night in the city we heard the knock of axes, the distant crash of falling trees, in the woods north and east of the city. Next morning the woodcutters were busy hauling in wood for pyres outside the walls.

One pyre was built up high and separate for my mother. She was carried out on a white litter, dressed in the delicate white palla she had woven and called my wedding gown. Everyone in the city who could walk followed the procession.

The closest relative of the dead lights the fire, with face averted. I lit her fire. When the fire had done its work I picked out of the fierce smoking ashes a bone, a little finger bone, to bury in the earth, so that her soul need not wander. Then my father stood and called out her name three times, as is our custom, and I and all the people called her with him: *Amata! Amata! Amata!* And silence after that.

THE OLD GUARD VERUS WAS DEAD, AND AULUS. EVERY ONE OF the young men who had been my suitors was dead. My mother was dead. Almost every household in Latium grieved for a father or brother or son killed or crippled. I think one cannot be left alive among so many deaths without feeling unendurable shame. They say Mars absolves the warrior from the crimes of war, but those who were not the warriors, those for whom the war was said to be fought, even though they never wanted it to be fought, who absolves them?

In the evening of the day of my mother's funeral, I called Maruna, Sicana, and others of the chief women of the Regia to come with me. Old Vestina was too broken with grief to do anything but crouch on the floor in my mother's room and rock herself, crying without tears, making a little moaning like a sick child.

We walked down through the streets to the altar of Janus, where I made offering of meal and incense to the power of beginning and ending. People of the city gathered round. No one spoke. The silence of the city after the noise of war brought awe into us all. In our loss and fear we craved the acts of religion, the ceremonies that allow us to admit our helplessness, our dependence on the great forces we do not understand. When I had made the offering to Janus, I went, followed by my women and many people, to the doors that stood ajar in their high cedar frame nearby, the War Gate, the gate that led nowhere whether it was open or shut. I pushed at one of the doors, then the other. I could not move them. Standing open, they had sagged from their hinges and rested on the stony ground. My women helped me, and men came forward to join us. We finally forced the gates shut, and Sicana and one of the men lifted up the squared beam of oak and slotted it through the thick iron staples of the lock. Then I spoke to the gate: "Stay shut. The treaty holds!" I felt as if I were speaking to an enemy, defeated for the moment, but never anything but an enemy. The people murmured after me, "The treaty holds."

AENEAS DID NOT COME TO LAURENTUM FOR NINE DAYS, THE period of mourning. This was simple decency. Coming sooner, he would be perceived and resented as the conqueror enforcing his triumph. No matter that he had sworn to leave the crown and the sword to Latinus and bring only his gods to Latium: we had seen that promise twice broken in the making.

Still—"The new king's in no hurry to come, is he?" people said. Even my women called him that, though I told them it was disrespectful to our true king. Word got round that the Trojan had been wounded and needed to recover, and people said with some satisfaction, "So Turnus nicked him after all." Yet they told with admiration how he had hunted Turnus across the battlefield for two hours with an arrowhead in the muscle of his thigh. When he did come he walked lame, and looked rather drawn and gaunt.

He sent a messenger ahead to prepare us, and arrived with a troop of only ten or twelve men, all mounted, dressed in what finery they had—their armor, mostly, cleaned up and polished, and maybe a cloak or tunic that had been handsome before the long voyage from Troy. A couple of splendid Etruscan princes were with them, but none of the Greeks: in grief and bitterness of heart at his son's death, Evander had called all his men back to Pallanteum. Aeneas rode a horse that had been one of my father's gifts to him at the very outset, that day when the first treaty was made, when I was promised to him. The fine dun stallion, well trained but lively, scented his old friends the mares in the royal stables as he passed and set up a lot of whinnying, which of course the mares answered with neighs and squeals; so that part of their entrance was fairly noisy. The guards stood aside for them at the gates of Laurentum and they rode quietly up the Via Regia. People came running to look and crowded on the roofs, but they too were quiet.

The men dismounted at the house door. I hurried down from my spy post above the door and came round to enter the council chamber from the back. But Gaius, who had taken over Verus' position as chief of the king's guards, stopped me at the doorway. "The king says please to wait until you are sent for, queen," he said.

He was the first to call me that. I am not sure he knew what he was saying. He was a silent, shy, grave old man, embarrassed at having to stop me.

So I had to wait at the doorway, unable to hear most of what they were saying. My father was on his cross-legged throne. I could see his back, and several Trojans, but not Aeneas. There was some speech making. The Etruscan Tarchon asked Latinus' pardon for bringing his men to fight against the Latins, explaining that the people of Caere had resolved to take the tyrant Mezentius from Turnus in Ardea to punish him as he deserved, but an oracle told them they must have a foreign leader for such an expedition, and Aeneas had turned up at exactly the right moment. Latinus accepted this apology as gracefully as it was offered. He wanted no quarrel with Etruria. Drances did a great deal of the talking. He had been utterly odious to me since Turnus' death; there was no reason in it, but I could not help it, and I clenched my fists in loathing as he droned on. Then one of the Trojans said something and an Etruscan answered, and everyone laughed, which changed the mood; and I heard a quiet, resonant voice: "I bring a gift for your daughter, King Latinus."

"That is most gracious, noble Aeneas," my father said. "And she will bring to you a dowry worthy of our wealth and pride."

"I have no doubt of that, my king. But what I bring, I wish to give her with my own hands."

My father nodded, and said to Caesus who was attending him as page, "Send for my daughter Lavinia."

Caesus was just turning to fetch me as I came forward with Gaius. I arrived with unseemly speed. My father looked a little startled.

At last I could see Aeneas. He had been hidden from me before because he was seated—my father had had a folding stool brought for him, since he was still lame. But he stood up as soon as he saw me, and we looked at each other at eye level. He was much taller than I, but I was up on the dais.

Seeing him made me happy. It brought me joy. I thought I saw a gleam, a reflection of my pleasure in his face.

We bowed our heads in formal greeting, and then a dark man with a keen, kind face, Achates, brought a big pottery vessel up to the dais and rested it there. It was made of heavy red clay, undecorated, broad at the bottom, broad-shouldered, with a sealed stopper. Aeneas put his hands on it, large, scarred hands, with a formality of gesture that came naturally to him, and also with a kind of affectionate tenderness.

"Lavinia," he said, "when I left Troy I could not bring much with me: my father and my son, some of my people, and the gods of my household and my ancestors. My father is with the lords of the underworld; my son Ascanius stands there, and with him are my people, ready to do you honor as his mother and their queen. And my Penates and the sacred things of my ancestors I give you now to keep and cherish on the altars of our house, in the city that will bear your name. They have come a long way to your hearth and heart."

I knelt down and put my hands on the vessel too. I said, "I will keep and cherish them," in a thin voice.

"Where shall we build Lavinium?" he said, energetic, smiling now with open pleasure, looking from me to Latinus.

"We must go about the country and see what will suit best," my father said. "I thought of a region in the foothills, up near the father river. Good growing land, and good timber above it."

"Down the coast," I said. My voice was still weak and hoarse. "On a hill, in a bend of the river that comes down from Albunea."

They all looked at me.

"I saw it there, the city," I said. "In a dream."

Aeneas continued to gaze at me, and his face grew grave and intense. "I will build your city where you saw it built, Lavinia," he said. Then he drew back a little, though we both still kept our hands on the pottery vessel. He smiled again and said, "And did you dream the day of our marriage?"

"No," I whispered.

"Name it, King Latinus," Aeneas said. "Name it soon! Too much time wasted already, too many deaths, too much grief. Let us not be wasteful, from now on."

My father did not ponder long. "The Kalends of Quintilis. If the auguries be good."

"They will be," Aeneas said.

THEY WERE, OF COURSE.

The Trojans had only what was left of June to start their city

and build us a house, but they were amazingly hard workers, better disciplined than we Italians and not used to taking so many
holidays. By the first day of the fifth month, the town of Lavinium
existed. A bend of the little river Prati half encircled the steep rocky
hill that was the citadel. Around the west and south sides of the
hill, sloping down more gently, was a ditch and rampart; higher up,
a wooden palisade showed where the city wall of tufa rock would
be built. Within that the streets were laid out. The main road went
up to the citadel with a sharp turn on a steep ramp just before
the gate, an excellent defensive position, as all the old soldiers said
with satisfaction. A small stone house stood on the hilltop, facing
the gate: the Regia. That house, the only one completely finished,
looked out over the tents and huts and scaffoldings that made up
most of the other habitations, and across the palisade to the water
meadows of the Prati and the sea dunes a couple of miles to the
west. East of the city the forests of oak and pine rose up and up
towards the old volcano, the long mountain, Alba.

Early in the morning of that first day of Quintilis, my last day
in my father's house, I was arrayed as a bride. I who had so often
ornamented the sacrificial lamb or calf was now ornamented, and
my role, like theirs, was meekness. Vestina parted my hair with a
bronze spear blade into six tresses and wound each with red wool
fillets; I put on the wreath of good herbs and flowers I'd picked
before sunrise in the fields outside town; a woolen sash was tied in
a complicated knot round the waist of my tunic, Vestina and old
Aula arguing for a long time about exactly how to tie it; and over all
went a large, long, light veil, dyed red-orange. It was the flame veil
my father's mother Marica had worn when she was married, and
her mother before her. Then I joined the three young boys waiting
for me in the courtyard, all carrying lighted white thorn torches.
The flames were invisible, a mere tremor in the brightness of the

midsummer day. Caesus walked in front of me, the other two boys walked beside me, and their mother Lupina, a respectable towns-woman, came behind me as my matron of honor. After us came my father with his counsellors and what was left of his guards, and an honor guard of Trojan soldiers sent by Aeneas, and everybody else who wanted to be in the wedding.

We went down the Via Regia and people joined us all along the way, all shouting out the wedding word nobody knows the mean-ing of, "*talassio! talassio!*" and throwing nuts about and making dirty jokes. The dirty jokes are part of the marriage ritual, which seemed to surprise the Trojans. There was plenty of time to tell them, since the whole lot of us walked all the way to Lavinium, at least six miles. The wedding torches had to be relit or replaced several times, and people got hungry and began eating their walnuts and filberts instead of throwing them about. Water sellers with their tiny, heavy-laden donkeys did a good business all the way.

It was strange to me to walk inside the flame veil, looking out at the world through it. All that path I knew so well, all the hills and fields and forests, were a little dim, and colored faintly as if with sunset light. I felt set apart from all things, all people, alone, in a way I would never be alone again.

When we came at last to the front door of the house on the hill in the new city, Caesus turned round and with a whoop waved his burning torch and threw it end over end as high as he could into the crowd massed behind us. There was a scramble for it and a lot of yelling, as people burned their hands grabbing at it to carry off for good luck.

Then they all quieted down again and watched me as I rubbed the posts of the doorway with the lump of wolf's fat Vestina had carried and given to me to use—it was brownish, stale, with a rank smell. Then she gave me some red wool fillets, and I tied them around the door posts, murmuring worship to Janus the Door-keeper.

All this time tall Aeneas stood in the shadow inside the door-way, silent and unmoving, watching me.

When I was done, I stood still and looked up at him.

He asked the question that is asked: "Who are you?"

And I gave the answer that is given: "Where you are Gaius, I am Gaia."

Then with a sudden, wide smile he moved, he picked me up and swung me high over the threshold of our house and set me down inside it.

So I was made his wife, the mother of our people, his and mine.

AS A WIFE, I NEVER FELT THAT GRIEVING ANGER THAT I USED TO feel and once spoke out to my poet in Albunea, asking why must a girl be brought up at home to live as a woman in exile. Indeed my exile was a small matter, since I went only a few miles from my old home, my father, the dear Regia with its laurel tree, and the Lar Familiaris of my childhood. But there was more to it than that. Men call women faithless, changeable, and though they say it in jealousy of their own ever-threatened sexual honor, there is some truth in it. We can change our life, our being; no matter what our will is, we are changed. As the moon changes yet is one, so we are virgin, wife, mother, grandmother. For all their restlessness, men are who they are; once they put on the man's toga they will not change again; so they make a virtue of that rigidity and resist whatever might soften it and set them free. But in giving up my girl self and taking on the obligations of womanhood I found myself freer than I had ever been. If I owed duty to my husband, it was very easy to pay. And as understanding grew between us and we came to trust each other, there were no restraints on me at all but those of religion and my duty to my people. I had grown up with those, they were part of me, not external, not enslaving; rather, in enlarging the scope of my soul and mind, they liberated me from the narrowness of the single self.

I did not bring the Penates of Laurentum with me. My father had manumitted his slave, Maruna's mother, to be their servant and guardian in my place. When I first entered my new house in Aeneas' arms, the Penates of his father's house in Troy stood on the altar at the back of the atrium: they were the gods of this house now, my family's gods, and I was their servant and guardian. A very old bowl of thin silver, worn and dented, stood near them, ready for the sacred meal. The lamps were of polished black clay. On our dining table was a plate painted red and black and on it was a little mound of dried fava beans, the food that must always stand on the table for the gods who share it with us, and near it the salt cellar: all as it should be. And on the hearth Vesta, the holy fire, burned small and clear.

Aeneas was about twice my age when we married. When I first saw his whole body, all muscle and sinew and bone and scar, I thought of the lean splendor of a wolf Almo and his brothers had caught and kept caged for a while before they killed it as a sacrifice to Mars. Aeneas' body had been made in a hard school. But the man was no wolf, nor a hard man. I knew he had loved two women before me and grieved for them both. Although he knew me first only as an item in a treaty, he was disposed by nature and by practice to treat me as a wife, intimate to his own being. At first I think my youth awed him. He was afraid of hurting me. He praised my beauty with incredulous delight. He honored my ignorance, but I was impatient with it and ready to learn from him, as he soon learned. As often as we made love I remembered what my poet told me, that this man was born of a goddess, the force that moves the stars and the waves of the sea and couples the animals in the fields in spring, the power of passion, the light of the evening star.

I WILL NOT, I CANNOT TELL MUCH IN DETAIL OF THE THREE years of our marriage, for my mind holds me back from speaking much of those doings and undertakings that seemed of such importance to us and filled our days so full. And indeed they were important both to us and to our people; and they have filled my life, not only then but ever since, completing me, so that though I knew the bitter grief of widowhood, I seldom felt the utter emptiness. I think if you have lost a great happiness and try to recall it, you are only asking for sorrow, but if you do not try to dwell on the happiness, sometimes you find it dwelling in your heart and body, silent but sustaining. The purest, completest happiness I know is that of a baby at the breast and the mother giving suck. From that I know what perfect fulfillment is. But I cannot regain it by remembering, by speaking, by yearning. To have known it is enough, and all.

I knew how little time Aeneas had to live, and he did not. Or I think he did not. I do not know all the prophecies he may have heard during his voyage, or when he went among the shadows. If he did know, the knowledge did not weigh on him or make him shorten his view or shrink his hope at all. He looked forward fearlessly and sought to shape the time to come; he was a man building a city, founding a nation, working in every way he could for the well-being of his people, his family, himself. His shield hung in our entrance hall, full of images of the time to come, the kings, the templed hills, the heroes and their wars. He had carried the future of his people on his shoulder into war. Now he meant to found that future in peace.

After ten years of war in Troy, war had met him again unlooked for, unwanted, here on the Italian shore. He wanted never to meet it again. He was determined to make an enduring peace, as Latinus had done. His first and strongest purpose was to establish the rule of law, the custom of negotiation and arbitration, the superiority of rational patience over mindless violence, among his Trojans and the Latins who were building Lavinium with them, and among all our neighboring peoples.

It did not take me long to realise, as the first year passed, how his mind dwelt on the ending of the brief war here in Italy, how that had shaken and reshaped all his idea of who he was and what his duty was. Not the war itself; that had been unavoidable; once Mars rules men, Mars must be obeyed on his own terms. It was the ending of it that weighed on Aeneas: the manner of Turnus' death. To him, that put all the rest into question.

He saw it as a murder. He saw himself as a murderer. He had withheld his sword, giving Turnus time to surrender to him fully and courageously, and yet after that, dismissing the obligation to spare the helpless and pardon the conquered, in a fury of vengeance he had killed him. He had done *nefas*, unspeakable wrong.

We talked in the summer mornings before we got to work; we talked in darkness, in our marriage bed, in the lengthening autumn nights. He learned that he could talk to me as I think he had never talked to anyone, unless perhaps Creusa long ago, in the dark years of the siege of Troy, when he was young. He was a man who thought hard and constantly about what he had done and what he ought to do, and his active conscience welcomed my listening, my silence and my attempts to answer, as it struggled for clarity. And my ignorance welcomed his questioning, which taught me what is worth asking.

"You were angry," I said. "You should have been! First Turnus challenged you, then he deliberately ran away from you, kept you chasing him, knowing you'd been wounded, to wear you out. It was a coward's tactic."

"If it was a tactic. All's fair in war."

"But he broke the truce!"

"It wasn't his doing. He let his sister talk, and Camers, and that Tolumnius, who threw the spear. Believe me, I have no regret at all for killing Tolumnius . . . But Turnus didn't speak, then or later. Not till the end. He acted like a man under a spell."

"That's what Serestus said," I said. "The owl he saw—just before you met with Turnus—he said he doesn't know if he saw an owl flying around Turnus' head, beating at him with its wings, or if he saw something Turnus was seeing, that wasn't actually there."

I could feel Aeneas shudder slightly. He did not speak.

After a long time I said, "I think there was some evil in Turnus' heritage. In my mother's family. Something frantic. A madness. A darkness. It ran in their blood like a black snake, a fire without light. Oh, may the powers of all goodness and the Earth Mother and my Juno keep it from me and our child!"

I knew by then that I had conceived; and I too shuddered as I spoke, and held to Aeneas for courage. He soothed me, stroking my hair.

"There is no evil in you," he said. "You are as clear of soul as the springs of the Numicus, up there in the hills, as pure and clear."

But I thought of the springs of Albunea, silent, pallid, under their stinking bluish mist.

"Turnus was young, ambitious, impatient," he said. "But what was evil in him?"

"His greed," I said at once. "Greed, selfishness—self, self! He saw the world only as what he wanted from it. He killed the Greek boy for his sword belt. And killed him cruelly, and boasted about it! That was what you couldn't bear—seeing that belt on his shoulder."

"I killed the Etruscan boy Lausus. Cruelly."

"You didn't boast about it!"

"No. I grieved about it. What good did that do? He was dead."

"But Aeneas, nobody spared anybody in that battle, not even when they begged for their lives—you said so." Later, I remembered that it was not Aeneas who had told me that, but the poet. But neither Aeneas nor I noticed at the time, and I went on, eloquent in my desire to spare him his anguish— "You were fighting to the death, not just you and Turnus but all of you. It doesn't matter if you were crazy with bloodlust or cold as seawater, you did what you had to do. Pallas tried to kill Turnus and so Turnus killed him. Lausus tried to kill you and so you killed him. Turnus tried to kill you and so you killed him. It was a challenge to the death between you two. Nothing else could have ended the war. That is the order—the *fas* of war. Isn't it? And you obeyed it. You did what you had to do, what had to be done. As you always do!"

He said nothing for a while, and then very little. I thought he was struck by my argument. He was stricken by it.

It was only much later that I saw I had taken from him the self-blame that allowed him some self-justification. If he could not see his battle rage as the enemy of his piety, as fury for a moment overcoming his better self, if he could not see his killing Turnus as a fatal instant of disorder, then he had to see the fury as part of his true nature, part of the right order of things, the order he had spent his life trying to uphold, serve, preserve. If that order held his killing Turnus to be a righteous act, was it, itself, righteous?

Turnus' death ensured the victory of Aeneas' cause, but it was a mortal defeat for the man Aeneas.

As he struck, Aeneas had called the killing a sacrifice. But of what, to what?

I did not know what kind of courage I was asking of my patient hero. We did not speak again of the matter. I went on thinking that I had unburdened his mind of an unnecessary guilt, comforted him, relieved him of the need for courage. Young wives can be great fools.

Our city grew up around our little Regia so quickly that it sometimes seemed unreal, a vision, like my dream of it; but to look out from our door and see the thatch and tile roofs all around, and smell the cooking smoke from them rising, and hear the voices of the people, a young Latin wife calling to her Trojan husband, a workman shouting to his helper, a child singing a jumping-game song—that was all real, every morning and evening, and vivid and cheerful. Lavinium looked much like any other city of our coast, though its citadel stood higher than many, on its ridge of tufa over the little dark river Prati. Left to themselves, the Trojans might have built the houses differently, but the carpenters were Italians and did things the way they always did things. And I insisted that every tree within the walls that could be left standing should stand. The Trojans thought that odd at first, but they admitted the virtues of shade in midsummer, and came to take pride in the oak or laurel or willow grove that sheltered their house. We had less shade than most, in the Regia, but I had brought a scion of the laurel of my father's house in our courtyard, and in a year it was already above our heads. And we planted a wild grapevine to climb out over a lattice and shade the south end of the courtyard.

There were a great many weddings that first year. Not many Trojan women had come from Sicily on this last leg of the long retreat from Troy. The men were eager to take a wife wherever they could find one. By winter there was hardly an unmarried girl left in Latium, and unmarried Latin men complained about it copiously. My Silvius was the first baby born in Lavinium, but before that May was over there were five more little Trojan-Latins wailing in cradles around town, and the powers that attend childbirth were busy all that year and the years that followed.

Local families that acquired Trojan sons-in-law were drawn to the city by the bonds of kinship, and workmen came attracted by the need for their crafts. Many of them settled down, liking the new town and its king. Before long there were more Latins than Trojans in Lavinium. The hardy warriors who had come so far with Aeneas found themselves living as Italian householders among Italian householders, farming beside the native farmers, their great city a legend, their noble lineage meaningless, and all their battles, adventures, storms, and voyages sunk in daily domesticity at the fireside of a small house in a small city in a foreign land.

It was hard for some of them, the younger ones particularly. The men over thirty were mostly glad to be done with hardship and salt water, to have a hearth of their own and a bed with a wife in it. But Aeneas kept an eye on the men in their teens and twenties, giving them the hardest work to do; anything dangerous in any way was for them; and he kept up a series of drills and athletic games in which they competed for championship in one skill or sport after another, while older men and children looked on and cheered. Young Latins were welcome to these games, and many joined in them with strong competitive spirit. There were various Trojan holy days to be marked by games, and Aeneas added every Latin festival he could to the calendar, so the young men were always in training for one event or another.

My stepson Ascanius had learned to ride in Africa and was an excellent horseman, usually taking the lead in any displays of riding and training. In other sports, archery, racing, leaping, wrestling, throwing the stone, or military drills with sword and spear, he was not naturally among the best, but he thought he ought to be and drove himself desperately to excel. When he came in sixth, or fifth, or even second, he was angry and ashamed, and would dispute the judgment, or go off scowling to berate himself. If he was not the huntsman who killed the boar or stag, he came home from hunting sad and sullen. He had his father's seriousness and sense of duty, but not his sense of proportion or his patient strength. Their young prince had naturally been the darling of the exiled Trojans during their wanderings, and I think when they were in Carthage the queen had spoiled him, for he was always talking about what Dido had let him do and how splendid it had been in Africa. If he noticed how his father's face darkened at such talk, he never asked why. With me, only a few years older than he was, he was wary and reserved. I could not be the cherishing mother he had lost. I seemed to him, and even to myself, more like an elder sister, a powerful rival for the father's love. He was jealous of his baby half brother. No father could have loved a son more than Aeneas loved Ascanius, but Ascanius had not yet grown into the generosity of heart that would let him simply accept that love; he thought he had to earn it by proving himself superior to it. He was restless and unhappy, and his unhappiness troubled his father. Fortunately he loved hunting, and so he was sent with a hunting party up into the mountains as often as he liked. Our flocks and herds were not yet plentiful, and game was a great treat for us. Ascanius could feel himself needed, a hero, worthy of his father, when he strode in with a feast's worth of meat and a bearskin, the rack of a great stag, or the tusks of a mountain boar as trophy.

My son Silvius was born the day after the May Kalends, a little early by our calculations, not a large baby, but a fine one. Even when his little red face was as flat and slant-eyed as a kitten's I could see his father's features latent in it, the strong brow line and eminent nose. He smiled unmistakably at less than a month old, and wept real tears soon after: again taking after his father, a good-humored man, easily moved to tears. Silvius suckled insatiably, had almost no colic, slept a great deal, and when awake was wide awake and full of good cheer. There is not much you can say about a baby unless you are talking with its father or another mother or nurse; infants are not part of the realm of ordinary language, talk is inadequate to them as they are inadequate to talk. Silvius was a fine baby and gave his mother and father infinite delight, let that suffice.

There was not much hard feeling against Aeneas' people among the people of Latium. As the Latins saw it now, they had been used by the Rutulians to fight a war that was more in Turnus' interest than theirs. They had been humiliated and were glad to put it all behind them. My father Latinus was held in more honor now than ever, as his people saw his effort to keep the peace justified and his prophecies fulfilled. He welcomed their goodwill; but he was a man bereft of joy in life. His health often failed. The war, brief as it was, had made him old. More and more often he called for Aeneas to come up to Laurentum, or came to Lavinium to advise and consult with him on matters of government and land use, decisions about planting, harvesting, trade. He made it clear that Aeneas was his son, the next king of Latium, and that his counsellors must keep Aeneas' favor or lose his. He was immensely generous to us, opening up his royal lands to our farmers, stocking our pastures with the best of his own flocks and herds, so that Lavinium could grow and flourish from the start.

Within a couple of years the new town was drawing people away from the old one. People said to one another, "Things are lively down there on the Prati; what if we set up shop there?" So Laurentum began slowly to become the town it now is, a very small, sleepy, silent place, its gate unguarded, the neglected houses shaded by immense trees, no one at all in the Regia but a few old guards and their wives and slaves to care for the house gods and sit spinning by the pool under the great laurel.

If most of the Latins kept no grudge against Aeneas' people, old Tyrrhus did, and his one son who had survived the war, and his daughter Silvia. They did not forgive the Trojans, would never forgive them. The old man defied Latinus openly, calling him a coward who'd sold his kingdom and his daughter to a foreign adventurer. Why don't you Latins rise up and drive out the usurpers? he shouted. Look what the king is doing, giving away our cattle to these robbers!— Latinus let him shout, let him keep his position as royal herdsman, did not punish or reprove him at all. That shocked people like Drances, who said the king endangered his dignity and power by permitting treasonous speech, but Latinus ignored Drances as well as Tyrrhus. Since his rant brought about no response, people came to dismiss Tyrrhus as only a bitter old man, raving in his unassuageable grief. As for Drances, Aeneas trusted him no more than I did; he and Latinus let him talk, and let his talk die away into nothing.

The stag Cervulus that Ascanius shot did not die of the wound, but lived on some years, lame and timid, always staying close to the farmhouse; so people in Laurentum told me. I sent to Silvia once to ask if I might visit. She sent me no reply. Cowardice kept me from going there. I was afraid the old man would rage at me and insult my husband. I was afraid Silvia would turn her back on me. She married late, a cousin who had come to help her father and brother with the herds. So she never left her own Penates, but lived all her life on the home farm. I never saw her again.

Outside Latium, among our allied and neighbor kingdoms, the war had left hard feelings and sore hearts. Every people that had sent warriors to aid Turnus had seen them limp home beaten, their kings and captains dead. The conduct of the war itself had been so erratic—a treaty no sooner made than broken, then remade, then broken again in the making—and its aims had been so unclear, that they hardly knew who was to blame. It was easy to lay it to Turnus' ambition. But then, Latinus had allowed his people to fight alongside Turnus as if it had truly been an alliance of Italians to drive the foreigners out. And the Volscian and Sabine kings and captains had been slaughtered not by Italians but by Trojans, Etruscans, Greeks. Everybody knew the Etruscans were seeking dominion over the southern states; Greeks were never to be trusted; and who were these Trojans who had sailed in claiming all Italy as their inheritance?

For word of that prophecy had got out. Though Aeneas never spoke of it in public, some of his people did: they told how he had brought them here, guided by omens and oracles, to rule the whole country, to found a glorious, everlasting empire. Ascanius talked about it to the Latin youths who were now his intimates. He brought them into our atrium to show them Aeneas' shield with its mysterious foreshadowings of mighty buildings and endless wars. "Those warriors, those kings are my descendants," he said to his friends. As he spoke, I passed by carrying little Silvius on my shoulder, as Aeneas had carried the shield.

IN THE SECOND SPRING, LATE IN MARS' MONTH, A BAND OF Rutulians and Volscians met in secret outside Ardea and coming across country at night made an early morning assault on Lavinium. Our walls were built solid by then, but they were not guarded against attack; closed at nightfall, the city gate was opened before dawn to let shepherds and herdsmen in and out with their animals. Our first warning was a couple of farm boys who came pelting up the ramp shouting, "An army! An army is coming!" The gate-keepers set up the alarm. In an emergency, Aeneas moved like a cat: he was up and outside, calling to Ascanius and Achates, Serestus and Mnestheus, to get the men together under arms, before I understood anything at all.

When I went up on our roof to look out over the walls and saw the mob of men drifting across the fields like a dark cloud shot through with the gleam of spear points, swift and almost silent, terror gripped me. It was war again, it was Mars coming again to break down the doors, blood and death and ruin, the end of everything. I held Silvius close to my breast, crouching so that we were sheltered by the roof-parapet, and moaned like a hurt dog. I had lost the courage of virginity. I was a cowering, weak-kneed woman like the rest of them, fearful for my child and my man. Fortunately Maruna was not. Just as when we had thought Laurentum was to stand siege, she began to speak to me about supplies, water, wood for the cookfires, and so brought me out of my fit of cowardice. I went down with her and said the morning prayers, and then saw to what was to be done.

The attackers never got into the city: our men poured out of the gate to meet them, Aeneas and his old captains at their head, the Trojans and the young athletes armed with sword and shield, spear or lance, and the householders brandishing hoes, mattocks, scythes, and sickles. The two mobs met face to face on the outer wall of the encircling earthworks, where they fought savagely but briefly. Several young archers up on the gate tower shot at the attackers as they scattered, turned, and fled. Most of our men gave chase, some of them stopping to catch a horse from the herds kept in the near paddocks, but Aeneas brought his Trojans and all the young men he could back into the city. I was waiting in front of the house as he came up the street with his troops and turned to talk to them. "How's that for a lively start to the day?" he said, in his voice that that you could hear through all other voices, even when he spoke quietly, and they all laughed and cheered. "I think they've had their lesson," he went on. "We're in a good position to practice restraint. The less men they lose, the less revenge they'll need to take. The whole thing can be quickly forgotten. Who was leading them? Did anyone see?"

"Camers," several Latin voices answered, "young Camers of Ardea."

"Well, they won't be apt to follow him again soon. Were they all Rutulians?" He could not yet tell peoples and tribes one from another as we natives could, but even if he had identified the attackers he might have asked for information; he knew that people like to be asked, like to be the ones who know.

"Volscians, there was a whole crowd of Volscians," the Latins called, with various descriptions of Volscian character and anatomy—"them with horses' arses on their hats," one man shouted. The townsmen were excited, elated with their sudden, easy victory. Small wounds were exhibited proudly. Householders and young men came back with trophies of enemies they had chased down and killed or forced to surrender—breastplates, swords, helmets. Lavinium was a noisy city all that day and night, and a lot of green wine was drunk. Aeneas was genial with the boastful revellers, keeping open house at the Regia for them till very late. "It's brought them together," he said to me as we stood apart from the crowd, near the women's side, before I went to bed. "My people and yours. They're all Lavinians now. Since this had to happen, it happened fortunately."

"But is it going to go on and on?" I asked him, stupidly. "Will it happen again and again?" The awful fear I had felt that morning had never left me, it was like a thin narrow coldness in my bones.

He looked at me with the eyes that had seen his city burn, that had seen the world of the dead. He held me gently. "Yes," he said. "But I will keep as much of it from happening as I can, Lavinia."

He was able to stave off most of it, for a while. The rout of the would-be besiegers sent a clear message that Lavinium could defend itself, and he followed up on that with energetic efforts to strengthen our alliances with the Sabines, with Caere and other cities of Etruria, and with King Evander in Pallanteum.

Evander, still sunk in grief for his son, held Aeneas responsible for not protecting the boy in battle; his welcome to our visit was reluctant. I had not been there since my visit with my father when Pallas and I were children. It was very sad to see the little settlement grown poorer, the houses settling into the mud of the riverbank, the women and children looking thin and weary. I looked around in wonder, for this was the place where my poet had said the great city of our descendants was to be. Among the thickets up on those rough hills were to stand the shining palaces and altars pictured on the shield; great crowds, great rulers were to walk on marble pavement, here, between the thatched huts and the wolf's deserted cave, where a few lean cattle wandered seeking forage.

Aeneas was in a heavy mood that night when we were alone in the room given us in Evander's low, dark house. Evander's sorrowful rancor was hard for him to bear. Seeking some way to cheer him, and with my head full of those images, I said, "You said I have a gift for knowing where to build a city." For he had often praised my choice of the site of Lavinium.

"Yes, you do."

"Well, this is the best site of all."

He looked at me from under his brows, waiting.

"I saw it in . . . call it a dream." I had never come so close before to speaking of the poet to him, and felt I was treading on a dangerous edge, but I went on, cautiously. "The city on your shield, the great city—"

He nodded.

"It will be here. Just here—and up on those hills, the Seven Hills. I think it will be called by one of the father river's sacred names. The Etruscans say Ruma, we say Roma. It will be the greatest city in the world." I looked over at the baby, who was sound asleep in his travel basket. "Full of little Silviuses," I said. "Thousands of them!"

After a moment he smiled. "Lucky town," he said. "You saw this?"

"On your shield, mostly."

"You know how to read it," he said thoughtfully. "I never have."

"Guesses, dreams."

He stood over the baby's basket, brooding, and presently reached down and stroked the soft wispy hair with the back of his forefinger. "You'll carry it," he whispered to the baby.

"Let it not be in battle," I said.

"Wherever he must . . . Come then, my dear. We'll sleep in the great city tonight."

Evander's alliance was grudging and he had not much assistance to offer us, but word of our friendship with the Greeks of Pallanteum reached the Greeks at Arpi, a much larger and wealthier colony in the southeast, ruled by a man Aeneas had known long ago and far away: Diomedes, a Greek captain at the siege of Troy. There was little cause for love between them. Achates told me why—Aeneas himself never talked about the war with the Greeks. In combat, in the last year of the siege, Diomedes had killed Aeneas' charioteer, and while Aeneas stood over the body to save it from the Greek looters, Diomedes brought him down with the throw of a great stone, hitting him in the hip joint, bringing him to his knees. Diomedes' sword was raised for the death stroke, when Aeneas threw dust up into his eyes and got away—an escape so unexpected it was uncanny, and added a good deal to Aeneas' reputation as a fighter. Diomedes, furious, went looking for him through the battle. When he finally found him, lamed, he rushed at him to kill him, but the great fighter Hector came to Aeneas' defense, bringing the whole Trojan line back into battle around him.

Achates told me this story when we were discussing the Greeks and their colonies. I told him in turn how Diomedes had refused to join Turnus' alliance, warning Turnus to beware of Aeneas, for he was under the protection of great powers. Achates nodded and said, "A wise man, Diomedes. Wiser than he was, anyhow. He used to be a great brawler. He'd take on god or man . . . I wouldn't mind seeing him again, after all these years."

And not long after we returned from Pallanteum, an envoy arrived from Arpi with a gift of ten fine mares and a proposal from Diomedes of an alliance between his people and the Latins "under their kings Latinus and Aeneas."

Latinus was entirely in favor. He said, "Go on. Go on down there and seal a treaty with the man. That puts the Rutulians and Volscians between him and us. In the nutcracker."

"There's a saying," Aeneas said: "Keep an eye on Greeks when they offer gifts." He spoke wryly. "Horses, particularly."

"I'll keep the horses, then," my father said. "You go make the speeches." He was in a mellow mood, that summer; his health had improved and he had come to Lavinium several times, to do worship at the altar of his grandson, as he said.

Aeneas did not take me down to Arpi with him. It was a long way through unsafe country, and he was not sure if he could trust Diomedes. I worried about him while he was gone, but not very much. It was only the second summer. It was not time to worry, yet.

He and his well-armed troop of companions came back safe and sound after twenty days. He said he and Diomedes had a good talk and fought the whole Trojan war over. They had sealed a treaty of peace and assistance at the altar with the sacrifice of ten boars, ten oxen, and ten rams, for Diomedes was rich.

On the way home, the last night out, Aeneas spent the night at the Alban Mountain. "That's a sacred place if I ever saw one," he said. "It made me think of Mount Ida. But nobody lives there."

"It is sacred. Father's been there for the winter solstice, when a gap in the rim of the crater points to the sun. And when there's drought, or rain out of season, or if lightning strikes somebody dead, people go to Alba to pray and worship. I don't know why it's empty. Maybe the land's not good."

"There's a village up by the lake, they said, but there ought to be a real town there. The soil is pale, though."

"It's white ash," Ascanius said. "Ash is good for vines."

Aeneas went north early in the autumn to Caere by ship, taking with him as fine a gift as we could offer Tarchon and his people for their help in the war: three white bulls, three white rams, and a pair of stallion colts with grey coats that would whiten as they aged. The horses had splendid gear of gilt leather and gilt bronze, given by my father. It was not a mighty gift for two kings to give, but it was fitting to our present status. There was no use our pretending to equal the Etruscans in wealth, or power, or the arts of living. They knew it and we knew it. They made Aeneas welcome in Caere, and he stayed over a month in Etruria, visiting Falerii and Veii, well received everywhere. He sailed home pleased with his journey.

I did not want to spoil his pleasure, but when we were in our room away from everyone else and I could speak my mind I burst out, "Oh never go away again for so long, Aeneas! I beg you! Never go away again at all!"—and to my surprise I began to cry.

Of course he soothed me and quieted me and asked what had worried me, and of course I could not tell him that only this winter and the next summer and the next winter were left to us together.

I said, "I know you have to make these journeys. But maybe you can put them off till later—when Silvius is a year or two older?— Not this year. No more traveling this year. Or even two years? And not for so long— Not for a whole month—"

It made no sense to him. How could it? He worked at it, and finally said all he could possibly say: "I won't travel unless I must, Lavinia."

I nodded, trying to repress my weeping, and hot and red with shame at my weakness and my efforts to deceive our fate.

"I cannot bear to see you cry," he said. His own eyes were full of tears.

THERE WAS ANOTHER CAUSE OF MY DISTRESS AT HIS LONG absence, which I did not mention any more than the other: Ascanius' behavior while he was gone. Aeneas had left him in charge of the household and all affairs at Lavinium, as was right. The eldest son and heir should be getting experience in taking responsibility. Understandably, Ascanius found it frightening to take on his father's authority, was anxious, and overdid it. He ruled with a heavy hand. People were ready to make every excuse for his youth, but he was uncommonly tactless even for a boy his age. He was hasty, willful, pompous; he sulked at any setback, and disdained any advice, even from Achates—especially from Achates, perhaps, because Achates was so faithful a lieutenant and friend of Aeneas. Pining for combat in order to prove himself fearless, or fearing it and therefore stumbling into it, I do not know which, Ascanius sought a quarrel wherever it could be found. In the month Aeneas had been gone, he had stirred up resentment and ill-feeling in almost every person or group he had had to deal with, done damage which would take months to repair.

Try as I might, I could not forgive Ascanius for spoiling both the peace of his father's rule and his father's peace of mind. I so much wanted Aeneas' brief reign to be a true reward for all his travails, a haven of happiness. I longed to see my son of the evening star shine out at last in tranquillity. While Aeneas was in Etruria I had thought I should tell Ascanius what I knew: that his father's life had not much longer to run. Surely if he knew that, natural piety would make him wish to spare his father trouble and grief, and his competitive spirit could control itself for a year or so. But Ascanius was so suspicious and jealous of me that I could not bring myself to trust him with that knowledge. He might even scoff at it. He tended to look down on all things Latin, including our oracles and sacred places; and I had heard him say that the best thing about the Greeks was that they knew how to keep women in their place. Though I told myself it was just a boy talking, and believed Ascanius had a good heart under all his bluffing and sulking, still I could not trust him with my knowledge. I could not trust him not to use it against Aeneas, in anger, or as a show of power.

Ascanius and I kept out of each other's way as best we could.

Aware, now, that his wife and his son did not get along, Aeneas was careful not to put either of us in a false position with the other. Though people often confuse it with weakness or duplicity, tact is a great quality in a ruler, whether of a country or a household; awareness of the other allows respect, and people respond to it, returning the recognition and the respect. Aeneas governed with tact, and was beloved for it.

He had to exercise it actively that winter and spring, mending fences with landowners and tribesmen and neighboring peoples whom Ascanius had offended—including my father. Rebellious as Ascanius might be, his pride in his ancestry and father was as naive as a child's, and he simply could not accept the doddering old chieftain of a province on the far western edge of the world as an equal, let alone as his king. During Aeneas' absence he had dismissed a messenger from Latinus without answer and had issued orders contrary to Latinus' orders. My father said nothing at the time, but spoke to Aeneas after his return. He suggested—Latinus had a good deal of tact, himself—that the boy be given a domain to rule, away from both Laurentum and Lavinium. (My father called Ascanius the boy, and greeted him as son of Aeneas; whereas he called his grandson Silvius, and greeted him as little king. His tact did not prevent him from being very stubborn.)

Aeneas acted promptly on the suggestion. He offered Ascanius the governorship of the region of the Alban Hills, Lake Albanus, the village of Alba Longa, and the old city of Velitrae. He told him that his job there was to keep the peace with restless neighbors, so that the religious festivals of Mount Alba, to which people came from all over south Italy, could be held in safety, and to see to the improvement of agriculture and the training of a loyal body of farmer soldiers in the service of the Latin kings. He told me he had been blunt with his son, warning him that if he stirred up trouble instead of preventing it, he would be summoned back to Lavinium and deprived of command.

Ascanius went off with his bosom friend Atys, and a tiny army, all mounted on good horses and well armed, helmet plumes nodding, proud and handsome. He stayed in Alba Longa, and sent satisfactory reports to his father. The experiment appeared to be successful.

It was a great relief to me to have him gone. I would have Aeneas to myself and unworried by his son, all the rest of the summer, the autumn, the winter. I did not think about the spring. Spring would come. Janus would open the gates and Mars would bring it in as ever. I need not think about it.

Cattle rustlers and bands of brigands, poor men from Rutulia and the hill country east of Latium, were a perpetual threat to outlying farms; the Aequians and Sabines, who lived up the Tiber and its tributary the Allia, harassed Evander's settlement and sometimes sailed down the father river in their war canoes, hoping to raid the salt beds, so that Aeneas had manned ships anchored at his old camp at Venticula to chase them off. But these were no more than the troubles my father had always had, and Latium was as much at peace again as when I was a child. Aeneas could give his mind to building and farming and flocks and herds, to hunting, which he loved as his son did, and to the ever-recurring rituals, which he loved as I did.

We who are called royal are those who speak for our people to the powers of the earth and sky, as those powers transmit their will through us to the people. We are go-betweens. The chief duty of a king is to perform the rites of praise and placation as they should be performed, to observe care and ceremony and so understand and make known the will of the powers that are greater than we are. It is the king who tells the farmer when to plow, when to plant, when to harvest, when the cattle should go up to the hills and when they should return to the valleys, as he learns these things from his experience and his service at the altars of earth and sky. In the same way it is the mother of the family who tells her household when to rise, what work to do, what food to prepare and cook, and when to sit to eat it, having learned these things from her experience and her service at the altars of her Lares and Penates. So peace is maintained and things go well, in the kingdom and in the house. Both Aeneas and I had grown up in this responsibility, and it was dear to us both.

He and Latinus divided their royal duties harmoniously, the younger man always deferring to the old man but ready to take the burden from him if he tired. Not all our Latin customs were familiar to Aeneas the Trojan, but he took up our rituals as if born to them and performed them with a ready grace. I remember him as he led the Ambarvalia, that spring, the bright spring.

Every farmer was doing the same rite on his own land, leading his own household through the ceremony; Latinus would be going to his land under the walls of Laurentum while Aeneas led the procession down from Lavinium to the royal fields. During the days before, we had done a good deal of work in the house to prepare, washing the white clothes everybody wore—they must be washed in running water, which meant a lot of trips down to the river—and gathering good herbs, lucky herbs, and weaving them into garlands for both people and animals. Everyone who participated was supposed to refrain from sex the night before and come to the ceremony chaste.

The silence was what I had always loved best about Ambarvalia. Nobody spoke. People, like animals, walked saying nothing. It wasn't actually a requirement, but because any word spoken would carry unearthly weight, and a word said amiss might bring disaster

to the crops and beasts, it was easier and better not to speak at all.
Only the king and his assistants in the ceremony spoke "with the
lucky tongue," almost inaudibly repeating the litanies which old
Ferox lined out for them a few words at a time, his voice soft and
expressionless. Ferox had farmed this piece of land long before
we built Lavinium near it; he had known the litanies and led the
circumambulation of the fields for sixty years. He was the true lord
of the rites.

Aeneas followed him, leading a white lamb wreathed about with
the leaves of fruit trees and wild olive, and we all followed after,
clear around the field three times, from boundary stone to boundary stone, facing Janus and turning our backs on him as he faced
and turned his back on us. We walked in silence, so that we heard
the sound of our garments, and our bare feet on the plowland, and
our breathing, and the birds singing the spring in, up in the oak
groves.

Then Aeneas led the lamb to the old stone altar topped with a
fresh turf of grass, and made the sacrifice. You can tell a great deal
about a man from how he performs sacrifice. Aeneas' hands on the
leggy ram-lamb were calm and gentle, his knife stroke sudden and
sure; the lamb went down softly on its knees and then its side as if
it were lying down to sleep, dead before it could be frightened.

During the sacrifice old Ferox prayed aloud, telling the spirits
of the place that as we now with our gift of life increased their
numen, their power itself, so we asked them to give us increase and
keep harm from the planted fields. And then, with other old men,
loud and harsh, he sang the Arval Song:

> *Be with us, Lares, help us!*
> *Let no harm come,*
> *no harm come, Mars!*

Mars of the Wild, eat your fill,
eat your fill, Mars, leap on the boundary stone,
eat your fill, Mars, stand on the boundary stone,
call the Interceders to plead for us!
Be with us, Mars!
Dance now, dance now, dance now, dance now, dance!

So we had drawn the silent circle of protection around the fields, and prayed to the implacable power of the place and season, and now came the dancing, and the feasting, and the carols and love songs.

Of that song Ferox and the old men sang, Aeneas told me he had never heard anything like it, nor had he known the Mars we know. The Mars of his people was a bringer of war and disorder only, not a guardian of the herds and flocks, not the power that holds the thin boundary between the tame and the wild. He asked the old men about the song and about Mars, and I know he pondered over what they said.

He had not known the song in far-off Troy, but my poet had known it in far-off Mantua, across the mountains, in the dark of time to come, hundreds of years after I first heard it sung. That night in Albunea when we talked about our households and our ways, I asked the poet if his people kept Ambarvalia, and he smiled at me and sang, to the tune that was ancient even when I knew it, *Enos Lases iuvate!*—Be with us, Lares, help us.

MARS' TIME IS THE SEASON OF THE FARMER AND THE WARRIOR: spring and summer. In October the lances and shields of the Leapers are put away. War ends as the harvest comes home. That year Latinus held the October Horse ceremony, the only time we sacrifice a horse except at the funeral of a king. People came from all over Latium for it, grateful for the peace of the realm and the excellence of the harvest. It was the last great ceremony held at Laurentum.

We went there to stay several days, and Aeneas assisted my father in the rites. I could no longer do so, since my marriage, for I was not the daughter of his household any longer, being the mother of my own. But little Silvius, Latinus' heir, was allowed to take the plate of sacred food from the table to the hearth after dinner and cast the food into the Vestal fire. Maruna's mother went with him and prevented him from dropping the plate as well as the food into the fire. "Only the beans, Silvius," she whispered, and he, very solemn, said, "Ony bees." He was supposed to say, "The gods are favorable," but we said it for him.

That was a good autumn, rich and mild, and the winter rains were long and soft. In the press of daily occupation and obligation, and the continual delights and anxieties of caring for Silvius, and the unfailing joy and pleasure of Aeneas' companionship and love, I lost track of the passage of the days; they were all one day and long, blessed night. But once in a while I would wake for no reason deep in the winter darkness, my body and soul as cold as the ice on the river's edge, thinking: This is the third winter.

Then I would lie awake and my mind would gnaw and gnaw at the puzzle I could not solve. The poet had told me that Aeneas would rule for three summers and three winters. Was the summer we married the first of the three summers? I thought that because it was half gone before he came to rule in Lavinium, the count of three summers and three winters should begin with the winter of that year, and the summer that lay before us now would be his third—his third and last. But at least he would have till the sum-mer—through the summer—he would not die this spring!

But why must he die? Perhaps the poet had not meant that at all. The poet had not said he would die, only that his reign would be three years. Perhaps he would give up the kingship, give it to Ascanius, and live on, a long life, a happy life, the life he deserved. Why had I not thought of that before?

The idea filled my mind and dazzled me so I could sleep no more; and in the morning when he woke I could scarcely keep myself from bursting out to him, "Give your kingdom to your son, Aeneas!"

I had sense enough not to do that, but in a day or two I did ask, trying to speak lightly, if he had ever thought of laying his rule aside and living as an ordinary man.

He looked at me quickly, a flash of his dark eyes. "That choice wasn't offered me," he said. "Priam's nephew, Anchises' son."

"But now you're in a land where your fathers are less important than your sons, perhaps."

"If I grant that," he said after considering it, "what then? I was sent here to be king. Hector came from his grave, Creusa rose from her death, to tell me what I had to do. I was to take my people to the western land, and rule. And marry there, and have a son . . . You can't say I don't do my duty, Lavinia." He had spoken somberly at first, but he ended with a half-suppressed smile.

"No one would ever say that of you! But you *have* done it— you carried out the prophecy—you fulfilled your destiny—hard as it was, voyaging over sea, the storms, and shipwrecks, and losing friends, and having to fight a war when you finally got here— And you have reigned, and founded your dynasty. Do you never think of saying: Now I've done that, now let me stand aside—let me rest a while, now I've come to harbor?"

He gazed at me for some time, a direct, mild, thoughtful gaze. He was thinking why I said what I had said, and finding no answer. "Silvius is still rather short to stand aside for," he said finally.

It made me laugh. I was very tense. "Yes, he is. But Ascanius—"

"You want Ascanius to rule Lavinium?" He was surprised into sternness for a moment, then his expression changed, became tender; he thought he knew why I was asking him to step down. "Lavinia, dear wife, you mustn't fear for me so much. It's less dangerous to be the king than to be a common soldier. Anyway, the day of our death isn't in our hands. There is no safe place. You know that."

"Yes, I know that."

He came to hold and comfort me, and I held him close.

"Truly," he asked, "you'd give up being queen, to spare me the trouble of being king?" I had not in fact actually thought about that aspect of my plan. He went on, "Who would take your place? We'd have to get Ascanius married off." He was teasing me, by now. He knew that the idea of handing over my people and my Penates to a strange woman would be dreadful to me. I was distressed and ashamed, feeling I had been caught in a lying trick, a stupid ruse. I could not speak, but blushed the way I do, turning red all over. He saw and felt that and kissed me, gently at first, but with arousing passion. We were in the small courtyard of our house, no one about. "Come on, come!" he said, and still red as fire I followed him into our bedroom, where the conversation took a different form.

But after that day I was never able to put the poet's words wholly out of mind. They were always in my thoughts, underneath my thoughts, like the dark streams that run underground. There must be some way in which the words did not mean that Aeneas was to die after three summers and winters as king in Latium, but meant only that his rule would end. Maybe he would conquer a neighboring country and rule as king of the Volscians or the Hernici. Maybe

he would take me and Silvius back to his own country, and rebuild
the beautiful city of Ilium that Achates and Serestus told me about,
with its walls and towers and high citadel, and rule there as king of
Troy. Maybe he would not die, only be very ill, weakened by illness,
so that Ascanius must come and take on the active role of kingship
for him, and be called king—but Aeneas would live on with me in
Lavinium, and have joy in his son and in his life—he would live, he
would not die. So my mind ran from possibility to possibility like
a hare dodging hounds, while the three old women, the Fates, spun
out the measured thread of what was to be.

THE WINTER WAS MILD BUT LONG. JANUARY WAS ALL RAIN
and mud. A portent occurred in Laurentum: the doors of the
War Gate, which my mother had opened and I and Maruna and the
men of the city had closed, three years ago, swung open of themselves. People came to Janus' altar in the morning of the Kalends
of February and found the gates hanging ajar. The bolts of the iron
hasps that held in place the great locking beam had rusted through,
so that the hasps gave way and let the beam drop. The hinges also
were rusted and askew, so that the gates could not be closed. Latinus was gravely troubled by the omen. He did not think it right
to interfere, to repair the hinges and the hasps, until the meaning
of the event became clear. No one knew why they had been made
of iron, the unlucky metal, never used in sacred places. He had his
smiths make new hasps and bolts and hinges of bronze, but he did
not mend or close the War Gate yet.

Troubling news was coming in from east and south of the
Alban Hills. Farmers and villagers along the border reported am-
bushes, barn burning, cattle thieving, and harassment, carried on

by both sides, Latin and Rutulian. And young Camers of Ardea, who had led the inept attack on our city two years before, sent to us to complain that his city was being threatened and its farms and pastures constantly raided, by men from Alba Longa.

I watched Aeneas master his bitter, disappointed anger. He was like a man mounted on a powerful horse that fights the reins and plunges, nose to feet, and kicks, twisting its body, and finally is brought to stand white with sweat, shaking, ready to obey.

My heart felt as if it was being squeezed in a fist of fear; but now that the time had come, my empty imaginings of escape all died away and left me to face what there was no escaping. When he said, "I must go down to Ardea," I made no protest and tried to show no undue fear. He went fully armed and with a strong escort. He was not taking any unnecessary risks, only necessary ones. I kissed him good-bye and held up Silvius for his kiss, and smiled, and bade him come home soon.

"I will come home soon," he said. "With Ascanius."

My best friends among Aeneas' friends, Achates and Serestus, had ridden away with him; I was left with my women. They were of great comfort to me. They helped me keep everything in the household and the city running on as it should. Serestus' wife Illivia had just had a baby, and we could forget our worries playing with him. My father sent a man down daily to ask if we had news and if we needed advice or help. He did not come himself, for he had been troubled with a cough all winter, and the weather was foul, with hard rains and the ways deep in mud. Nor did I go to him, for I was needed in my city.

Those were nine long, dark days and nights.

At evening of the day after the Ides of February, a troop of wet men on wet horses tramped up out of the rainy dusk to the city gate. The guardsmen cried out, "The king! King Aeneas comes!" He rode in, his sword on his hip and the great shield on his shoulder. Behind him rode Ascanius, unarmed; then Aeneas' men, all armed.

My relief and joy at seeing him, embracing him, was so great it set all else aside. I felt that night that to have known such fulfillment was to be, in some part of my being, forever safe from absolute despair, from the ruin of the soul. Joy my shield.

I do not know if that is true, but I would not deny it, even later, even now.

Everything was bustle at first, getting baths and food for the tired men. Aeneas had time to tell me that he had patched up a month's truce with Camers and brought Ascanius back "to talk about what went wrong." Serestus and Mnestheus were left in charge of Alba Longa and the restive borderlands.

Ascanius had indeed caused most of the trouble, by claiming as Latin ground certain winter pastures used by the Rutulians, and putting settlers in a stream valley the Rutulians considered their summer pasture, and sending his soldiers to harass any Rutulians who crossed the border. Since the border was a vague one in many places, and traditionally porous, these were sure means of rousing bad feeling. Camers' attempts to protect Rutulian farmers by sending out armed men had resulted in some bloody skirmishes and much menacing talk from Ascanius about leveling the walls of Ardea, to which Camers responded by threatening to annex Velitrae and obliterate Alba Longa.

Achates told me about the meeting with Camers. He praised Aeneas' peacemaking skill, which as he described it consisted in saying almost nothing. Camers had wanted to come round, but could not admit it. His failed attack had left him sore, chastened, ready to let well enough alone; but Ascanius had been making boasts and threats which he would not endure. Aeneas listened patiently to a long list of offenses, without either apologising for them or justifying them, before he could even suggest a truce. Achates said he had been so patient and so firm that Camers, who was not much older than Ascanius, ended up talking to him, the man who had killed Camers' father in the battle before Laurentum, as to a father.

So the truce was made, and made in good faith, though both Achates and Aeneas thought that Camers would have a problem controlling the rough farmers of his borderlands. Aeneas' problem, evidently, was how to control his son.

Although Ascanius had been brought back in apparent disgrace, nothing was said of it that night: he was made welcome at the impromptu feast we set out for the homecomers. He showed neither shame nor defiance, but behaved much as usual. He had been very well trained in manners, and they stood him in good stead at a time like this. He must have been puzzling over the question of what Aeneas was finally going to say or do. So was I. But the evening went off cheerily enough, and father and son embraced as they used to at parting for the night.

And the question continued unanswered. Aeneas had done what he had said he'd do: deprive Ascanius of command and bring him back to Lavinium. And that was all. He said nothing. He was not a man to waste words. He did, and let be. He spoke when he had to.

Ascanius stewed quite a while, fretted, sulked, and once or twice tried to bring the situation to a head. Aeneas evaded his attempts. The nearest he would come to discussing Ascanius' position was through a kind of running conversation they had about virtue. Manly virtue, that is, in the original sense of the word—manliness itself, manhood. Ascanius said one day, with his youthful pompousness, that the only true proof of manhood was in battle: true virtue was skill in fighting, courage to fight, will to win, and victory. Aeneas said, "Victory?"

"What's the use of skill and courage if you're dead?"

"Hector had no virtue?"

"Of course he did. He won all his battles, till the last one."

"We all do," Aeneas remarked.

That was a little beyond Ascanius, perhaps, and the subject was dropped; but Aeneas brought it up again soon, at dinner one day.

"So a man can prove his manhood only in war," he said meditatively.

"A certain kind of manhood," Achates suggested. "Surely wisdom is as much a virtue as battle prowess?"

"But perhaps one that isn't limited to men," I said.

I will say here that the Trojans had not been used to including women in conversation, nor were any Greeks I ever met. For men and women to sit together at table and speak as equals was our Latin custom, which I think we may have learned from the Etruscans. As queen, I could have my way in such matters. Some of the rougher Trojans needed a lesson in respect, in table manners, which they got both from Aeneas and from me. But others like Achates and Serestus took to this as to our other customs without any trouble. When I invited them to the Regia, their wives came with them and sat with us above the salt, and often I invited the women to come when their husbands were away.

"Indeed. Women can gain wisdom," Ascanius announced, with his irritating, touching pomposity. "But not true virtue."

"But what is piety?" Aeneas asked.

That brought a thoughtful silence.

"Obedience to the will of the powers of earth and sky?" I said at last, making my statement a question, as women so often do.

"The effort to fulfill one's destiny," Achates said.

"Doing right," said Illivia, Serestus' wife, a calm, forceful woman from Tusculum, who had become one of my dearest friends.

"What is right in battle, in war?" Aeneas asked.

"Skill, courage, strength," Ascanius answered promptly. "In war, virtue is piety. Fighting to win!"

"So victory makes right?"

"Yes," Ascanius said, and several of the men nodded vigorously; but the older Trojans, some of them, did not. Nor did the women.

"I cannot make it out," Aeneas said in his quiet voice. "I thought what a man knew he ought to do was what he must do. But what if they're not the same? Then, to win a victory is to be defeated. To uphold order is to cause disorder, ruin, death. Virtue and piety destroy each other. I cannot make it out."

Even Ascanius had no answer for that.

I doubt if anyone there knew what was on Aeneas' mind, when he said that to obey one's fate might be to disobey one's conscience. Only I could know how the death of Turnus weighed on his soul. I know Achates thought he was speaking of the Greek victory over Troy in a war which, though they might be justified in waging it, brought almost as much ruin on the Greeks as on the Trojans. Perhaps he was.

At any rate, he did not let Ascanius' definition of manhood as battle courage rest. He returned to the discussion next day. We had no visitors, and the three of us had gathered around the hearth after the day's work was done, I with my distaff, Aeneas with a little whetstone and my small ritual knife, which had grown dull. He drew it lightly and patiently across the stone. "If a man believes his virtue can be proved only in war," he said to Ascanius, "then he sees time spent on anything else as wasted. Farming, if he's a farmer—government, if he's a ruler—worship, the acts of religion—all inferior to prowess in war."

"Yes, just so!" Ascanius said, pleased, thinking he had convinced his father.

"I would not trust that man to farm, or govern, or serve the powers that rule us," Aeneas said. "Because whatever he was doing, he'd seek to make war."

Ascanius got the drift now, and recoiled uneasily. "Not necessarily—," he began.

"Necessarily," Aeneas said, with grim finality. "I spent my life among such men, Ascanius. I proved my virtue among them."

"Yes, you did, father! You were the best, the best among them all!" There were tears in Ascanius' eyes and his voice trembled.

"Except for Hector," Aeneas said. "And on the other side, Achilles, the great hero, and Diomedes, who both defeated me. I would probably have lost to Odysseus, big Ajax, maybe Agamemnon. I think I could have beaten Menelaus. And what if I had? Would I be a better man for it? Would my virtue be greater than it is? Am I who I am because I killed men? Am I Aeneas because I killed Turnus?"

He was leaning forward; the firelight gleamed in his eyes; he did not raise his voice but spoke with terrible intensity. Ascanius cowered back from him, catching his breath.

"If you are to rule Latium after me, and pass it to your brother Silvius, I want to know that you'll learn how to govern, not merely make war, that you'll learn to ask the powers of earth and sky for guidance for yourself and your people, that you'll learn to seek your manhood on a greater field than the battlefield. Tell me that you will learn those things, Ascanius."

"I will, father," the young man said, in tears.

"Much depended on me," Aeneas said, more gently. "Much will depend on you. In the end, I did ill. You have begun ill, but I count on you to do well in the end. So, give me your hand on it, son."

Ascanius put out his hand, and Aeneas drew him into an embrace; they clung hard to each other.

I sat with my distaff, my face turned to the fire. I could not weep.

A FEW DAYS LATER, JUST BEFORE THE MARCH KALENDS, AENEAS sent Ascanius back to the Alban Hills. He said nothing about honoring the truce with Camers; there was no use saying more; he could only hope. He looked a little grim, those early days of March, when the Leapers were in the streets shaking the sacred spears and singing *Mars, Mavors, macte esto!* But Serestus and Mnestheus came back from Alba Longa reporting that everything was quiet and that Ascanius seemed resolved to keep it so.

It was a warm spring, after the wet winter. Everything was early to bloom and bear. The walnut trees in the forests were beautiful in their quick flowering. Barley and millet came up tall, with heavy heads, and the grass was as thick and tender in the meadows and on the hillsides as I ever saw it. Our flocks and herds had a good increase, and Aeneas was particularly pleased with the crop of new foals in our stables. He had bred a very fine mare to the stallion Latinus gave him, and the bright chestnut colt she bore was his pride. "He'll be Silvius' horse," he said. And he introduced the boy child and the horse child quite solemnly. He let Silvius lead the mare about and see how the colt followed her, and finally set him up on her back for a ride. Silvius was transfixed with terror and delight, clutching the mare's mane with one hand and his father's hand with the other, and making a soft noise, "oo! oo!" like a pigeon as they paraded round the stable yard. After that every morning he would ask his father, timidly, "Wide?" And Aeneas would go with him to the stables for his ride.

Our people, my Latins of Lavinium, called Aeneas father. "Will that fence do, Father Aeneas?"— "Father, the barley's in!"— They spoke to Latinus the same way, and young as I was, I was Mother Lavinia, for we use the words not only for our parents but for those who take responsibility for us. Often a soldier calls his captain his father, and rightly, too, if the captain looks after his men as he should. But Aeneas' people used the word to him in a particularly affectionate way, caressingly, claiming him. The duty that had been laid on him to lead his people had isolated him as their leader; after his father's death he had had to make the decisions alone, take responsibility alone; so this bond of affection meant a great deal to him. He tried to deserve it. He took his actual fatherhood with the same seriousness and deep pleasure. It was beautiful to see him walk with Silvius, shortening his stride to the child's, ever careful of the child's dignity.

I knew he had greatly honored his own father. He never spoke of his mother and I do not know if he ever knew her. It was with some caution that I asked him about his own early childhood.

"I don't remember much," he said. "I was with women, in the woods, on the mountain. A group of women living in the forest."

"Were they kind to you?"

"Kind, careless. They let me run about . . . I'd get into trouble, and one of them would come and laugh and scoop me up. I was wild as a bear cub."

"Then your father came for you?"

He nodded. "A lame man. In armor. I was afraid of him. I remember I tried to hide in the thickets. But the women knew my hiding places. They scooped me up again and handed me over to him."

"So after that you lived with him?"

"And learned farming and manners and all that."

"When did you go to Troy?"

"Priam had us come, sometimes. He never liked us."

"He gave you his daughter," I said, surprised.

"He didn't exactly give her," Aeneas answered, but he did not want to say any more about Creusa, and I did not press him. After a little while he said, "It's a good place for a child, the woods. You don't learn much about people, but you learn silence. Patience. And that there's nothing much to fear in the wilderness—less than there is on a farm or in the city."

I thought of Albunea, that fearful place where I had never been afraid. I almost asked him to come there with me, but I did not. Though it was so nearby, I had not been there since our marriage. I wanted to go and yet it did not seem the time. I found I could not imagine being there with him. So I said nothing of it.

The weather was so mild in late March that we went over to the coast, a walk of a couple of miles. I wanted Silvius to have a first sight of the ocean. Aeneas carried him perched on his shoulder most of the way. We were a large group winding through the dunes, slaves carrying picnic food, several families, a few extra young men as guards. Everybody, slave and free, children and grown, scattered out on the pale yellow beach as soon as we got there, wading, gathering shells, enjoying the sunlight. Aeneas and I wandered off from the others, leaving Silvius with a group of adoring women and Maruna to keep them from spoiling him. We walked a long way down the shore. I could seldom get out to walk as I used to these days, and it was a wonderful pleasure to step out barefoot on the sand, splashing through the small streams that ran down to the sea, keeping pace with my husband's even, untiring stride. The sea made its emotionless lament to our right. Looking out over the low breakers to the wave glitter that dissolved in the mist of the horizon, I said, "How far you came! Across that sea—the other seas—years, miles."

"How far I came to come home," he said.

After a while I said, though until the moment I said it I had not been perfectly certain of it, "Aeneas, I'm carrying a child."

He walked on for a while, a smile slowly spreading over his face, then stopped, and stopped me by taking my hands, and took me in a close embrace. "A girl?" he said, as if I would know, and I rashly answered, "A girl."

"All I want you give me," he said, hugging the breath nearly out of me, kissing my face and neck. "Dark one, dear one, wife, girl, queen, my Italian, my love." There were some rocks running down from inland that would hide us from anyone coming down the shore, and we tugged each other towards them. In their shelter we made love, rather hastily and with a good deal of laughter at first because of sand where it was not wanted, but with a rising wild passion, so that at the height of it I felt that he had made me one with the sea and its tides and its deeps. When we came back to the world he lay there on the sand by me, and he was so beautiful I could not look away from him. I touched his breast and arms and face softly with my fingertips, and he lay half asleep in the sunlight, smiling.

We got up and walked out into the water, waist deep, hand in hand, till the cold struck through and the tug of the waves began to take us off our feet. "Let's go on, let's go on," I said, but I was frightened, too. Aeneas suddenly swung me round, half carrying me back to the shore. Then we wandered back to the others. Silvius had fallen asleep under a little awning the women had made out of scarves. There was sand in his small, arched eyebrows, and his

face in the pale radiance under the white cloths was very serious. I
lay down by him and whispered his name to him, the name I called
him secretly, "Aeneas Silvius, Aeneas Silvius."

I cannot tell any more of our happiness.

Early in April Aeneas went down to Alba Longa overnight, and
reported that all was well there. Late in April my father came to
visit us for some days. May came. The day came that I was at the
mouth of Tiber three years ago at dawn and saw the dark ships turn
and come up the river one by one.

That day Aeneas went, with Achates and our chief herdsman
and four or five young men, looking for a small herd of our cattle
that had escaped their pasture east of town, crossed the Numicus
at the ford, and were thought to be wandering down towards Troia.
These were our finest cows and heifers and we did not want them
scattered or lost. The men found the herd and drove them back
to the river. A group of men from Rutulia had stolen the cattle,
or perhaps was following them to steal them. These men attacked
Aeneas and the others while they were at the ford of the Numicus.
They were armed with spears and staves. Several of Aeneas' men
had weapons, and though outnumbered, fought back fiercely, killing two of the outlaws at once. The Rutulians fell back and ran,
all but a young man whom Aeneas had pinned down, his sword
at the man's throat. The young man begged, "Don't kill me, don't
kill me!" Aeneas hesitated, then turned his sword aside and said,
"Go on." The young man struggled up and ran off. He stopped
and picked up a spear another man had dropped. He turned and
threw it. It hit Aeneas in the back and went through his chest. He
fell to his knees and then facedown in the shallow water of the
ford. He did not die at once, but he was dead when they carried
him into Lavinium, into the Regia, into the courtyard, where I was
looking through our new cloth, the winter's weaving, that had been

bleaching on the grass outside the walls. I had picked out a fine piece as a toga for him. Unaccustomed to wearing the toga, he often found it cumbersome. I was folding the light, soft, pure white cloth when I heard them calling out his name and mine.

Go on, go. In our tongue it is a single sound, *i.*

It is the last word Aeneas said. So in my mind it is spoken to me, said to me. I am the one to go, to go on. Go where?

I do not know. I hear him say it, and I go. On, away. On the way. The way to go. When I stop I hear him say it, his voice, Go on.

IN LAVINIUM ALL THAT NIGHT THEY CRIED HIS NAME ALOUD, calling him father, lamenting in the streets.

Achates, Serestus, Mnestheus gathered the men of Troy at first dawn and rode to Ardea, scouring the countryside on the way: they did not find the cattle thieves, but Camers of Ardea knew who they were and where to look for them. He rode with the Trojans. They rode the men down and killed them all. They were farmers' sons from northern Rutulia, led by a couple of Etruscans who had come with Mezentius to Ardea, bitter, leaderless men living in exile.

I had sent a rider on our best horse, Aeneas' horse, to Ascanius in Alba Longa. Ascanius arrived in Lavinium on the second day, and late that day the Trojans came back. Our house that had been full of weeping women was full now of grim, armed men.

I did not let them put armor on Aeneas. All that gear of bronze and gold and the great shield that held the fearful future should go to Ascanius and then to Silvius. I washed his body, noble and terrible in death, scar-seamed. I clothed him in the toga of our people, the fine white one I had chosen for him.

When many die, as in plague or war, we burn the dead, but our older way is burial under earth. I ordered that Aeneas' grave be beside the road above the ford of the Numicus. There he was carried, the torches flaring and smoking in the rainy wind of a May morning. Latinus spoke the ritual words. Men heaped up the river rocks into a great barrow over the grave. When all was done I stood and called his name aloud three times, *Aeneas! Aeneas! Aeneas!* And the other people called his name with me. Then in silence, carrying the dead torches upside down, we walked back to his city.

On the ninth day after his death, Latinus performed the sacrifice of kings, killing the beautiful stallion he had given Aeneas by the tomb of rocks. The horse was buried by the tomb.

On that day also he named Ascanius king of Latium, to share the rule with him as Aeneas had. It was necessary that Latinus lend this succession all the weight of his authority, and that I too demand that my people recognise Ascanius as king: for they did not want him. He had antagonised them from the beginning. It was he who shot Silvia's deer. They never forgot that. He had been arrogant, quarrelsome, aloof, seeming much more a foreigner than his father. My people in Lavinium wanted Latinus to rule them, wanted me there in the Regia, bringing up Silvius, their little one, their prince, their king to be. They stood sullen, with tear-streaked faces, while Latinus proclaimed Ascanius king.

In the days of mourning Ascanius had for the first time appealed to me for support; he found I could give it to him, and he came to me to weep. During the ceremonies he looked and acted what he was, a boy overwhelmed by grief, dismayed, distressed, terrified by the responsibility he must bear. Accepting the kingship and making his vows to the people and the land, he spoke in a barely audible voice, trembling. At one point I had to say to him softly, "King of the Latins, hold up your head!" He obeyed.

I do not know what the strength was that carried me through that time. I suppose I am one of my people, made of oak. Oaks don't bend, though they can break. And I had known what was coming. I had lived with Aeneas' death a long time, from the time I first saw his face, high on the ship's prow, dark in the twilight of morning, gazing up the river in prayer and eager hope. Three years, the poet had said. Three years to the day it was. The three old women who spin and cut the thread had measured exactly, to the inch, nothing to spare. No gift of summer days.

IN THAT FIRST YEAR OF AENEAS' DEATH HIS CAPTAINS AND OLD companions, particularly Achates, were my mainstay. Though my dear Maruna, the women of the household, and friends such as Illivia gave me most generous, loving sympathy and support, I wanted most of all to be with Aeneas' friends, because it was a little like being with him. It was the tone of the male voice, the way they moved, what they talked about, even the Trojan accent, that comforted me. Among them he did not seem so far from me.

Achates had loved him—I will say this, though my heart resists—as much as I loved him, and for years longer. I am sure Achates came very near suicide that summer. He blamed himself for the incident at the ford: he should have insisted they wear cuirasses, he should have been closer to Aeneas during the fighting, he should not have let Aeneas release the young man, should have followed the young man and kept an eye on him, should have seen the weapon lying on the ground—everything that he could blame himself for, he did.

It was Achates who had first told me, when they brought Aeneas home, what happened at the ford. Now I found that by letting him tell it over, he could talk out some of his shame and rage, and strange as it may seem I wanted to hear it again, to hear it told over and over, till I could see it as if I had been there, as if I were Achates, as if I had knelt by Aeneas, had pulled the terrible blade out of his back, and held him in my arms, and watched his blood color the shallow water that ran among the rocks. "He was not dead. He held on to me, but I don't think he saw me," Achates said. "He was looking up at the sky. When we picked him up to lay him on the litter, he closed his eyes. He never spoke." He never spoke, but he was not dead, then. So long as Achates told me the story, Aeneas was not dead.

Ascanius, almost distraught with his new responsibilities, was at first jealous of my being with the Trojan captains: they were his men, not mine, he needed them for advice and to do his bidding, and they had no business loitering around the Regia with women. He ordered Achates to go up to Alba Longa and govern there. Achates accepted his order without a word, but I was afraid for him. I went privately to my stepson and asked him to send Mnestheus or Serestus, who knew the settlement better and would have no objection to leaving Lavinium. "Let Achates stay here, at least till next year," I said. "He goes daily to Aeneas' tomb. Let his grief heal. He has no heart to go to Alba Longa."

"You want him here with you?" Ascanius asked, drily.

I have noticed that some men whose sexual interest is in men not women believe that all women are insatiably lustful of men. I don't know whether this is a reflection of their own desires, or fear, or mere jealousy, but it fosters a good deal of contempt and misunderstanding. Ascanius tended to look at women that way, and his ardent wish to keep Aeneas' memory unsullied led him to suspect me with every man. I knew that already. It outraged my honor and disposed me to feel some contempt in return for Ascanius, but neither anger nor scorn would do me any good. I said, "I wish I could keep all Aeneas' friends, and his elder son, here with me. But I've been afraid Achates may take his own life in his grief. I beg you to let him stay here with you, at least through the winter, and send someone else to Alba Longa."

"I wish I could go myself," Ascanius said.

He strode up and down the room we were in; he did not look much like his father, but sometimes he moved like him.

"I meant it as an honor for Achates," he said. "The chief city of Latium is going to be Alba Longa, not Lavinium. The situation is infinitely better—higher, better land—and central to where our power will be when I finally get real control over Rutulia. I thought Achates would take it as an honor. But if he is as broken as you think, I'll send Mnestheus and Atys. So, you need not kneel, mother." For I had been ready to go down in the formal posture of supplication, holding his knees. I knew he would not have held out against that. He was not a hard young man, but kindly by nature, and easily swayed, though rigid about hierarchy, formalities, anything that supported his uncertain self-esteem.

And it was not easy for him to keep up that self-esteem here in Lavinium, where the people endlessly mourned Aeneas, honored old Latinus, loved me as daughter and widow of their kings, and resented him. Trying to emulate Aeneas' authority, he was harsh in manner and often arbitrary in judgment. It was a difficult year for him, even though the harvest was superb and all Latium remained peaceful, with little of the raiding and boundary jumping we had all feared might follow the death of a king at the hands of outlaws.

The winter was a dark one, with long, cold rain, snow up on the hills and even on the piedmont farmlands. I learned at last to weave well, that winter, for if I had no work to keep my hands and mind occupied I could do nothing but hide in my room and weep. I feared for the first time that I had my mother's weakness, her madness. At night I went into dark places in my mind. I went down underground among shadows and could not find the way up and out. In my room in the darkness I heard babies weeping underfoot. I dared not take a step lest I step on a baby.

I have not told this all in order as it happened. It is still hard to speak of. A month after Aeneas' death I lost the fetus that might have been my daughter. Only my women knew that I had been pregnant and that the pregnancy miscarried. Only my women and Aeneas knew. I went with Maruna in the dark before dawn and we buried the tiny scrap of life that had not lived, deep under the great stones of Aeneas' grave.

ASCANIUS WENT OFTEN TO ALBA LONGA, AND IN THE SECOND summer after Aeneas' death, not long after he celebrated the Parentalia for his father with all due ritual, he moved there. Trouble had flared up on our borders; he wanted to govern from Alba, a more defensible position. He took with him the Penates of Troy, and Silvius and me. He left Mnestheus and Serestus in charge of Lavinium. Achates chose to stay there, as did most of the older Trojans. The men who followed Ascanius were his particular friends and intimates among the young Trojans, such as Atys who had been his childhood sweetheart, and the group of young Latins who formed his guard and captained his forays. Many of these men were still unmarried; if they had wives they brought them and their household along to settle in Alba. I was allowed to bring twenty women as my retinue. As Ascanius had no wife, we were given all the woman's side of the Regia, a much bigger and finer house than the small one Aeneas had built in Lavinium. Ascanius' high house was imposing, and the site of it was more than imposing. It was like living in the sky. From the walls and roofs of the citadel you looked right down on the great lake and across it to the eastern wall of the crater. Farther down the mountain the young vineyards were thriving, as Ascanius had predicted, and the town that sprawled out below the citadel was thriving too, full of activity, building, the coming and going of armed men.

I felt exposed there, always; there were too many great ashen slopes, too much sky, no shade. The water of the lake did not move, did not speak, like the waters I knew, but lay silent, blue, hard. I felt isolated there. I felt useless.

I ran the household for my stepson, of course, obtained and trained slave women to do the housework and cooking and cloth making, and saw to the rites and festivals as always. I would have attended councils and dinners with the men as I had done in my father's house and my husband's, but I was not wanted there. Nor did I belong there. Mars ruled in Alba. The talk was all of war, even in the winter season when there was no fighting.

It was not that Ascanius sought to be continually in arms, but he seemed unable to avoid combat, and combat was continually offered along our southern and eastern borders. He met every threat or challenge at once with counteraggression; he followed victory with vengeance, defeat with renewed attack as soon as possible. Truce was rare, peace was gone. He provoked even old Evander to break the alliance. I think he might have been crazy enough to quarrel with the Etruscans, if my father had not prevented him. Latinus kept up a strong friendship with Caere and Veii. He let Ascanius know that if he imperiled that bond, he might have to prove his claim to co-rule western Latium. He was deeply angry with Ascanius, not least for dragging me and Silvius off to Alba.

He came once to visit us there. It was a hard trip for him, for he was an old man and lame with old wounds. He had given Aeneas and me most of his valuables; he came in what state he could, with what few were left of his companion guards, late in December. He accepted Ascanius' welcoming honors stiffly. He sat with the young men at the feast table and hardly spoke, the servants said. Whenever he could he would come sit with us in the courtyard or at the fire in the weaving hall, and talk with me, and study his grandson.

Silvius' favorite toys at the time were two big acorns and their cups and a curious litle knot of wood he had found that looked slightly like a horse. With these he was playing most intently down on the hearth, whispering a story about them under his breath. Now and then we could hear a bit of it: "Go on, drink. No. The fat one said not to . . . Look, is it a house?"

"This is a fine boy, Lavinia," my father said.

"I know," I told him, laughing at the lovably predictable.

It was good to laugh. There was little to laugh about in that house.

"You bring him up well." It was a statement, not an order, but it had a sound of command or warning in it.

"I hope to bring him up as Aeneas would."

Latinus nodded vigorously. "Right," he said. "Stay with him."

"I do, father."

"Your husband was a great warrior, but he sought peace."

I had thought myself past it, but the tears welled. I fought the sob and did not speak.

"His son might govern well enough in peace," Latinus said. "But he hasn't the patience to fight wars. Don't let him have the training of your son."

How could I prevent Ascanius from taking over Silvius' up-bringing, if he wanted to? I had no power.

"I wouldn't have come here if I could have stayed in Lavinium," I said at last, trying to keep my voice from pitiable quavering.

"I know, daughter. It was best that I not interfere."

I nodded agreement.

"But if the time comes that you must, that you know it right to go—then take your gods and your child and go! Will you?"

"I will."

I thought he was telling me to come to him, but he said, "Tarchon of Caere would take you in, and treat you with honor."

"Oh—surely it won't come to that!" I said, staring at him, shocked and startled.

"I don't know what it will come to. If *he* learns a few lessons of war and draws in his horns, all may yet be well." *He* was Ascanius. "I tried again last night to tell him to leave Evander and Pallanteum alone. The old man is dying. The Etruscans will move in when he dies and take over the Seven Hills. In peace. No reason why they should not. Except *his* impatience. Oh, I was a fool as a young man, but never fool enough to take on Etruria! The best allies we could have. How can I make him see it?"

"You can't, father."

"Oh look, oh look," came Silvius' little whisper, "they're giving him a golden bowl!"

My father watched the child with a half smile, but his eyes were sad. "Patience!" he said. "I need it as much as he does."

It was the last time I saw my father. He took cold, walking out in his crop lands in the rain, and it went to his lungs; he died a few days later, the day after the Ides of January. I ordered horses and a few men to escort me and Maruna and Sicana to Laurentum. Ascanius, busy up on our border fighting the Marsi near Tibur, knew nothing of what had happened. I did not take Silvius with me, for he had had a cough and fever for some days, and the weather was bitter with icy rain. The great laurel stood in its winter darkness over the fountain in the courtyard of my old home. The War Gate still hung open, rusted on its unlucky hinges. All the people in Laurentum seemed old; there were no young faces or voices. I stayed only long enough to bury my father by the roadway into his city. I could not stay the nine days of mourning. I had to go back to my son in the city of my exile.

ASCANIUS WAS SOLE KING OF LATIUM NOW. NOT ALL THE LATIN farmers were happy about it, but they made no protest or resistance; the pressure on our borders was insistent, and they wanted a single leader during war. And war was our lot for years to come. The Volscians and the Hernici, hoping Latinus' death had weakened the kingdom, harassed the border farms and towns constantly. Before long Camers of Ardea, who had come to see Aeneas as an ally and almost a father, took offense at Ascanius' arrogance; he began letting his Rutulians make raids and forays into Latium, and rebuilt his alliance with the Volscians. And, though it did not yet bring any increase of fighting, the Etruscans of the great inland city Veii were sending groups of farm families to colonise the Seven Hills on the Tiber. They did not occupy the little Greek settlement, but simply moved in all around it, building on both sides of the river, where Janiculum had been and up on the hill they called the Palatine, clearing the forest along the riverbanks and pasturing their fine cattle all through the valleys. Many of the younger Greeks of Pallanteum moved to Diomedes' city in Arpi, others came to settle in Alba Longa. Latium had long laid claim to the region of the Seven Hills, and all the south side of the father river as far up as Nomentum. Ascanius was bitterly irked by this quiet takeover, but he remembered Latinus' warnings and didn't defy Etruria. The Veiian colonists offered excellent terms to us for salt from our salt beds at the river mouth, and showed no sign of wanting to expand

234 Ursula K. Le Guin

further into our lands. They called the new settlement by their name for the river, Ruma.

Aeneas' shield hung in the entryway of the high house of Alba Longa. Ascanius did not wear it when he went out to war, or the greaves and gilt cuirass, the helmet with its maimed red crest, and the long bronze sword. Once he said in my hearing that these forays by farmers, these squabbles with petty barbarian kingdoms, didn't deserve such mighty weapons but should be settled with hoes and mattocks. I think the armor was too heavy for him.

I saw Silvius standing in front of the shield, looking up at it steadily. He was six or seven years old. I asked, "What do you see there, Silvius?"

He did not answer for a while and then said, in a small voice as if from far away, "I'm watching all the people in the great round place."

I stood with him and gazed. I saw the mother wolf, the burning ships, the man with the comet over his head, soldiers killing soldiers, men torturing men. I saw a splendid thing: great arches of white stone that strode down from the mountains across valleys to the city with its hills and temples. The city Rome.

I was afraid of the shield, but the child was not; the power that had made it and dwelt in it was in his blood. He put out his hand to the golden cuirass, following the curves and decorations with palm and fingers, smiling.

"You'll wear it one day," I said.

He nodded. "When I know how," he said.

Silvius had a good deal of strength, for a child. He was not boisterous, and rougher boys often mistook his quietness for meekness or timidity. If they presumed on it, they found out their mistake. He ignored verbal attacks, but he met physical bullying or threat with instant resistance and retaliation: hit, he hit back hard.

He was competitive; he loved all sports and games, rode and hunted whenever he could, and was a diligent pupil of Ascanius' old teacher of swordplay, spear throwing, archery, and the other arts of battle. With boys and men he was serious, silent, and reserved. Only with me and my women and the little children of the women's side did he go off guard. The Silvius of the courtyard was merry, affectionate, mischievous, greedy for sweets, patient with babies, impatient with ritual duties, fond of jokes and silly riddles and nonsense rhymes. Everybody liked him. Even Ascanius liked him, half unwillingly.

In those early years of his reign, barely out of his own boyhood, Ascanius lived in the glare of his father's name, forever trying to find his own glory, always outshone. He was too adoring of Aeneas' memory to be able to resent him, but he was envious and resentful of any other power or popularity, particularly mine. He felt that he must outdo his father, striving to be a brighter sun, and here was I the moon, effortlessly shining with the sun's reflected light, effortlessly beloved by my people, because I was one of them, and because they had loved Aeneas. However modestly I lived, hidden like a captive in Ascanius' house, he perceived me as a constant threat to his dignity, and believed I undermined his decisions. Our people were increasingly unhappy with the endless warfare that kept young men in danger and left the farms for old men to plow—how could they be happy with it? But Ascanius blamed their protests and reluctance on me. I poisoned his councils, I whispered with the women, I turned the Latins against him. In vain I behaved as a Vestal, not a queen, doing nothing at all but look after the household and the altars: still I was at fault.

It was a dull life, not a bitter one, but dusty, dust dry, with no spring of life in it except my beautiful, bright, thoughtful boy. He grew, and thrived, and gave me a vein at least of tenderness and hope.

There came a March when we Latins struck out at last at the Volscians and Rutulians, driving their armies right down to the coast, taking Ardea and Antium and reducing them to beg for terms and accept our domination. Our men came back from that campaign in time for the April plowing, and were home all the summer. The harvest was good. In the knowledge of victory, Ascanius began to relax and show the benevolence that was his original nature. He invited me several times to feasts in his great hall, treating me with formal honor. A few times he even talked with me informally, very cautiously, but beginning to show a glimmer of trust. It was then that he told me a strange story, a prophecy I had not heard before. I will tell it as he told it.

It was in the time when Turnus was gathering armies to drive the Trojans out. Aeneas was making ready to sail up the Tiber to ask help from Evander. In the morning of that day, Ascanius said, he and his father saw lying on the riverbank a great white wild sow with thirty white piglets suckling her. At once Aeneas called for a sacrifice, and at the altar he announced the portent: his new kingdom was to be founded in the place called White, that is Alba, and his heir would rule there for thirty years.

Neither he nor my poet had spoken to me of this prophecy. I knew only that he had been bidden to build a new city in Italy and name it for his wife. I did not speak of that, since Ascanius cherished this portent of the sow as justifying his move to Alba Longa. It weighed strangely on my mind. I dreamed more than once thereafter of albino piglets who trotted by one after another endlessly, though their throats were cut and gaped open bleeding dark clots of blood, and of a huge white creature gasping and wallowing on the grass, who had been bled dry and yet was not dead and could not die.

The next year was a peaceful one, but then the Sabines joined with the Aequians against our northeastern towns and farms, burn-ing, looting, and taking slaves as far into our territory as Tibur and Fidenae. Two years went in fighting those peoples. Ascanius defeated them decisively in a long battle late in the year in the hills above the Anio. All the old Trojans fought with him there, Achates, Mnestheus, Serestus, men who had fought before the walls of Troy when they were young. It was their last battle. The soldiers came home in the winter rain, lean and lank as old wolves, but victo-rious.

Again Ascanius was genial and gracious in triumph. He sum-moned the Trojans from Lavinium to receive special honors in Alba Longa, and made sure that his younger captains treated them with respect. Though there had been little profit from this defensive war, whatever booty had been taken he shared out among all the men who had fought for Latium, and he sent lavish gifts to Gabii and Praeneste in thanks for their aid.

Along at the time of the dark solstice he came back from a brief trip down to Ardea. He sent for me and said to me, "Mother, I know your heart has never been here in Alba Longa."

"My heart is where my son is," I said.

"And beside your husband's tomb, I think." He said it gently, and I nodded.

"You have ruled my household with grace and wisdom, and many here will grieve for your going, if you go. But I say to you now, if you wish to go, you may. I have asked for the hand of Camers' sister Salica, and she will come here as my bride in April. If you were here to show her the ways of the house and teach her the skills of housekeeping in which you are so outstanding, you would have our undying gratitude. But if you feel that it may not be wise to have two queens under one roof, or simply if you wish to return to Lavinium, which is your home beyond all question, built for you by my father, I wish you to feel free to make whatever choice you please."

The pompous awkwardness and the good intent were very like Ascanius. I was sorting out his words, and a glow of hope was just beginning to rise in me and warm my whole soul, when he went on, "And I'll keep Silvius here, of course, for his training. It's time I was a better brother to him—I who stand in a father's place to him."

"No," I said.

He stared.

"If you are bringing a wife here, it's right that I go. She should rule here. I'll go back to Lavinium willingly, gratefully. But not without Silvius."

He was puzzled, displeased; he had thought his offer entirely reasonable and generous.

"The boy is eleven, is he not?"

"Yes."

"It's time he was brought up among men."

"I do not leave my son. He is my charge from Aeneas."

"You cannot be his mother and his father."

"I can. I am. Ascanius, do not ask this of me. You will not part me from Silvius. I am grateful for your brotherly care for him. Have no fear, in Lavinium he'll be brought up in all the ways and arts of men by his father's companions and your Latin captains there. I think you know I haven't coddled him. Is he unskilled for his age, or lazy, or cowardly? Is he in any way unworthy of his father?"

He stared again. I was the she-wolf on the shield now. He saw my teeth.

He said at last, "This is unseemly."

"That I should refuse to give up my son?"

"He will be here with me. A few miles from Lavinium!"

"Where he is, I am."

He turned away, baffled, repeating, "This is most unseemly."

Few people, I suppose, had openly opposed his will since he became king of Latium. He had forgotten that there was still a queen.

I stood silent. He said at last, "We will speak of this again." And as he left the room, he said hastily, almost shrewishly, "Consider your position. You cannot have your way in all things."

He could not bear contradiction; he did not have the strength that allows opposition. He could be generous only when his will prevailed. I saw even then that he would be immovable. I had justified his suspicions. He knew now that he had been right to suspect me all along, all the years I had done his bidding, served his household, bowed my head and held my tongue. I was a woman, therefore never to be trusted, never obeyed. I must be disregarded, or defeated.

When I went to my rooms in the women's quarters that evening my head felt as if it were fuller of thoughts than my skull could hold, yet I could think only of the one thing. Ascanius had ruled my life for nearly ten years. I had done his will not my own, and he had taken that for granted, as if I were a slave. Now he meant, without malice but without need or reason, to take from me the use and purpose of my life. He was not the man to bring up my son, Aeneas' son. My father had said so, and I knew it was so.

"Is there something wrong?" Maruna asked me when we were out in the urinals together, and I said, "The king's sending me back to Lavinium."

Maruna's face lighted up.

"He means to keep Silvius here."

She was silent.

"I won't go without him," I said. After a moment, going to the basin to wash, I said, "And I won't stay here. Enough is enough!"

She came to stand by me, and I called to the girl, "Maia, come bring us fresh water, child!" The ten-year-old came with a pitcher and poured cool water over our hands, while her little sister ran in with towels. They were Sicana's granddaughters, not pretty children but very bright. "You'll come back with us to Lavinium, you two," I said to them, and they made big eyes, wondering what I meant.

"I will go," I repeated to Maruna, drying my hands. It helped calm me to say it aloud. "And with Silvius. Maruna, am I like my mother?"

As usual she paused before she answered. "In many ways," she said at last.

"Because I know how she went mad. I know I could go mad as she did. Tell me if you see me going mad. Promise you will."

"I will."

"I have my father in me too. I think if I knew the madness was taking me over, I could stop it. But not if I lost Silvius."

She nodded.

I did indeed understand something of how my mother's mind worked in her frenzy: the ceaseless whirl of ideas, plans, schemes, the terrible irritation with anything that turned thought from its obsession and with anyone who did not understand it, and the curious sense of waiting in ambush. I remembered two pale gold eyes that shone of their own light. I was the she-wolf in the cave, standing stiff-legged, silent, in darkness, ready.

PREPARATIONS FOR THE MARRIAGE OF ASCANIUS AND SALICA went forward at the same time as my preparations to leave the king's house of Alba Longa. I and my women left everything in readiness for the new queen, every grain bin filled, the chests of bedding and clothing full of clean, folded, fine-spun woollens and supple furs and fleeces, the sacred meal made ready, the altars dusted and the floors swept. There was not a moth, not a mouse among the stores, and every snowy lamb's-wool rug on the floor was fresh. I had my pride. And also I wanted Salica to feel welcomed and at home. She was young, just eighteen, and though Ascanius would never mistreat her, I did not think he would be a good husband. He had no sexual interest in women and did not like them as companions. He was marrying because people think it strange if a king does not take a wife, and because he wanted an heir to prove his manhood, perhaps to bolster his unadmitted rivalry with Silvius.

I had spoken at once, of course, to Silvius about our departure, and we talked the matter over, for he was a thoughtful and intelligent child, and children have a wisdom of their own. I had thought he might volunteer to stay at Alba Longa, not wanting to quarrel with Ascanius, and because he saw obedience to his king and older brother as his duty. But he did not. He said, "Let Ascanius rule here and leave us free to rule Lavinium. I'm Latinus' heir as well as Aeneas'. I want to live in the west and learn my lessons from my father's friends. Ascanius doesn't really want me here." After a while he added with a regretful sigh, "But Atys says the horses here are a lot better than the horses in Lavinium."

"Your father chose a colt for you, sired by his own stallion. I think that horse is there in the royal stables."

He lit up at that.

"So you see Latium with two kings again?" I asked him.

"If need be," he said, grave as a man of forty, and then, "I don't want to be here without you!"

"And I won't leave you here. So that's settled."

"Him and his sow and his thirty pigs," said Silvius.

"When we're in Lavinium, I will take you to the forest of Albunea," I told him, with a deep swell of anticipated joy in my heart.

"Where your grandfather Faunus may speak to you from the darkness of the oak groves in the night, as he spoke to your grandfather Latinus."

"Tell me about Picus," the boy said, and so I told him once again about the grandfather who became a woodpecker. He loved to hear the stories of his land and people here as well as he loved to hear the old Trojans tell over their war with the Greeks.

We were so content with our arrangement and imaginings that I persuaded myself Ascanius would see reason as I saw it. But when I went to him to ask formal leave to depart for Lavinium with my son, he was extremely angry and made no attempt to hide it.

"You may go," he said. "Silvius stays here. As I gave you to know last month."

There was nothing for it but supplication. "Son of my husband, king of Latium," I said, and went down on my knees and took hold of his legs at the knees— "I who am daughter and wife and mother of kings ask you to honor my will in this. Aeneas left me Silvius to bring up, and I will obey his sacred charge. You lose nothing in letting your brother go with me. You gain our love and gratitude. Reign here and over us, with your wife, and your children to come—and may the powers that guard the wombs of women be favorable! Let Silvius live in his father's house among his father's old fellow-warriors, and grow to manhood there. Then he will be worthy to come to you and serve you, if fate wills and allows it."

It is very difficult to stand while someone is clasping your knees and pleading eloquently at you from below. The clasp puts you off balance, and your position is acutely embarrassing, all too much as if you were allowing oral sex. Perhaps some people are gratified by receiving a supplication, but I always hated it, and hoped Ascanius might find it as unpleasant as I did. I bowed my head down after I spoke till my forehead was on his feet. He could move only by kicking me. He tried to shift his feet, but didn't kick. We were in his council room, and ten or twelve of his friends and counsellors were watching and listening.

I should not have challenged him among other people. If I had sought him out alone he might have let me persuade him. But changing a command, giving way to a woman—he could not let himself be seen showing such weakness.

"The boy will stay," he said. He shifted around enough that I had to let go of his legs. I stayed kneeling some little while, silent. It was a deep and uncomfortable silence. His young courtiers were no friends of mine and most of them had no interest in Silvius, but most of them were Latins, and our people have a piety towards the bond of parent and child, as well as the habit of respect for the mother of a household. It was shocking to them to see me on my knees, more shocking to hear my stepson flatly refuse my plea.

I stood up and gathered my white palla round me, facing him. I put the corner of it up over my head, as in a sacred act. I said, "Our wills in this matter are different, king." And I turned around and walked out of the council room. As I gained the corridor I heard the men's voices break out in the room behind me, and as I went farther I could hear Ascanius' voice, high and loud, trying to dominate them.

I had defeated him morally; but that really made no difference. He was still in control. I must get out of his control. There was no time to ponder further or prepare.

I sent Tita to bring Silvius in from the exercise field, and Maruna and Sicana and I gathered our women—sixteen of the twenty who had come with us here nine years ago, and the children some of them had borne here, and a few others who had attached themselves to me—and told them to leave as soon as they could, to take different ways down through the hills, a few in each group, keeping unseen as best they could, and make their way to Lavinium. I sent for two light carts to be brought out and a pair of mules to pull each; we loaded a few garments and things precious to us in them. I put Rosalba and her newborn baby in one, along with old Vestina, who was very frail now and living in a twilight of the mind. Silvius and Maruna and I rode in the other cart. Silvius stood up with the driver and ordered him to put the mules into a trot. We were off, down the steep white road, within an hour of my interview with Ascanius.

The short February day was ending when we drove into Lavinium. The little walled town with its citadel above the river looked very quiet and grey in the low light from the west. The narrow river reflected the sky like a shard of glass.

Some of my young women, running cross-country the way Silvia and I used to do, had got there before us. They had roused the few slaves who looked after the Regia, got the doors open and fires lit on the Vestal hearth and in the kitchen and royal apartment. But the widowed house was cold and dank and dusty. All the clean bedclothes and soft furs and fleeces were back there in Alba Longa, and all the fresh food too. The wheat and millet in the granaries was scant and stale. There was not room for all of us as we kept arriving, and several women had to seek the hospitality of families in the town. But as word went round among the townsfolk, they got up a real welcome for us, bringing us all kinds of food and drink and comforts. "Little queen," they called me, the way they had when I was a child. "Little queen, have you come back to us then? Will you stay, will you stay in your own city? And the king, our little king, Aeneas Silvius, look how he's grown!" By the time Achates arrived to bid me welcome, I could give him at least a good fire and a bowl of warm wine thickened with meal and honey.

Of all Aeneas' old comrades I had missed Achates most; he was the kindest of them, the most brotherly. He had come up to Alba Longa often to visit with me, and I always rejoiced to see him and found him a wise counsellor. For all his loyalty to Ascanius, I felt that he was secretly on my side. It was a blow, therefore, when he said, "But Silvius cannot stay here if the king forbids it."

"The king," I said, "the king," and then I paused. At last I asked, "Who am I, Achates?"

He looked at me, taken aback.

I said, "I am your king's wife."

After a long time he said, "Widow."

He was a brave man.

"And your king's mother," I said.

"My king to be."

"You owe protection to your king to be."

"Ascanius intends him no harm, Lavinia."

"He intends no harm, but harm will come to Silvius there. He doesn't belong there. It's not his seat in the realm—this is. Ascanius will be busy with his new bride, and she with him. No one there will look after Silvius' interest. Some of them are intriguers and no friends of his. I will not leave my young ram-lamb unguarded among strangers!"

The image made Achates cock his handsome grey head. "Better say you don't want your wolf cub brought up in a barnyard," he said. Then he clearly wished he hadn't said anything so disrespectful to Ascanius, and frowned. "The boy's older brother is his proper guardian," he said stiffly. "I know it's hard for you to part from him—"

"Do me justice, Achates! When the time comes to part from him, I'll let him go! But the time has not come. He's young. He needs to be with true friends and teachers—like you. His father and his grandfather left him in my charge, and I will not give that up to anyone else."

I thought I could sway him, but I could not.

Nor would Aeneas' other old companions, when I talked with them in the next days, approve my keeping Silvius from Ascanius' court. I think they all thought that I was right, but could not admit it. The will of a widowed queen could not be openly allowed to overrule that of a reigning king. Ascanius had not treated them very well, he had left them to grow old away from the center of power, he ignored them except for the most formal recognition of their service; but they were Aeneas' men and he was Aeneas' son and his word was law. If Silvius had been older, they would have listened to him, for he was Aeneas' son too and they loved him dearly; but as grown men they thought they should not be swayed by the will of a boy of eleven.

Meanwhile, we waited for word to come from Alba Longa. Daily I looked out from the walls dreading to see a mounted troop ride down the hill road, soldiers with orders to take Silvius back with them, or Ascanius himself coming down from the mountain to play the sky father with lightning and thunder of wrath.

However, the wedding festivities were going forward in Ardea and Alba, all those days, and I think Ascanius found it undignified to be squabbling with his stepmother while welcoming his bride. He simply ignored us. So we had all the end of March at peace there in Lavinium, and I cannot say how often I wept with both pain and joy at being there again, in my home, where I and my love had lived.

I had brought Aeneas' armor and sword and shield in the cart—Sicana helped Silvius and me lift them down and carry them. Now they hung again in his own house, where they should hang.

And we waited to hear from the house of Ascanius.

In midmorning one day while I was at my loom starting a new piece, the girl Ursina came running in. "A troop of armed men on horseback, coming down the way from Alba, queen," she said. "About a mile away now. One leads a riderless horse."

For Silvius.

I had made a hundred plans for what to do when Ascanius sent for Silvius, but they fell to dust under the hooves of those horsemen. There was only one thing to do, and it was what I had done already—run. Run and hide.

"Send Silvius to me," I told Ursina, a girl of fifteen or so, wild and tawny as a lioness, Maruna's niece. She darted off. I went to my room and tied up a few things in an old palla, and when Silvius came panting in I told him we were going to the forest to escape from Ascanius' men.

"I'll get horses," he said.

"No need, we're not going far. And horses are hard to hide. Get your cloak and good shoes and meet me in the kitchen."

I gathered up a cook pot and some food in another bundle, Silvius came, and we were off. Maruna met us in the doorway of the house. I said, "I hope he will not punish you!"—meaning all my women and the people of the house. "Tell the king's men: the queen went with her son to the great oracle of the springs near Tibur to ask guidance of the oracle. That will keep them busy a little while."

"But you . . ."

"You know where to look for me, Maruna. The woodcutter's."

She nodded. She was desperately worried for us and I was worried for her, but I could not hesitate. Silvius and I went down the street, slipped out through the postern gate of the town, and struck across the fields, across the last pagus, following the course of the

Prati into the wooded foothills northwest under cover of the new-leaved oaks. In time we came to the old path from Laurentum to Albunea, winding along under the hills.

Silvius wrinkled his nose. He could scent like a hound.

"Rotten eggs?" I asked. We had not spoken at all, hurrying along in fugitive silence.

He nodded.

"That's the sulfur springs."

"Are we going there?"

"Nearby."

We came to the forester's cottage where Maruna used to spend the night while the poet and I talked in the sacred grove. Trees had grown up and closed in on the high round hut, and I almost passed it without seeing it. The clearing and what had been the kitchen garden were rank with brambles and tall weeds. I called out. No one answered. I went to the door and saw the house was desolate. The woodcutter and his wife had gone elsewhere, or were dead.

Silvius was into the hut and all around it with a child's quick curiosity. "This is a good place," he said. He put down his bundle on the doorstep. I had noticed how unwieldy it was as he walked with it, and it went down with a thud and a clank. "What did you put in that?" I asked. He looked at me a bit askance, and opened up the bundle. He had brought his short bow, arrows, a hunting knife, and the short sword he used for battle practice.

"For wolves," he said.

"Ah," I said. "Well, dear son, I think maybe we are the wolves."

He thought it over and the idea clearly pleased him. He nodded.

"Come and sit down a bit," I said, sitting on the doorstep and pushing the weapons aside to make room. A shaft of sunlight struck through the gloom of the pines and oaks all around and made it warm there. Silvius sat down next to me. I looked at his thin brown boy legs and the shoes that were too heavy for his feet. He leaned his head against me. "They don't want to kill us, do they, mother?" he asked, not with terror but for reassurance.

"No. They want to part us. I am certain in my heart that it's wrong for me to let you go. But there's no way I can keep Ascanius from taking you to Alba, except by hiding you so he can't."

He thought for a long time and said, "I could go live on a farm somewhere off in the country and pretend to be a farm boy."

"You might. It would put the farmer's family at risk, though."

He nodded shortly, ashamed of not having seen that.

I was ashamed too of involving him in any deceit. I said, "Listen. I lied about going to the great oracle at Tibur. But I do want to consult the oracle. Ours, my father's, my forefathers' oracle, here, at Albunea. Maybe it will tell us what to do. I don't know if it will speak to a woman, but it might speak to you. Grandson of Latinus, of Faunus, of Picus, of Saturn . . ." I stroked his hard, slight shoulder, still sweaty from our quick walk. "Son of Aeneas." I kissed him.

He kissed me back. "I won't leave you," he said. "Never."

"Oh, never and forever aren't for mortals, love. But we won't be parted till I know it's right that we part."

"That's never, then," he said.

A bird sang out sweet from the dark trees, a long trill brimming with the lovely ignorant happiness of spring.

"Is this where we're going to stay?"

"Tonight, at least."

"Good. You brought fire, didn't you?"

I showed him the little clay fire pot I had filled from Vesta of the Regia and brought in a wicker sling. "Lay a fire on the hearth and say the prayers," I told him. I swept out the hut while he did so, and we kindled the hearth fire together.

"Your father grew up in the woods on a great mountain, Ida, did you know that?" I asked him. Of course he knew it, but he wanted to hear it again, and listened intently while I repeated to him the little that Aeneas had told me of his childhood. Then he went off with his bow and arrows to see if there were any unwary rabbits or quail about. I went on cleaning out the hut, and made us beds of young pine boughs I tore from saplings. There was no rubbish in the hut, only the tiny leavings of spiders and woodmice, and some fallen thatch. Poor people have little to leave. There was half a broken earthenware bowl on a shelf; it had been kept, it was of use. I put in it the handful of salt I had brought from home and set it on the shelf that would serve as our table.

Silvius shot nothing, but had planned where to lay snares for quail in the morning, and brought four crayfish he had hand-caught in a streamlet. We garnished our millet porridge with crayfish. I wished only that I had been able to carry water from home, for the water of the streams all around the sulfur springs is vile to the taste.

We slept rolled up in our cloaks. I slept long and well. At Albunea, even outside the grove as we were here, I was always spared from fear. Or rather I felt fear but it was entirely different from the sharp dread of losing Silvius, and from the endless alarms and anxieties of living; it was the fear we call religion, an accepting awe. It was the terror we feel when we look up at the sky on a clear night and see the white fires of all the stars of the eternal universe. That fear goes deep. But worship and sleep and silence are part of it.

Silvius was away all next day exploring the forest heights above the springs. I did not worry about him; he was a sensible boy; there

were no boars or bears this near the farmlands, and here in inner
Latium no enemies were near. Along in the afternoon, Ursina appeared at the edge of the clearing, quick and silent as a mountain
lion. "Aunt Maruna sent me," she whispered. She brought a jug of
good water, a bag of dried fava beans, and a packet of dried figs
and raisins—Tita had put that in for Silvius, having great sympathy
for his love of sweets.

"What did the men from Alba Longa do?" I asked.

"They asked about you. Aunt told them you had gone to
Albunea of Tibur. The others think you did. The men went back
to Alba yesterday. Aunt said to tell you this: they ordered Lord
Achates and Mnestheus to bring Silvius to Alba when you come
back to Lavinium."

I kissed her and asked her to bring a little wine for sacrifice
tomorrow. She slipped off again as quietly as she had come.

I sat on the half-decayed wooden doorstep in the spring sunlight and pondered.

If I went back to Lavinium, faithful Achates would obey Ascanius' order.

I could take Silvius back to Alba Longa myself and stay with
him there, an unwelcome, unwanted, unwilling guest in Ascanius'
court, struggling to protect my son from neglect, envy, and harm.

I could do as my father had suggested years ago: make my way
to Caere in Etruria and ask King Tarchon to take us under his protection and help me bring up Silvius as a king's son.

That was a truly frightening thought to me, but I made myself
consider it.

I was still thinking when I heard the little sparrow whistle that
was our signal, and Silvius appeared. He was dirty, thorn-scratched
and tired, had snared a big hare, and was proud of himself. He
washed, I skinned and cleaned the hare, and we made spits of green

willow and toasted the meat over the small fire in the hut, an excellent dinner.

"Tomorrow evening we fast," I told Silvius. "We'll spend the night in the sacred forest."

"Can I see the cave and the stinking pools?"

"Yes."

"What do people take as offering?"

"A lamb."

"I could go get a lamb from the royal flock there by Lavinium—I'd make sure nobody sees me—"

"No. We can't go near town, neither of us. We'll make what offering we can, tomorrow. The grandfathers will understand. I've gone there before with empty hands."

The next day, as the sun hung red above the sea mist in the west, we followed the narrow path into the grove of Albunea and came to the sacred enclosure. It looked as derelict and lonesome as the woodcutter's hut. Its oracle spoke chiefly to those of my father's lineage, and there were few of us left now—some old cousins still living in Laurentum, and myself, and Silvius. No one had done sacrifice there for a year or more. The remnants of fleece on the ground were mere black shreds. We cut a turf for the altar, and Silvius poured out the flask of wine as offering while I prayed to the ancestors and powers of the place. It was already too dark to go to the pools. We had brought our cloaks. My son laid his out just where my father had slept when we were here. I took my old place near the altar where I had sat and talked to the poet. We sat in the darkness for a long time, silent. The stars burned white through the black leaves of the trees. When I looked over, I saw Silvius had lain down, curled up in his cloak; he looked like a lamb asleep in the starlight. I sat awake. The creatures of the night made separate sounds, rustlings and scratchings, near and far on the forest floor;

an owl called once, from the right, far away up on the hillside, a long quavering *i-i-i.* I felt no urgent presence of the spirits of the place. It was all silent, all sacred.

After a long time, when the constellations had changed, I spoke to the poet, not aloud but in my mind. "Dear poet, all you told me came to be. You guided me truly, up to Aeneas' death. Since then I've let others lead me. But I go astray. I can't trust Ascanius: he doesn't know his own enmity to Silvius. I wish you were here to guide me now. I wish you could sing to me."

No voice spoke. The hush had grown very deep. I sighed at last and lay down, overcome by sleep. Sleep made the ground seem soft and the cloak warm to me. Words and images drifted through my mind. The words were, *Speak me!* Then they turned and seemed to reverse themselves as they drifted away: *I say your being.* I saw Aeneas' shield very clearly for an instant, the turn of the she-wolf's head to her bright flank. I felt myself lying on a vault like a turtle's shell of earth and stone that arched over a great dark hollow. Below me lay a vast landscape of shadows, forests of shadowy trees. Out beyond those trees I saw my son standing in dim sunlight on the bank of a river, a river wider than Tiber, so broad and misty I could not clearly see the other shore. Silvius was a man of nineteen or twenty. He was leaning on Aeneas' great spear and he looked as Aeneas must have looked when he was young. There were multitudes of people all up and down the endless grassy bank. The grass was shadowy grey, not green. A voice near me, by my ear, an old man's voice, was speaking softly: ". . . your last child, whom your wife Lavinia will bring up in the woods, a king, a father of kings." Then I had so strong a sense of my husband's presence, his physical body and being, with me, in me, as if I were he, that I woke and found myself sitting up, bewildered, in the dark, bereft. No one was there. Only Silvius asleep across the clearing. The stars were fading as the sky paled.

SILVIUS HAD SLEPT WITHOUT DREAMING. IT WAS I WHO HAD the dream and heard the voice, but it was not my grandfather who spoke.

At dawn we rose and went to the spring. While Silvius explored about the cave, I sat on the rock outcrop and watched the sunlight strike across the pale water through the low mists that always hung above it. The stink of sulfur was less strong in the morning air. We bathed in shallow pools a little way downstream from the dead, muddy ground at the cave mouth. The water was warm and felt soft on the skin. It would be a good place to bring arthritis, or an old aching wound.

We went back to the enclosure, and having nothing else to offer in thanks we heaped the altar with sweet herbs, boughs of bay laurel, and what few flowers we found in clearings in the woods. When we had done that and said our thanks, before we left the sacred place, I told Silvius my dream. "I saw you, a grown man. Yet it was as if you were not yet born—as if you stood waiting to live. And beside me an old man was speaking. He was not speaking to me. He spoke of you to your father Aeneas. He said: *That is your last son, a king and father of kings, whom your wife Lavinia will bring up in the woods.* And then the dream ended."

We pondered it as we went back to the woodcutter's hut.

"It means we're to stay here, in the forest. Doesn't it, mother?" Silvius said at last.

It was what I had been thinking, yet my first impulse was to deny it, to say no, it couldn't be that clear and simple. I said nothing till we came into the clearing, and then, "It seems to mean that. But how . . . ? We can't lurk here like outcasts or beggars—living off what Maruna can send us."

"I can hunt, and snare, mother."

"You certainly can, and you'd better do it, too, if you want meat tonight. But in the long run . . . People will see us, everybody here knows us, after all! We can't just vanish into the forest."

"If we went farther, we could. Up in the hills."

"For how long, child? Summer, yes; autumn, maybe; winter, no. Life's hard for those who live apart from others, even if they have a sound roof and a full granary. You and I are too soft for it . . . But I will not take orders from Ascanius! If I obey him in this, if I give him you, even if I go with you, I will have given your kingship away. He must accept our sovereignty in Lavinium. Where can we go?"

"Well, what if people do recognise us? And find out where we are? Would anybody make us go to Alba? If we said we were supposed to live in the woods—if we told them the oracle said so?"

"I don't know."

"Well, let's find out," Silvius said.

It is pleasant when your child says what you want to say.

"His pigs told him to go to Alba," I said. "How can he argue with his grandfather, who tells us to stay here?"

I began to remember how, when Faunus told my father in Albunea that I must be married to a foreigner, Latinus had announced it right away to all and sundry. The more people heard it the more powerful it was. Everyone, not just the king, had heard the oracle.

"I think I should go to Lavinium today," I told Silvius. "You stay here. Get us a rabbit or quail if you can. If anybody but me comes here, disappear. I'll be back before evening."

So I walked back along the foothills and across the fields to my city, thinking hard all the way, and entered the gate in midmorning. I was relieved to find Ascanius had still not sent for Silvius. And I was surprised and touched by the welcome people gave me, crowding round me with greetings and caresses and anxious inquiries. I was the center of a whole throng by the time I had climbed the street to the Regia.

Here's my chance, I thought. So I turned round there before the house doors, while people of the household came crowding out behind me to make me welcome, and called, "People of my city!" They quieted down to hear me, and I spoke out, hardly knowing what I was going to say from one word to the next. "Last night in the forest of Albunea, in the place of the oracle of my forefathers, I lay down by the altar to sleep. And the voice of King Anchises, father of our King Aeneas, spoke to me in dream, prophesying that his grandson Silvius was to live with me in the woods of Latium. In obedience to this foretelling, I will neither send my son to Alba Longa nor keep him here in Lavinium, but he and I will live in the forest until the signs and portents bid us do otherwise. The voice in the dream called Silvius king and father of kings. May you rejoice in that knowledge as I do!" They put up a great shout at that, which heartened me, and I ended—"But till Silvius comes to the age of rule, Ascanius rules alone, and my city will continue to be governed by Ascanius and by his father's friends."

"But where will you go off to in the wilderness, little queen?" some old fellow in the crowd called out, and I answered, "Not far, friend! My heart is in Lavinium, with you!" That made them cheer again, and I entered my house amid a considerable tumult, my heart beating very hard. Achates was there to meet me. Riding the goodwill of my people, I forestalled what he might have said, saying to him, "My friend, I know Ascanius ordered you to bring Silvius to Alba Longa. As your queen, I ask you to obey me, leaving Silvius with me, letting the prophecy be fulfilled."

He accepted that with a slow bow of his head, saying only, "You saw the Lord Anchises?"—incredulous yet wistful, urgent, wanting to believe me.

"No, but I heard a voice, that spoke as if to Aeneas. I took it to be his father's voice. The fathers speak, in Albunea."

Achates hesitated and then asked, "Did you see him?" *Him* was Aeneas, of course, and Achates spoke with such love and longing that the tears came into my eyes. I could only shake my head, and after a while I said, "He was there with me, Achates. For a moment."

But as I said it I knew that it was not true. Aeneas had not been there with me as a man in the flesh, nor had Anchises spoken. It was the poet who spoke. It was all the words of the poet, the words of the maker, the foreteller, the truth teller: nothing more, nothing less. But was I myself any more, or less, than that?

And this was nothing I could say to any living soul, or ever did, till now.

I HAD BEEN RIGHT TO COUNT ON ASCANIUS' RESPECT FOR portents and oracles, which he had learned from his father but exaggerated almost to superstition. He was rigid in all observances; he longed to be called pious, as Aeneas was. Piety to him meant a man's obedience to the will of higher powers, a safe righteousness. He would never have believed that Aeneas saw his victory over Turnus as his own defeat. He did not understand that in his father's piety lay his tragedy.

I may misjudge him; he may have come to share some of Aeneas' anguish of conscience, as he grew older. But I never knew Ascanius well.

At any rate, when Achates and Serestus took word to him of my decision, he entertained them without berating them for obeying me rather than him, and sent back no clear message at all to me. I think he felt himself forestalled by the combination of forces I

258 | Ursula K. Le Guin

had brought against him—the sacred oracle of the Italians speaking with the hallowed voice of the Trojan grandfather. By silence he gave consent.

So began the period of our "exile," no exile at all compared to that of the old Trojans forever homesick for their fallen city, our "living in the woods," which turned out to be a pretty easy life. I sent for some carpenters to come brace up the woodcutter's hut and thatchers to replace the rat-infested, rain-rotted roof. They ended up rebuilding the whole thing, adding on a second room and building a proper hearth, while volunteers swarmed in the clearing chopping brambles and spading and putting in a kitchen garden with every herb and vegetable that grows in Latium, even a sapling walnut tree and a full-grown Sicilian caperberry bush. They wanted to put a fence around it all, but I forbade it. "Wolves, queen," old Girnus said—"bears—!" And I said, "There are no bears in Albunea, and if a wolf comes here I will call him brother." They took that saying back to Lavinium, and some people called me Mother Wolf, after that.

The way from town to the woodcutter's hut soon became a beaten path, and I had to limit the number of volunteer workmen and visitors to a few and only on certain days, or we would have had no peace there at all. When, late in summer, all the workmen were done and it was quiet again, it was very quiet. Silvius was off all day in the forest or at his lessons—for the old Trojans took his education in hand with vigor, and put him through a merciless daily schedule of exercises, military drills, weapons training, music, recitation, and equitation. When I had cleaned my house and tended my garden, I had little to do, and being used to having a great household to run, I was bored and lonely at first. I felt myself useless, a fraud. The Regias I had managed with such hard work and endless care in Laurentum, in Lavinium, in Alba Longa, were all going on perfectly well without me. Maruna, with Sicana as her second in command, kept the house in Lavinium, and did the worship as I had trained her long ago to do; so I could not ask her to be with me in the forest.

But after a time I began to like my solitude. I lost the wish for any visitor or voice to break the silence of the trees, threaded always with the singing of insects and birds and the sound of wind in leaves. I gardened, and spun, and wove on the big loom set up in the second room, and was content with silence, until my son came back at evening to eat with me and talk a little, quietly, before sleep.

And so the years passed.

There were some border incidents, but Ascanius seemed to have lost his unhappy knack of stirring up wars. His marriage had been celebrated with great ceremony, his Rutulian wife kept his house in royal fashion, and they were said to be a happy couple. But they had no child. After a few years, Ascanius called in wise women and soothsayers. The wise women said that Salica was in perfect health and there was no reason she should not conceive. The soothsayers all foretold that she would die barren. They gave no cause or cure, and their prophecies were cloaked in images and cloudy language, for if the fault was in Ascanius they did not wish to say so.

I heard this and other news as gossip from Illivia and other women who came to visit with me, and from my Latin and Trojan counsellors who ruled Lavinium and the northwest of Latium in Ascanius' and my name. Achates, and Silvius too, saw to it that these men came to consult with me on matters of importance, so that I knew well enough what was happening in the country and around it, though I kept my advice to a minimum, and entertained no guests at all. If an important traveler, king or trader, came to Latium, he was entertained at Alba Longa. He was told that Queen Lavinia was living with her son in the forest in obedience to an oracle and so could not be seen. I had to turn away even Tarchon of Caere, who came to Lavinium, and whom I longed to see; I let Silvius go to him once, but I had to refuse myself, or else my exile became a mere mockery. But I could trust Achates and Mnestheus to entertain him as befitted a great Etruscan king and a true friend of my husband and my son. Tarchon did not go on to Alba Longa, which signified pretty clearly that if Ascanius wanted his friendship he must earn it.

Unfortunately, Ascanius chose to test it severely, by provoking the Veiian Etruscans at Ruma. Their colony there was growing larger. Latins in Fidenae and Tibur and around Lake Regillus were now patrolling the outlying borders of their farmlands, since there had been the inevitable episodes of cattle rustling, sheep stealing, quarrels at terminus stones. Mars was ready, as ever, to dance on the boundary lines. Ascanius had every right to defend his subjects' property, as Latinus had done when Evander's Greeks first settled there. But Latinus had a low opinion of the Seven Hills as a city site, thinking the river bottom unhealthy and the hills unfit for plowing or grazing, so he did not begrudge the territory to Evander. Ascanius did begrudge it.

He had got on with the Etruscans thus far only by ignoring them. He thought them arrogant, perfidious, incalculable. He said a treaty with Etruscans was worse than useless, for they would not keep it—though the only one he made with them was when they helped him fight the war on the Anio, and they had kept it. Holding himself superior to all Italians as a Trojan, son of the divine Aeneas sent by fate to rule in Italy, he resented finding himself actually inferior to the Etruscans in wealth, manpower, weaponry, and the arts of life. His prejudice made him see them as all of one kind. In fact Caere and Veii were old rivals. Tarchon did not like to watch the other city-state expanding south of the Tiber; he had come to

Lavinium to feel us out about the settlement at Ruma, and would have joined with us to put pressure on Veii to keep the settlement small. Achates and Serestus understood this and counselled Ascanius to court Tarchon. Ascanius brushed their advice aside.

In March, soon after the Leapers danced, he decided to teach Veii a lesson. He sent a small army to a disputed boundary between Ruma and Lake Regillus and drove the Etruscans, mostly shepherds, back almost to the Seven Hills. As they got closer to the settlement, reinforcements met them, and they began to turn and fight. Men were killed on both sides. To Ascanius' soldiers, their losses justified them in keeping the flocks that fell into their hands. But by the end of a second day, they had to fall back all the way to Lake Regillus, letting go the sheep they had taken. The Rumans rounded up their flocks and stayed on armed guard all across the uncertain border.

As if scornful of his enemy, Ascanius had not gone with his army. He put it in charge of his boyhood friend, Atys. I had known Atys as a handsome, warmhearted, rather childish man, who was kind to Silvius when we lived at Alba and gave him riding lessons. Retreating with his army, Atys had taken off his helmet, hot with the bright spring sunlight; a stone an Etruscan shepherd threw struck his head and knocked him from his horse, and he never recovered consciousness. They brought his body and those of five other soldiers home to Alba Longa.

Ascanius broke down. He threw himself on Atys' body weeping, and could not stop his tears. When his wife tried to console him and lead him away, he turned on her with cruel, senseless insults, screaming that she had whored with half his army and was barren because she was a whore. He could not be torn away from Atys' corpse until his weeping exhausted him, sobs becoming convulsions and then a kind of swoon from which he could not be roused. All this was in the great courtyard of the Regia, witnessed by many. Word of it came to Lavinium within hours. Silvius told me when he came home in the evening from his lessons.

Everyone was shocked, puzzled, alarmed by this inordinate show of grief. Atys had been Ascanius' boy lover, but that was long ago. If Atys was so dear to him why had he sent him on this mission? After all, he had experienced captains who knew the ground better, like Rutilus of Gabii, who had grown up there. Among the talk and speculation Sicana and the others brought me next day was a persistent tale that some time ago Ascanius had been overheard quarreling with Atys, shouting that he was ashamed of him. Atys' friends wondered if he had been sent to lead an inadequate army into danger as punishment, or to get rid of him. And many were now saying that Atys and Ascanius had never ceased to be lovers, that even on the eve of Ascanius' wedding they had met, and ever since. Amid such sad and shameful gossip Ascanius lay still stricken in his room, seeing no one.

His wife Salica was turned from his door. Humiliated past endurance, she went with a group of her women to her family home in Ardea.

I was fated, it seems, to live among people who suffered beyond measure from grief, who were driven mad by it. Though I suffered grief, I was doomed to sanity. This was no doing of the poet's. I know that he gave me nothing but modest blushes, and no character at all. I know that he said I raved and tore my golden tresses at my mother's death. He simply was not paying attention: I was silent then, tearless, and only intent on making her poor soiled body decent. And my hair has always been dark. In truth he gave me nothing but a name, and I have filled it with myself. Yet without him would I even have a name? I have never blamed him. Even a poet cannot get everything right.

It is strange, though, that he gave me no voice. I never spoke to him till we met that night by the altar under the oaks. Where is my voice from, I wonder? the voice that cries on the wind in the heights of Albunea, the voice that speaks with no tongue a language not its own?

Well, these are questions I cannot answer. I will tell you now of another question I cannot answer, and a thing not many people believe. You will not believe it either, I know, but it is the truth.

I had nothing to do with the Penates of Troy leaving the altar of the king's house in Alba Longa and coming to Lavinium.

I gave no women orders to spirit them away by night, or men either, or children. Because it was an act that might have been calculated for political effect, there will always be suspicion, even open assumption, that it was planned and executed by me, or by someone else who wished to weaken Ascanius' authority. I do not think it was. I think the gods knew when it was time to come home.

Maruna came to me at Albunea, early in the morning, out of breath, and bade me come with her at once to Lavinium, to the Regia. I had not entered the gates of my city or my house for five years, but I knew Maruna would not summon me without cause. She hurried with me across the April fields, through the city gate, through the doors of the house, to the hearth of Vesta at the back of the hearth room, where the Penates of Latium had stood ever since my father's death. And I saw standing with them the figures of clay and ivory, the gods of the house of Anchises, that Aeneas had brought with him across the lands and seas from Troy.

I gasped and stood in awe, my legs trembling. I was shocked, incredulous, frightened.

Yet the fear did not go very deep. I could not be terrified, because I could only see it as right that our gods should be here, in our house.

So the others perhaps saw me as less amazed than I might have been, and thought my surprise and my questions a pretense. And indeed I did not ask many questions. I thought it impious to question mortals about a matter that had apparently been carried out by greater powers.

Of course some of my women were capable of spiriting the Penates out of Alba and into Lavinium. But as I thought about it I could not imagine any of them actually doing it. All of them seemed utterly surprised, dismayed, even terrified when they saw the figures on the altar; and they were honest women. I would not let them be interrogated. If indeed I found that one had done it, what was I to do with her? Punish? Praise? Best leave the inexplicable unexplained. As for the men, I left them to Achates, Serestus, and Mnestheus, who I knew were themselves incapable of plotting an act of sacrilege, however welcome its implications. They found no suspects and no hint of how or even when the strange event had occurred. The first to see the gods had been Maruna herself, coming for the morning worship.

I stayed in my city, that day, among my people. I sent for Silvius, and ordered a triple sacrifice, a lamb, a calf, and a young pig. Silvius presided, with the old Trojan captains to assist him. With the lifeblood and roasted meat of the good animals we thanked and blessed the Lares and Penates of Troy and Latium and asked their blessing. Maruna read the entrails as the Etruscans do, and foretold from them great and lasting glory for the house of Aeneas.

And then I went back to the little house in the forest. But my son stayed in the Regia that night, guarding his ancestral gods, seeking their blessing.

In Alba Longa there had of course been great dismay, horror, when the absence of the old Penates was discovered. A little camillus, a helper, a boy of nine, who first raised the alarm, had been beaten nearly to death by horrified women who blamed the mischief on him. Queen Salica, who might have calmed them, no longer lived there.

They carried the news to King Ascanius with fear and trembling. He came out of his rooms, then, for the first time since Atys' death. He walked across the great court to the Vestal hearth and stood gazing at it. Only the Penates of the old village of Alba Longa stood there, few and humble as the gods of a poor man's house. Vesta herself, the body of sacred fire, burned up clear and bright as ever.

Ascanius cast a little salted meal into the fire. He lifted up his hands to pray, but he could not speak; tears began to run down his face; he turned and went back in silence, weeping, to his rooms.

ASCANIUS MADE NO EFFORT TO FIND A HUMAN AGENCY FOR the Penates' return to Lavinium. To him, as to me, it was a pure sign of the will of the powers greater than us. We accepted it as such. But while it was a miraculous joy to me, and a portent of divine favor to Aeneas' younger son, to the elder son it was an almost fatal blow.

I do not know whether his marriage had been such an unhappy mockery as—now—everyone was saying. All the women's quarters were abuzz with talk about how unhappy Salica had been from the very beginning, how she suffered from her husband's distaste for her, how she hid her humiliation even from her closest companions (except of course the one telling the story). If all that was true, Ascanius had also worn a public mask and never let it slip, all these years. I think it likelier that something little by little went wrong in the marriage, Ascanius' sexual discomfort with women perhaps driving him gradually back to seek the tender simplicities of his first love; and Atys, poor loyal soul, was there to offer them. Poor souls all of them.

But fate was hardest on Ascanius. He lost his lover and a battle at one stroke; at the next, his wife; and then his father's gods. His choice of a capital was, it seemed, wrong. Everything he had built up to support his image of himself as Aeneas' worthy successor slipped away from him, like mud crumbling softly from a riverbank into the water.

He could not pull himself together for a long time, so long that his war captains, despairing of getting any orders from him, came down to Lavinium and asked the counsel of the old Trojans and the young king.

For so Silvius was openly called now. He would be seventeen in May. He had lived in the forest, following the oracle; he had served his term of exile. The return of the ancestral powers to his house was a clear sign. The young king and the gods had come home on the same day.

The people of Lavinium and all western Latium made him a heartfelt, joyful welcome, bringing tribute unasked and overflowing. Soon from Gabii, Praeneste, Tibur, Nomentum, people were arriving to see and greet him and offer him their white lambs, their fine colts, their service in arms. There was a sense all over the country of a darkness lifting, a better hope. No mortal hope is ever fully satisfied, I know, but this overflow of good feeling and confidence secured much of its own fulfillment: the Latins saw themselves as a people again, they held up their heads. Only a fool could have spoiled so promising a start. Not being a fool, Silvius was cautious and often almost incredulous of his good fortune, and relied very much on the counsel of people he had learned to trust; but being seventeen years old, he seized every advantage, accepted every gift, rejoiced in his popularity, offered love for love, and rode the fair wind, as long as it blew, like a happy young hawk.

When the captains came from Alba Longa, he called a council, and he called me to it.

I demurred, privately, to him. I was so unused to being among people, after five years in the forest, that the idea appalled me. "I don't belong there," I said.

"You sat in your father's council, and my father's."

"No. I sat at the back and listened, sometimes."

"But you are the queen."

"Queen mother."

"A queen is a queen," said my son, regally.

He did look a good deal like Aeneas, but there was something of Latinus and myself, something Italian, in the way he stood and the way he turned his head. He knew how to occupy space. He would be a handsome man at twenty-five, but an absolutely beautiful one at fifty. Such maternal thoughts distracted me. I was staring at him as a cow stares at her calf, with mindless, endless contentment.

"You are the queen here, mother, and you can't do anything about it, unless I get married. Then you can retire, if you insist. But I don't plan to marry any time soon. If you aren't the queen then you're my subject, and I command you to attend the council."

"Don't be childish, Silvius," I said. But he had won the game, of course. I attended his council. I sat at the back and never spoke. There was no use shocking Ascanius' captains. They were worried enough as it was.

They had information that Veii had been sending armed men to Ruma ever since our ill-fated border raid. It looked as if the Etruscans planned either forays into our territory or an all-out attack on Gabii or Collatia. The chiefs of Alba Longa had sent all the men they could raise into the area to guard it, but it was a long border, and our soldiers were spread thin. They had strict orders not to attack, only to defend.

"But we don't know what they'll be facing," said Marsius, a young general. They were all young. Ascanius had not liked to have older men about him.

"We could double the army easily," Mnestheus said. "There's great spirit among the people here."

"We could get in touch with Tarchon of Caere," said Silvius.

The Albans looked blank, frowned. "An Etruscan?" said Marsius.

"Tarchon was here not long ago, and it seemed he had in mind an alliance to contain Ruma."

Serestus spoke: "But we were not then at liberty to discuss it with him."

There was a silence.

"I know you remember that Tarchon of Caere helped you, or your fathers, put my father on the throne of Latium," Silvius said. He said it mildly, not chiding or reproaching. I saw Achates look at him with a half smile. He was hearing his king speak. We all were.

We sent messengers to Caere, recruits and volunteers to strengthen the Alban forces encircling the Seven Hills. In April Tarchon's army moved eastward from Caere, cutting off the route from Veii to the Tiber. There were some skirmishes in Etruria, none in Latium. The colony at Ruma withdrew all forces from its borders; its men ceased to threaten our farms and cities, turning back to plowing and harvesting. Silvius had won his first war without fighting it.

At the end of that summer he rode to the woodcutter's house on his handsome chestnut stallion, and said to me, "Mother, I think you should come back to your city." I had been thinking the same thing, and merely nodded.

It was a great pleasure to live again in the high house of La-vinium, to sweep Vesta's hearth and prepare the salted meal for my gods and Aeneas' gods, to look after a great storeroom and a busy household, to have children about underfoot and women to talk things over with and the deep ring of men's voices out in the stable yard.

In that life, which had been all my life till we went to the forest, the years slipped away. Silvius went up to Alba Longa often, meeting amicably with his brother, sharing the duties of rule, though now Ascanius took second place, deferring to the younger king. He came a few times to Lavinium for festivals or councils, a sad-eyed, heavyset, stooped man who fussed over trifles. His wife lived on in Ardea in her brother Camers' household. Silvius, who frequently crossed the Tiber, cultivating amity with Etruria, married the Caeran lady Ramtha Matunae, a beautiful and noble woman. We held a great wedding in Lavinium.

The children began to come: a girl, a boy, a boy, a girl. Then I was the grandmother queen in the noisy courtyard, where the laurel tree I had planted when I came there with Aeneas towered over the walls.

When Ascanius had ruled thirty years in Alba Longa, he gave up his crown. Silvius, called Aeneas Silvius by his people, ruled Latium alone.

He moved then to Alba, for it was in truth a better center of rule than Lavinium. He begged me to come with him and Ramtha and the children, but I was not going to leave my city again, or not in that direction. He did not try to move his Lares and Penates, for they like me had shown their will was to stay where Aeneas put them.

So I lived on as the old queen in the old Regia, within the threshold my husband carried me across on our wedding day. Sicana died at last, and Tita, but Maruna was with me always. Now and then we walked, or rode in a donkey cart, to sleepy Laurentum of our girlhood, and spent an afternoon there by the fountain under the old laurel. Once we went on to the mouth of the father river and filled our cart with the grey, dirty, sacred salt. Often we walked down from Lavinium to the Numicus, and watched the water run, and coming home stayed a while by the great stone tomb where Aeneas lay in state near his daughter who might have been, a shadow in shadows. Now and then we walked to Albunea, and Maruna slept in the woodcutter's cottage while I went on alone into the forest, bearing fire for the altar, and an offering of fruit or grain and wine, and the fleece of a dark-colored ewe, on which I lay down in the sacred place to sleep. I heard no voices in the darkness among the trees. I saw no visions. I slept.

Maruna fell ill; her heart failed, she grew weak, and could not rise to sweep the hearth. One morning I heard the women wailing.

Silvius came for Maruna's ninth-day ceremony. No one wondered that a king should come to the funeral of a slave. He asked me again to come to Alba, to be with him, but I shook my head. "I will live here with Aeneas," I told him. There were tears in his eyes, but he did not press me. He was, as I had thought he would be, a splendid man at fifty, straight and strong-bodied, dark-eyed, with greying hair.

"You are older than he was," I thought, but I did not tell him my thought.

He had to be off; there was trouble from the Volscians, or the Sabines, or the Aequians. There would always be war on the borders, and often in the heartland. So long as there is a kingdom there will be another Turnus calling to be killed.

For a time after Maruna's death I did not go to Albunea. I could not bear to go with anyone but her, and having grown somewhat lame was timid about walking across the fields and up into the woods alone. At last, weary of my cowardice, I sent for Maruna's niece Ursina, whom I had given a farmstead on the Prati. She walked with me to the woodcutter's house, then back to her farm to see to her animals, and returned for me in the morning. She was still a lioness, a walk of four or five miles was nothing to her. So I could go to my forest when the need came on me.

Once when I went there in winter, sleeping out on the fleeces in the cold, though it hardly rained at all, I got up very stiff at dawn and found myself feverish. I stayed in the woodcutter's house that day, but the doctors in Lavinium insisted on bringing me back to town where they could torment me more easily. It may be that that happened more than once. As I speak now I feel my voice fail, as Maruna's heart failed, growing weak, so that even at the base of her throat one could hardly find the pulse. Even in my throat I can hardly feel the vibration of the voice.

But I will not die. I cannot. I will never go down among the shadows under Albunea to see Aeneas tall among the warriors, gleaming in bronze. I will not speak to Creusa of Troy, as I once thought I might, or Dido of Carthage, proud and silent, still bearing the great sword wound in her breast. They lived and died as women do and as the poet sang them. But he did not sing me enough life to die. He only gave me immortality.

I do not need to call on Ursina to come with me any more. Not for a long time. One must be changed, to be immortal. I can go from Lavinium to Albunea on my own wings. More and more I live there, hunting among the trees in twilight, in starlight. My eyes need little light to see their prey: to me the night there is luminous, a soft radiance. When the sun begins to rise and dazzle all the sky, I find the dark place in the hollow oak. That is my high house now. It does not matter that the Regia in Lavinium is only clay bricks in earth. In my dark bedroom I sleep the days away, near the pools of stinking, misty water that once were sacred. I wake as the sun goes down, and listen. My hearing is good. I can hear a mouse breathe among the fallen oak leaves. Through the noise of the water in the cave I can hear the roar and rumor of the vast city that covers all the Seven Hills and the banks of the father river and the old pagus lines for miles and miles. I can hear the endless sound of the engines of war on all the roads of the world. But I stay here. I fly among the trees on soft wings that make no sound. Sometimes I call out, but not in a human voice. My cry is soft and quavering: *i, i,* I cry: Go on, go.

Only sometimes my soul wakes as a woman again, and then when I listen I can hear silence, and in the silence his voice.

AFTERWORD

THE SETTING, STORY, AND CHARACTERS OF THIS NOVEL ARE based on the last six books of Vergil's epic poem the *Aeneid*.

For a long time anybody in Europe and the Americas who had much education at all knew Aeneas' story: his travels from Troy, his love affair with the African queen Dido, his visit to the underworld were shared, familiar references and story sources for poets, painters, opera composers. From the Middle Ages on, the so-called dead language Latin was, through its literature, intensely alive, active, and influential. That's no longer true. During the last century, the teaching and learning of Latin began to wither away into a scholarly specialty. So, with the true death of his language, Vergil's voice will be silenced at last. This is an awful pity, because he is one of the great poets of the world.

His poetry is so profoundly musical, its beauty is so intrinsic to the sound and order of the words, that it is essentially un-translatable. Even Dryden, even FitzGerald couldn't capture the magic. But a translator's yearning to identify with the text cannot be repressed. This is what urged me to take some scenes, some hints, some foreshadowings from the epic and make them into a novel—a translation into a different *form*—partial, marginal, but, in intent at least, faithful. More than anything else, my story is an act of gratitude to the poet, a love offering.

There have been one or two attempts to "finish" the *Aeneid*, justified by arguments that Vergil himself thought it incomplete (when he knew he was dying, he asked that it be burned), and that it ends with shocking abruptness in a scene that seems to put Aeneas' famous piety, even his heroic victory, in question. I think the poem ends where Vergil wanted it to end. This story is in no way an attempt to change or complete the story of Aeneas. It is a meditative interpretation suggested by a minor character in his story—the unfolding of a hint.

THE TROJAN WAR WAS PROBABLY FOUGHT IN THE THIRTEENTH century BC; Rome was founded, possibly, in the eighth, though there is no proper history of it for centuries after that. That Priam's nephew Aeneas of Troy had anything at all to do with founding Rome is pure legend, a good deal of it invented by Vergil himself.

But Vergil, as Dante knew, is a trustworthy man to follow. I followed him into his legendary Bronze Age. He never led me astray.

Sometimes I was puzzled, however. He was familiar with Latium (the region southwest of Rome), and I wasn't; but some of his geography seemed askew, or deliberately misty. Lavinium is now Pratica di Mare, that's all right; but at first it seemed a waste of time to try to be exact about the location of Laurentum, or the forest of Albunea, which couldn't be the sulfur springs near Tibur, now Tivoli, which Horace and other writers called Albunea; and the river Numicus or Numicius was as elusive in location as in name. But as a novelist I was uncomfortable not knowing how far my characters would have to walk from Laurentum to the mouth of the Tiber, how long it would take to drive a mule cart from Lavinium to Alba Longa. My friend the geomancer George Hersh, after burrowing into ancient sources on the Internet, found the modern map I needed for places and distances: *Lazio*, part of the *Grande Carte Stradale d'Italia*. There, in large scale, near Croce di Solferato, is Vergil's Albunea, properly convenient to Laurentum; and there it is, Rio Torto, the river that must have been the Numicus . . . It was deeply touching to me to find these places of legend on a highway map of the Touring Club Italiano. On the map and in the myth, they are real.

A later, equal joy was discovering *Vergil's Latium*, by Bertha Tilly, who walked all over the region in the 1930s with a keen mind, a sharp eye, and a Brownie camera. Tilly gave me infinite pleasure by rearranging some and confirming most of my sketch map. She photographed shepherds' huts built as they had been built for twenty-seven centuries. And she showed me how the coastline has changed at the mouth of the Tiber, and where the Trojans must have landed, sailing up the Tiber at dawn into the dark forest full of wings and birdsong.

MY DESIRE WAS TO FOLLOW VERGIL, NOT TO IMPROVE OR reprove him. But Lavinia herself sometimes insisted that the poet was mistaken—about the color of her hair, for instance. And being a novelist and wordy, I enlarged upon and interpreted and filled in many corners of his spare, splendid story. But I left out a good deal, too. The palaces and tiaras, the hecatomb sacrifices, the Augustan magnificence he gave to his setting, I reduced to a more plausible poverty. The Homeric use of quarrelsome deities to motivate, illuminate, and interfere with human choices and emotions doesn't work well in a novel, so the Greco-Roman gods, an intrinsic element of the poem, are no part of my story.

Free of the borrowed literary machinery of the pantheon, and authorised by some respectable scholars of religion, I found my characters following the sacred domestic practices of that profoundly religious people the Romans. Such ways of worship were centuries old in Vergil's day, and continued to exist in country places all through the Republic and the Empire, until the multiplication of imported deities and Christian intolerance finally suppressed them. "Pagan," meaning a worshipper of the gods, is a Christian usage; originally, pagans were simply the people who lived on the pagus, the Roman farm: hayseeds. Such country folk clung longest to the old, local, earth-deep religion. The song sung at Ambarvalia in my story is probably the oldest Latin poem known, yet it was written down as late as AD 218, by which time it was immemorially ancient and perhaps almost as strange to those who sang it as it is to us.

> *Enos Lases iuvate*
> *neve luae rue Marmar sins incurrere in pleores*
> *satur furere Mars limen sali sta berber*
> *semunis alternei advocapit conctos*
> *enos Marmor iuvato*
> *triumpe triumpe triumpe triumpe triumpe*

WHO WERE THE PEOPLE IN THE FOOTHILLS AND LOWLANDS of Latium in the eighth century BC—the Latins, the ancestral Romans? More knowledge than we used to have about them is coming to light, but still, I'm glad that my story is set in Vergil's semi-mythological, nonhistorical landscape, defined by a poet, not by the patient uncertainties of archaeologists. As for the historians, this early period is almost entirely frustrating to them. There is no reliable history of the Latins or of Rome itself until surprisingly late, well into the second century BC. The Roman historian Livy (who lived at about the same time as Vergil) is wonderful reading, but what he had to work with was almost entirely legend, myth, guesswork, tradition, contradiction, lists of festivals, names of consuls, fragments of enigmas; and we have less than he did, though our archaeology is more reliable.

Rome itself was probably a Latin settlement, almost certainly taken over for a while by the Etruscans and much influenced by them. But nobody is perfectly certain who the Etruscans were, though they left treasures of art and architecture wherever they settled, and we can decipher a certain amount—not all—of their language. They mostly lived north of the Tiber, in a league of twelve city-states that may have been considerably in advance of the Latins, culturally and economically.

The Latins and their neighboring peoples such as the Sabines, Aequians, Hernici, Volscians, all speakers of related Indo-European languages, had been migrating down from the north since before 1000 BC.

There was room for them. A great deal of Italy, back then, was forest. Where man goes, trees die; or, to paraphrase Tacitus, we make a desert and call it progress. By 800 BC the Latin-speaking people had moved into Latium, cutting trees and clearing their farm and pasture lands; and they may have been, as in my story, settled farmers and villagers (pagans), grouped by tribe or people under chiefs or kings. They probably weren't anywhere near as comfortable and civilised as I portray them. What is certain is that they were farmer-warriors, who spent a lot of time fighting each other. The Latins went on doing so with increasing success, for centuries, till they ruled all western Europe and quite a lot of Africa and Asia.

Like Vergil, I call the towns of the Bronze Age cities, and their people probably saw them as cities, but to us they might look like a walled or stockaded huddle of huts around a fort. Their people went out into the fields to herd sheep, goats, and cattle, and plant and tend barley and emmer wheat and vegetables, fruit and nut trees. They probably had no cotton or linen yet; the women carded, spun, and wove wool into the togas and pallas they wore (not all that different from a sari). It's possible that they knew only wild vines and the inedible wild olive, and couldn't afford to buy wine or olive oil from the Etruscans, who by then may have had them. But I couldn't imagine Italians without wine and olive oil. If it's any excuse, neither could Vergil.

I tried to give a glimpse of the countryside as it probably was then: a vast forest of oak and pine cut by steep river gullies running down to swampy grasslands and dune marshes near the coast. Settlements were mostly on rocky outcrops of the great volcanic complex of Mount Alba. The towns and their pastures and pagus fields were a small part of that wilderness. Each was a long way from the others. It would be a long time yet before they drew together to become Rome. People lived then in a wild world, a lonely one.

Vergil exaggerates the sophistication of that world, I play down its primitiveness: both of us, I think, because we want these people to be Romans—at least Romans in the making.

Ever since I first read about it I've been drawn to Rome, not the sick, luxurious Empire of the TV sagas, but early Rome: the dark, plain Republic, a forum not of marble but of wood and brick, an austere people with a strong sense of duty, order, and justice: farmers who spent half the year in the army, women who ran the farm meanwhile, extended families whose worship was of the fire in their hearth, the food in their granary, the local spring, the spirits of place and earth. Women were not set apart as chattel, and if only for that reason my imagination can be at home in an ancient Roman household as it cannot be in an ancient Greek one. They had slaves, as every people did then, but the slaves of the household, the *familia*, sat at table with the free. They were coarse, they were brutal, and they were tremendously different from us, but it is hard to feel them as essentially foreign when so much of our cultural heritage comes directly from them, half our language, most of our concept of law . . . and perhaps also certain homely but delicate values, such as the loyalty, modesty, and responsibility implicit in Vergil's idea of a hero.

I am grateful to W. Warde Fowler, author of *The Religious Experience of the Roman People*, and to H. J. Rose, author of *Ancient Roman Religion*, whose works, full of information and understanding, exemplify the nobility of scholarship. Bertha Tilly, in *Vergil's Latium*, and Alexander G. McKay, in *Vergil's Italy*, were invaluable guides. Karen Carr of the Portland State University Department of History shook some of the errors out of my Afterword and is not to blame for any that remain. My brother Karl Kroeber encouraged my reading of the *Aeneid* as a tragedy, but will probably rightly disown it. I am grateful to my editors Andrea Schulz and Michael Kandel and, as always, to the many people at Harcourt who work with me in so many ways to make a book what it ought to be.

—URSULA K. LE GUIN
2008